# *Alluring* TALES

## *Hot Holiday Nights*

*Also*

ALLURING TALES: AWAKEN THE FANTASY

# Alluring TALES

## Hot Holiday Nights

VIVI ANNA, SYLVIA DAY,
DELILAH DEVLIN, CATHRYN FOX, MYLA JACKSON
LISA RENEE JONES, SASHA WHITE

## red

**AVON**

*An Imprint of HarperCollinsPublishers*

HarperCollins books may be purchased for educational, business, or sales promotional use. For information please write: Special Markets Department, HarperCollins
Publishers, 10 East 53rd Street, New York, NY 10022.

FIRST EDITION

*Designed by Diahann Sturge*

Library of Congress Cataloging-in-Publication Data

Alluring tales : hot holiday nights / Cathryn Fox . . . [et al.]. — 1st ed.
    p. cm.
  ISBN 978-0-06-146317-4
  1. Erotic stores, American. 2. Erotic stories, Canadian. 3. Holidays—Fiction.
4. American fiction—Women authors. 5. Canadian fiction—Women authors. I.
Fox, Cathryn.
  PS648.E7A454 2008
  813'.01083538—dc22                                          2008026027

08  09  10  11  12    OV/RRD    10  9  8  7  6  5  4  3  2  1

# Contents

*To Jennifer Ray*
*for her honest reviews, enthusiasm,*
*and never ending support.*
*You Rock!*

# Peaches and Cream

## Cathryn Fox

# One

"My new guy's member is enormous and my mouth is so tiny." Tucked in the corner of Risqué, a members-only erotic club where Jennifer Angel bartended, Jennifer clicked through her in-box and read her messages out loud. Peeking over her laptop, she cast her best friend, Cat Nichols, a glance and said, "Jeez, you'd think spammers would have something better to do with their time." She moved on to the next message and blurted out, "Okay, I don't even have an erectile, so how can it be dysfunctional?"

With that, Cat laughed out loud. "Speaking of enormous members and erectile dysfunction, have you Googled him?"

Jennifer arched a questioning brow. "Googled him?" She kicked off her shoes, making herself more comfortable, and powered down her laptop. As she reached for her psychology textbook she asked, "Why would I Google him?"

Cat spun her laptop around on the small wooden tabletop, closed the article she'd been working on, and said, "Go for it. You'd be amazed at what you can find out about people on the Internet."

"Sam isn't going to hook me up with some psycho, gun-wielding, knife-throwing serial killer, is he?" Jennifer narrowed her eyes and scrutinized her friend. "Unless there is something I should know about your husband."

Cat chuckled. "Of course not." She held her hand up in honor. "I promise you that he's setting you up with one of the new research scientists who has just transferred in from the California branch. But go ahead and do it anyway. I Google people all the time."

"Of course you do. You're a reporter." Jennifer flipped through her textbook. "I'm a fourth-year psych student, no need for me to Google people. Within five minutes of meeting him, I'll have him all figured out."

"Have you ever Googled yourself?" Relaxing after a long workweek, and needing something to warm her up on this cool December day, Cat reached for her wine and took a sip.

Jennifer cocked her head and offered her friend a devilish grin. "*Uh,* yeah. All the time. Which is why you insisted I needed a man in my life."

Laughing, Cat nearly spewed her wine all over the laptop. "You're such a smart-ass, Jenn."

"It's a gift." Jennifer tossed her a lopsided smile and

then turned her attention to her open book, going over last night's lecture.

The ever persistent Cat pressed on, "Come on, just type his name in here, and you'll learn all about your mystery date."

Jennifer crinkled her nose and reached for her drink. The wicked gleam in her friend's eyes worried her. What the hell was Cat up to? "Why can't he get his own girl, anyway? What kind of loser agrees to go on a blind date?"

"Helloooo, you're going on a blind date, too, aren't you?"

"Yeah but that's different. I just don't have the time to find myself a good man," she scoffed and added, "Heck, forget *good*. Tonight I'd settle for a *hard* man." Although good *and* hard would certainly be a bonus, she mused. The truth was, as much as Jennifer wanted to, between work and school, she just didn't have the time to spice up her sex life—her very nonexistent sex life, save for her battery-operated toy, which she frequently *Googled* herself with.

"Besides, you and I both know what kind of deadbeat losers I attract," Jennifer lamented. "Which is the only reason I agreed to this setup in the first place. When it comes to instincts, I'm sure Sam's are better than mine. He's not likely to set me up with some *jackass*," she said, putting emphasis on that last word.

Never one to let things go, Cat insisted, "Go ahead and find out for yourself."

Needing to appease her friend so she could get some

schoolwork done before her blind date called to arrange a time and place for pickup, Jennifer grabbed the laptop and tossed Cat an impatient look. "Okay, okay, what did you say his name was again?"

"Jack," Cat said, unable to keep the grin from her face. "Jack Miller."

Jennifer rolled her eyes heavenward. "What were the odds?"

"But don't worry, Jenn. Sam assures me he's one of the good guys."

Jennifer grinned. "Like I said, tonight I'd settle for *hard*." She keyed in his name and gave a resigned sigh. "Oh, well, at least this will give us something to talk about during dinner." Since chatting about the weather was out—winter in Chicago hardly made for riveting conversation—this way she'd be armed with the basics.

After confirming that her impending date was a research scientist—an award-winning research scientist, to be precise—who ran sexy experiments on the female libido, Jennifer suddenly felt a surge of heat between her legs. She made a slow pass over her bottom lip as her thighs fluttered. Eyes alive with curiosity, she scanned the rest of the article and then went on to study the picture of Jack Miller.

Dark hair cut short gave him a boy-next-door look, but the sexy grin curling up the corners of his sensual mouth, combined with the smoldering heat in his gorgeous blue eyes, told her he was anything but. From the picture alone she couldn't tell what his body looked like, she'd have to wait until tonight to find out. As her gaze moved over his face, she fought back the urge to rub her hands in eager anticipation. Although something in her gut already told her this bad boy had a rock-hard physique that could torture her sex-starved libido in the most pleasant ways.

When she took a moment to entertain the idea, her body grew needy. Her nipples quivered and her pussy muscles tightened in heavenly bliss. Out of nowhere a burst of heat prowled through her, settling low in her loins. She clamped her knees and squeezed, merely adding fuel to the flames between her legs.

The one thing that Jennifer did know for certain was that there was something undeniably primal about Jack Miller that made her feel a little wild, and a whole lot wicked.

Once she finished the article, she gave in to impulse and decided to Google herself. Jennifer punched in her name, read the search results before her, and then rolled her eyes.

"Jesus, what were the odds?" she said. "I share my birthright with a stripper."

Jennifer Angel, AKA Peaches.

Cat chuckled. "That's one hell of a coincidence, Jenn. Just think, if Jack Googled you, and you asked him to pick you up here, he'd surely think that you're Jennifer Angel, AKA Peaches."

A little intrigued and a whole lot curious, she nibbled her bottom lip, wondering if her blind date had Googled her. If so, was he expecting a sex-deprived psychology student or an exotic pole dancer?

Her mouth twitched. Could a sexy mistake in identity lead to a night of wild, unadulterated sex, with Jennifer, AKA Peaches, living out her every fantasy?

How delightfully scandalous.

As she considered it further, her gaze raked over his picture again, her carnal thoughts taking her in an erotic direction, envisioning herself giving the sexy scientist his own exotic peep show.

A half smile lingered on her lips as a warm tingle worked its way through her bloodstream. Her pussy moistened and clenched as her body grew needy.

Perhaps it was her lack of male-induced orgasms or her inability to attract a decent guy that had her libido in an uproar and her mind conjuring up wild fantasies about her blind date.

Either way, she suspected the night ahead of her was about to get a whole lot more interesting.

"You're the luckiest son of a bitch I know," Brad Reynolds said, nodding his head in appreciation as he perused the erotic image on the computer monitor.

Jack grinned at his best friend and temporary roommate, then clicked his mouse to enlarge the picture on the screen. "Come on, no way is Sam going to set me up with a pole dancer," he said, unconvinced. "He told me she was a fourth-year psychology student."

Angling his head, Jack took great pleasure in Peaches's erotic pose, wondering if perhaps she could be both, a psychology student and an exotic dancer. Bent forward, her curvaceous ass was staring him straight in the face, begging to be spanked. And damned if he didn't want to be the one to spank it.

Jack fisted his fingers, his cock throbbing as he visualized himself doing just that.

His body vibrated as he mentally indulged in the sensual slideshow. There was something very sexy in an uninhibited woman, he decided.

Jack drew a sharp breath and let it out slowly, working to rein in his lust. He shifted uncomfortably, his jeans suddenly two sizes too small.

"Why not?" Brad asked, moving closer for a better view. "You moved all the way from California to Chicago to work with him on his latest sexual-research project. Maybe he wants to properly initiate you into the brotherhood."

Jack paused to consider things further. Perhaps Brad was right. After all, Brad had worked closely with Sam for the last year. "I guess you know Sam better than I do," Jack said, his voice husky with arousal. As Jack toyed with the idea, his cock throbbed with renewed interest. "He just doesn't seem the type. Then again . . ." His words fell off as he glanced at the clock.

"Then again *what*?" Brad asked.

With less than half an hour to meet Jennifer at their rendezvous point, Jack powered down his computer, climbed from his chair, and grabbed his coat. "Jennifer asked me to pick her up outside Risqué."

"Jesus, Jack. That's the city's hottest members-only exotic club—where anything goes. Or so I've heard. A friend of mine gave me a pass a few months back, but

I haven't had a chance to use it yet." Grinning like the wild man he really was, Brad raked his hands through his surfer-boy hair and studied the screen. "It has to be her. It just has to be."

Brad tore his focus from the computer and tossed Jack one of his signature playboy grins, one that had women shedding their panties, along with their inhibitions— Jack would know, he'd seen Brad in action and, in fact, had shared in that action when the two were in California together.

With a wicked gleam in his eyes, Brad pushed his hands into his pockets and angled his head. "If it is her, Jack, mind if I stop by for the show?"

Jack slapped his best friend on the back, thinking it had been far too long since they'd both spent the night pleasuring the same woman, and if things went accordingly, that's exactly what they'd be doing. Besides, since Brad had been kind enough to give him a bed until he closed the deal on his new condo, it was the least he could do.

Jack held his hand out and they punched fists. "To the brotherhood," they said in unison.

# Two

As Jack left Brad's condo and made his way to his Jeep, he noted that the earlier snowflakes had turned to rain. Picking up his pace, Jack ducked into his vehicle and blasted the heater, attempting to push back the damp cold. He'd only been in Chicago for one month and had yet to get used to the change in climate. Warm and dry, he was used to. Wet snow and high winds, not so much.

Less than half an hour later, he pulled up to the curb near Risqué, parking as close as possible to the front doors. He glanced at the building but the frosted windows prohibited him from viewing the inside. His gaze surfed over the streets, trying to see through the sea of multicolored umbrellas. He scanned the wet pavement, looking for some telltale sign of Peaches . . . *err* . . . Jennifer, he quickly corrected himself. *Jennifer.*

During their brief conversation earlier that day, after he'd agreed to pick her up outside the club, he'd told her what he'd be driving. Now he just hoped she would recognize his Jeep behind the stream of steady rain.

Jack played over their phone conversation and he took a moment to recall her sweet yet oh-so-seductive voice. Jesus, was it possible that his new coworker had set him up with an exotic dancer who worked at a club where anything goes? As a research scientist himself, had Sam instinctively known that Jack had spent the last year buried in his latest project, instead of burying himself in a soft, sexy woman? Fuck, he sure as hell hoped so.

A moment later he watched a woman push past the front doors of the club and pop open an umbrella. With determined strides, she cut through the congestion and rushed down the sidewalk toward him. Before she could reach his Jeep, a car sped by, its tires hitting the puddle a few feet away from her. Taking her by surprise, a wall of water hit her like a tsunami, stopping her dead in her tracks.

Jack could hear her curses from twenty feet away. Moving at breakneck speed, he killed his ignition, jumped from the driver's seat, and ran toward her. When he reached her side, he darted a glance over her wet clothes, registering every delicious detail of her drenched body.

As his eyes devoured the curvy woman before him, he took note of her open jacket, the way her nipples hardened beneath her breast-molding sweater and the way her snug jeans clung to her very long, very sexy legs. Despite the chill in the air, Jack could feel heat rising in him. A rush of sexual energy hit him so hard he nearly faltered backward.

He cleared his throat, hyperaware of his thickening cock and the way it was rising to the occasion, screaming for a woman's touch. But not any woman's touch. Oh no, not at all. Little Jack was clamoring for *this* woman's touch.

As Jack stood there taking pleasure in her most unfortunate situation, he berated himself. This probably wasn't the best time to be having erotic thoughts about, who he assumed, was his blind date. Not when she stood there gasping for breath and dripping like a sieve. Marshaling his lust-drunk mind, he commanded himself to focus on the situation.

When his gaze traveled back up her face, she looked up at him with the biggest, brownest, most expressive eyes he'd ever seen. Desire thrummed through his veins as their glances collided. The attraction between them was instant and all-consuming, hitting him with more force than a sucker punch. There was something about this sweet yet sexy woman that held his focus, and quite frankly, intrigued him.

A curtain of dark lashes covered her eyes when she glanced down at her soaked clothes. "Well, hell," she sputtered.

"Jennifer?" he asked, reaching out to cup her chin, bringing them face-to-face. When she blinked away a big fat raindrop, something inside him softened. An unexpected burst of warmth rushed through him.

"Yes," she managed to get out between clanging teeth.

"I'm Jack."

She shifted her umbrella to her other hand and lifted it higher, shielding them both from the elements. "Nice to meet you, Jack."

Even though her hair was plastered to her forehead and her makeup was running down her face, her eyes glimmered with dark sensuality when they locked on his. Lust jumped up and kicked him in the balls. Hard.

He wrapped his arm around her and anchored her against him, offering his warmth—the snug contact creating an air of instant intimacy. As she melted against him, her body reacted with a shiver.

"Let's get you warmed up," he said, running his hand up and down her arm, heating her with friction.

Brow knitting together in concern, she shook her head and pointed toward his Jeep. "I don't want to get your Jeep soaked." The soft warmth of her voice pulled at him. He drew her in closer and inhaled her alluring feminine scent, a heady combination of winter rain and . . . *peaches.*

Body igniting to a near boil, and his groin aching for a deeper intimacy, he clenched his jaw and bit back a moan. "I don't care about the Jeep. You're freezing."

Surprise registered in her eyes. With effort, she conjured a genuine smile. Silky soft lips curled at the corners, bringing light to her dark chocolate eyes. It did the weirdest things to his insides.

She glanced at his wet jacket. "Oh, hell. I'm getting you all wet, too."

Christ, she didn't know the half of it.

She stepped out of the circle of his arms and jerked her thumb toward the club. "I think I might have a change of clothes inside." Turning, she gestured for him to follow, her wet, lush ass dragging his focus. "I'd rather slip into something warm and dry before we go to dinner."

Clenching his fists, he bit back a growl of longing, and tugged her back into his arms. A pity, really, because he'd rather slip into something hot and wet before they ate out.

Despite looking like a drenched rat, Jennifer glanced up and watched the way Jack's smoldering blue eyes dripped with promise as they rolled over her body. Shivers of warm need traveled all the way to her toes as she let her glance roll over him in return, assessing him and taking great pleasure in his fine, athletic physique.

Locked under his muscular arm as he herded them down the sidewalk, she breathed in his intoxicating male scent, letting his spicy aroma curl through her blood and awaken all her senses. Thick muscles shifted as one strong arm pulled her in closer, carefully maneuvering them around a group of teenagers.

Oh yeah, no doubt about it, she mused, her mood lightening. Sexy Jack Miller had a rock-hard body that could undoubtedly torture her in the most pleasant ways. And boy, oh boy, did she ever want to be tortured.

In the most pleasant ways.

His gentlemanly gestures hadn't gone unnoticed, either. Jennifer couldn't remember the last time a guy had showed concern for her well-being—especially choosing her needs over his vehicle. Jack didn't care if she got his upholstery wet, or his clothes for that matter. Strange how that made her feel all warm and weird inside. Maybe, just maybe, he really was one of the good guys.

After they entered the unusually quiet, dimly lit club, Jennifer signed Jack in and gestured with a nod for him to have a seat at the bar. "I'll just be a minute," she said, and summoned Charlene to take Jack's drink order. Once Jack was comfortably seated, and quite happily watching Miranda's exhibitionist dance show, Jennifer made her way into the change room, hoping that she'd left a pair of jeans and sweater behind.

Marveling at the turn of events, she pushed back her wet hair, pulled open her locker, and surfed through her work attire.

"Dammit, there has to be something in here," she murmured to herself, especially since the club was like a second home to her.

Over the last couple of years, Jennifer had spent many hours working at the exclusive, members-only club, where private indiscretions remained . . . *private*, while finishing up her degree. Even though the pay was only modest and sometimes the elite, upper-class patrons were less than polite, she enjoyed her job. The truth was, there were other jobs she could take, but she liked bartending and listening to other people's problems. It was good hands-on experience for when she opened her own practice.

At least that's what she told herself . . .

Because deep down, she had to admit that working at the

club excited her, in more ways than one. So did the thoughts of climbing onto one of the many small stages and giving a sexy performance of her own while others watched. Heat curled a lazy path through her loins as she visualized it.

What would Freud have said about that one?

That she had exhibitionist tendencies.

That maybe she had asked Jack to pick her up outside the club on purpose.

That maybe she *did* want him to mistakenly think she was an exotic dancer.

And that maybe, just maybe, this was the perfect opportunity for her to step out of character, spice up her sex life, and live out one of her many, many fantasies.

She turned her attention back to her locker to discover that it only contained a spare work uniform, and some gym clothes, which needed washing. She stared at the clothes in dismay. Black pants and a crisp white shirt might land her a spot at a fine restaurant, but it certainly wasn't going to land her a spot between the sheets with her sexy scientist.

"Hey, girl. What's up?" Miranda asked. With her dance outfit in hand, Miranda closed the change room door behind her and pulled on a silky, cream-colored robe. The cream color looked incredibly sexy next to her gorgeous mocha skin. "Did you have a fight with a puddle or something?"

Jennifer pulled a face and frowned at her good friend. "Yeah, and the puddle won."

Voice sincere, Miranda, a very sexually empowered woman, who also happened to be the owner of Risqué, pouted her full sensuous lips in return and said, "Ah, poor baby. Here." She tossed Jennifer a fluffy cotton towel, followed by a nice soft robe.

"Thanks," Jennifer said, drying her face, knowing she could always count on Miranda to know exactly what she needed. Not only had Jennifer worked for Miranda for the past two years, they both took pole dancing classes down at the health club. Jennifer did it for strengthening exercise. Miranda did it to keep up-to-date with her booming business.

A moment later Miranda asked, "Hey, did I see you come in here with that hot guy at the bar?"

Jennifer nodded, knowing it was out of character for her. She normally didn't mix work and pleasure. Not that there had been a whole lot of pleasure lately, but still . . .

"We have a date but I can't go out looking like this." She squeezed the rain from her hair. "I'm a mess and I smell like dirty drain water." She gave a resigned sigh. "I'd go home and change but it will take a good hour for me to get all the way across town in this weather. Then it will likely be too late to eat out. I should probably just reschedule."

"Forget about it." Miranda's grin turned wicked as she reached into her locker. "Have a quick shower in the back room, put this on, and *eat in*."

Jennifer didn't miss the double entendre. She arched a brow and glanced at the sexy cheerleading outfit dangling from Miranda's fingertips. "Jesus, you can't be serious."

"Oh, I'm very serious." Miranda straddled the bench beside her and pulled on a body fitting sweater.

Jennifer took a moment to peruse her. Too bad Miranda was thin and Jennifer was curvy, otherwise they could have switched clothes.

Miranda's voice dropped an octave, her eyes narrowed. "You know you want to, Jennifer," she said, the tone of her voice daring her to deny it.

Okay, who was the psychology student here, anyway?

"I don't know what you're talking about, Miranda."

Miranda pulled her down onto the bench next to her and said, "It's quiet out there tonight. The weather's keeping patrons away. It's the perfect night for a new amateur act, to try out the moves we learned last week at dance."

Jennifer gulped air.

"Don't you think it's time to have a little fun, Jennifer? Time to spice up your sex life?" She snapped her fingers. "Because let me tell ya, baby. That guy out there looks like he's packing all kinds of delicious seasonings just waiting to spice up a hot little dish like you."

And once again Miranda knew exactly what she needed.

Jesus, could she do this? Could she put on a sexy cheerleading outfit and go out there and take it all off for her date? A man who fired her blood from simmer to inferno with one smoldering glance. A man who she instinctively knew would give her the best sex of her life. The thoughts of indulging in a wild, passionate affair with him—a guy who experimented on female libidos—had her thighs quivering with erotic delight.

She took a moment to mull things over and warm to the idea. Okay, maybe *warm* wasn't the right word, because the truth was, she felt downright hot.

Jennifer drew a fueling breath. Wasn't this the perfect opportunity to turn up the heat between them and live out a few secret fantasies while she was at it?

And since she never was one to let an opportunity pass . . .

# Three

*S*itting at the bar, nursing a cold beer, Jack glanced around, orienting himself, quickly understanding that the exclusive club catered to a specific crowd, those who liked to watch, and those who liked to be watched.

Couples were intimately gathered around the tables, all in various stages of dress, or rather, undress, completely engrossed in each other, or enjoying the various erotic shows throughout the room.

When the front door opened and the noise gained his attention, Jack turned. A wide grin split his face when none other than his best friend Brad strolled inside.

Jack waved him over just as a man and a woman took center stage. Exhibitionists that they were, they seductively undressed one another, indulging in each other's bodies while the voyeurs in the crowd perused the action with heated interest. Jack had to admit, he wasn't immune to the sexy show himself.

Brad cut across the wide expanse of floor and made his way over. With his damp hair touching his shoulders, and looking like the bad-ass playboy he really was, Brad angled his head and glanced at the stage, taking in the passionate show.

Jack summoned Charlene for another beer as Brad pulled up the stool beside him.

Brad blew a breath. "Christ, this is some place," he said, and then noted the empty seat on the other side of Jack. He furrowed his brow. "Where's your date?"

"She got washed out by a puddle and is out back looking for a change of clothes."

Brad grinned. "So she does work here, then?"

"Looks that way."

After his drink arrived, Brad thanked Charlene, took a pull from the bottle, and asked in whispered words, "Is she Peaches?"

"I can't tell." Of course, he wouldn't know for certain whether Jennifer and Peaches were one and the same. Sure she had the same long, wavy brown hair, but she'd have to slip into a G-string and bend over before he could make a positive identification. Jack's groin tightened at the visual image.

Just then a woman stepped from the back room. Tall, thin with gorgeous brown skin and dark, almond-shaped eyes, Jack immediately recognized her as the dancer who was onstage when he'd entered.

"Hey, boys," she said, offering them a sultry smile. "I'm Miranda." She cut her hand through the air. "I'd like to welcome you both to Risqué."

After a round of handshakes, Jack noted the chemistry between Brad and Miranda. Truthfully, the two looked damn good together. And they would be good together. For a while. Brad liked sex—heck, what red-blooded American didn't?—but what he didn't like was the idea of commitment. Jack knew it would take one hell of a spirited woman to tame a guy like Brad. Then again, it would take someone pretty damn special before Jack would ever consider anything long term, either.

Miranda took a seat beside Brad, caught Jack's glance, and said, "Jennifer wanted me to let you know she's almost ready." Voice teasing and eyes bright with mischief, she leaned in closer, handed him a condom and added, "The question is, are you?"

Jack was about to question her, but his jaw fell slack when the music changed and a sexy cheerleader replaced the couple on the dance platform.

Sweet Mother of God!

Jennifer's plump lips curled when she met his glance. Moving with innocent sensuality, she shimmied up next to the pole and ran her fingers up and down the metal rod, mimicking the action of what he was about to do to his dick—what he wanted *her* to do to his dick. If that wasn't enough to drive a sane man silly, with unhurried movements, she hooked one long leg around the pole, and tossed him the sexiest, most mischievous grin he'd ever seen.

*Goddamn . . .*

Jack's cock jumped in his pants, clamoring to break free and secure a front row seat. He gripped his bottle and took another slug of beer, needing to cool himself down before he erupted on the spot.

Taking her time, Jennifer paraded around the dance floor and shimmied against the pole. Rotating her curvy hips to the arousing music, she sensuously shifted from one foot to the other, her lush ass enticing him, begging to be spanked.

Jennifer bent forward and ran her hands up her legs, slowly, seductively, coming perilously close to her sex but never quite touching. Jack nearly sobbed as saliva pooled in his mouth, eager to get a glimpse of her hot little pussy. Her slow seduction nearly shut down his brain. Gaze riveted, pleasure resonated through his bones as he studied her every movement.

"Holy fuck," he murmured to himself, barely able to breathe, let alone think. A low hiss came from beside him as Brad also took pleasure in the erotic show.

With frank appreciation, Jack watched Jennifer sensuously slide her body up and down on the pole, taking in the aroused look in her eyes and noting with interest just how much she enjoyed putting on this sexy little act for him.

Flames surged through his body and he had to practically roll his tongue back into his mouth. His blood flowed thick and heavy when she slowly peeled off her top to reveal the most gorgeous set of pom-poms he'd ever had the pleasure of viewing. Full, round, and soft with pretty pink nipples beckoning his touch, his mouth.

When her eyes locked on his, his nostrils flared and he made a slow pass over his bottom lip. He was almost certain he saw her whole body shudder in response to his primal reactions. Fisting his fingers, he shifted in his seat. God dammit, he had every intention of finding out, every intention of making her as crazy as she was making him.

She leaned forward and went to work on her short skirt. Her dark hair, now dry, camouflaged her cleavage, driving his imagination and fueling his lust.

With seductive movements meant to entice, she wiggled her hips, lowered her skirt to her ankles and then kicked it toward him, leaving behind a pair of white lace panties that hugged her curvy hips to perfection.

She climbed up the pole, braced herself and then spread her legs wide open, giving him a sexy flash of her sweet pussy through the lacy material.

*Oh, fuck* . . .

Jack's breath grew shallow. His entire body trembled. Okay, that had to be the most erotic thing he'd ever seen.

In one fluid movement, she slid down the pole and crossed the small platform. Before he realized what she was doing, she lowered herself into a chair, tilted her head back, and pulled on a rope, dousing her body in water and shattering what little control he had left.

Okay, he was wrong, *that* was the most erotic thing he'd ever seen.

Brad shifted beside him. "Jesus, man. She's hot."

"Oh yeah," Jack agreed, his voice sounding tight. "She's hot, all right."

"Damn right she is," Miranda piped in. "Someone ought to cool her down."

Forget cooling her down. Jack had every intention of heating her up until she exploded all over him, again and again. His balls tightened and contracted in eager anticipation. He began sweating. Sweating, for Christ's sake. No woman had ever made him sweat before.

When Jennifer's gaze raced over him, the desire reflecting in her eyes became his undoing. Driven by need, Jack stood and took a step toward the stage.

Watching time was over.

It was time to play.

Brad's raspy voice stopped him. "Need a hand."

"Sure," Jack said, wanting to pleasure this wild woman and give her the ride of a lifetime.

When he turned back to Jennifer, she crooked her finger in a sultry invitation, motioning him forward.

In three long strides he crossed the floor and closed the distance between them. As he approached, he watched her wobble on a pair of too-high stilettos. Her cheeks were flushed and hot. Her body fairly vibrating. He moved closer and noted that even with the shoes on he still towered over her.

He gave her a crooked grin and brushed his knuckles over her warm cheek, pushing her wet hair off her shoulders to reveal her full, beautiful breasts.

"That was one hell of a show, Jennifer." Lust edged

his voice as his hands fell to her lush backside. He ran his palm over the curve of her ass and gave her a light slap.

She gave a little gasp. Her aroused smile nearly brought him to his knees. She went up on her toes. Her breath was warm on his face as she seductively whispered into his mouth, "You can call me Peaches."

His grin broadened. With exquisite gentleness he brought his hands to her breasts and with the pad of his thumb drew lazy circles around one puckered nipple. His fingers burned as they moved over her body.

"Peaches, huh?" he asked.

A shudder overtook her. Her rich, heady scent reached his nostrils. "Yeah, Peaches," she whispered with effort, arching into his touch.

Pleasure engulfed him as his glance panned down her curvaceous body, acknowledging the flare of desire between his legs before he brought his attention back around to her face.

"Why Peaches?" he asked.

When she opened her mouth, he pressed his finger to her lips and cut her off. "Wait," he said, a bevy of fantasies rushing through his mind. "There are some things I'd rather discover on my own." That little remark brought a smile to her face.

Just then Brad moved in beside her, sandwiching her small frame between them. By small degrees her body stiffened and her dazzling smile faltered. Surprise registered in her eyes as her gaze went from Jack to Brad back to Jack again.

Jack took note of her tense body language. "This is Brad," Jack said, addressing her concerns before she had a chance to voice them.

She tried for casual but her voice betrayed her. "A friend of yours?" she asked.

Jack narrowed his gaze, gauging her reactions. "Best friend," he said, wondering how she wanted to handle this. He suddenly sensed that he was pushing her past her comfort zone and that she wasn't at all who she said she was. But something deep in his gut instinctively told him it was a role she eagerly wanted to step into. "We share everything."

Her eyes widened with surprise and . . . *intrigue*. He felt a tremor race through her—it was a tremor from passion, not fear.

She swallowed. "Everything?" she asked.

"Yes, everything," he answered.

Jack was a considerate lover and had always taken his time to properly pleasure a woman, but for some inexplicable reason, Jennifer's needs and desires suddenly became more important than his very next breath. Knowing the two men could give her every pleasure imaginable and aching to do just that, Jack packaged her against his body, generating heat and need between them all.

"Do you want to play with us, Peaches?"

They exchanged a long heated look, one that caused a hush to fall over the crowd observing them, then he watched something in her expression change, darken. As her inhibitions ebbed away, her chest heaved with excitement and her eyes sparkled with lust.

"I knew you were trouble the second I set eyes on you, Jack," she whispered, then turned toward Brad, raked her fingers through his hair, and brought his mouth to hers.

When their lips connected, Jack threw his head back and growled out loud. Brad kissed her long and hard, devouring her with his mouth until the two of them were left shaken.

"Baby, you are so fucking hot!" Jack said.

Making no attempt at discretion, Jack cupped her elbow, pulled her back into his arms, and joined them hip to hip, her drenched body dampening his clothes. With his lips hovering only inches from hers, he followed the seductive sway of her body, loving the way she responded to him. Brad slipped in behind her, pulled her long hair from her shoulders and ran the soft blade of his tongue along the erogenous zone at the base of her neck.

"I'm getting you boys all wet," she whispered breathlessly, her body still quaking from Brad's hungry kiss.

Jack's laugh was darkly seductive and his whole body shook with sexual need, aching to explore the heat between them. "Yes, you are. How about you, Peaches? Are you wet, too?"

She set her full lips into a pout. "You know I am. I'm dripping." She shook her damp curls and murmured seductively, "Just look at my hair."

"It's not your hair I'm talking about."

"What—"

When he slipped his hand between her legs, pulled

aside her panties, and stroked her sopping-wet cunt, her voice broke off. Her unasked question morphed into a soft moan. Her sex muscles rippled with excitement.

"Ah, you're dripping, baby," Jack said, and with one quick tug ripped her panties from her hips.

Her eyes darkened and she pushed against his hand, making no qualms about what she wanted. As Jack continued to stroke her pussy, he exchanged a look with Brad.

Reading his intent, Brad anchored her back to his chest and ran his finger over her stomach until he reached her sex. He brushed his thumb over her swollen clit, and then widened her dewy lips.

"Ohmigod," she cried out, her head lolling to the side.

Forgetting all about the crowd, Jack dropped to his knees before her, and using his tongue, made a slow pass over her sweet pussy. He gripped her voluptuous curves, his fingers biting into her hips as a growl rose up from the depths of his throat. "*Mmmmm*, now I know where you got your name. You taste like peaches and cream."

Brad dipped a finger into her opening and brought his hands to his mouth for a taste. "*Mmmmm*, peaches and cream," he echoed in agreement.

Aching to pillage her with his hungry mouth, Jack stood, caught hold of her hand and guided her to the chair. "Why don't you have a seat right here and spread your legs for me, baby, so I can get a better taste," he whispered softly. When she gave him a needy sigh, he nudged her backward until her knees hit the chair. After she quickly lowered herself, she immediately widened her sleek legs, granting him entrance.

She looked so goddamn sexy sitting there bare naked, save for her high heels, her pussy spread wide open, his for the taking.

Smoldering brown eyes locked on his when he sank to the floor and insinuated himself between her thighs. His eyes shifted downward to take in her dampness. Using his fingers he pulled open her nether lips and took a long moment to just look at her gorgeous, passion-drenched pussy. His mouth went suddenly dry. Jack gave a lusty groan, bent forward, and licked her, hydrating himself with her cream.

Her hips practically came off the chair. Pitching forward, she gyrated under his tongue, took a deep breath, and whispered, "God, Jack. That feels so good." Her fingernails raked through his hair and held him to her. She made a sexy noise and shifted. "Don't . . . stop." Her voice came out broken, unstable.

Jack inched back and glanced up at her. His brain nearly stalled at the erotic vision. Dark curls framed her flushed face, her kiss-swollen lips were full and blood red. Heavy-lidded eyes were glossy, brimming with lust. His entire body trembled with longing as he perused her.

"You like that, baby?" Jack asked.

Her lashes fluttered, her lips caught between her teeth. She opened her mouth to answer but her words fell off when Brad moved in behind her, his palms racing over her skin before traveling to her breasts for a slow, gentle massage. She arched her back and moaned.

As Brad caressed her breasts, Jack turned his attention back to her pussy, feasting on her sweetness and priming her for his rock-hard cock.

Her pussy quivered when he deepened the kiss and pressed one finger to her opening. He could already feel the climactic clench of her muscles and was shocked at how close she was to release. Although he shouldn't have been too surprised, he was damn close himself.

She thrust her pelvis forward, forcing his finger in deeper. Her actions nearly took him over the edge. He drew a rejuvenating breath, needing to slow things down, to do this right, for her. Because deep inside him, something told him Jennifer, aka Peaches, was stepping out of character, for him and for her.

Jack listened to the hiss of Brad's zipper and the rustle of his clothes. Peaches made a small gasping noise. Jack lifted his head and shot them both a sideways glance.

Brad had moved to her side, and now offered her his cock. When he caught Peaches's glance, her warm fingers brushed over his chest and she looked at him with dark, questioning eyes.

"Do you want to suck him?" Jack asked.

She wet her lip, her body language conveying without words exactly what she wanted. The desire in her eyes filled him with need.

"Take him into your mouth, babe, and let me watch."

Peaches widened her mouth to accommodate Brad's thickness and then wrapped her lips around his head.

"Jesus," Jack bit out as his cock nearly jumped out of

his pants. He shifted uncomfortably, his dick hardening to the point of pain.

Blood pounded through his veins as he watched her work her sweet mouth over his best friend's cock. Raw desire seared his insides. Peaches whimpered low in her throat and it was all he could take. Aching to lose himself in her, he stood, tore off his clothes, and quickly sheathed himself. When Peaches caught his movements she turned to face him, making slow, sexy passes over Brad's dick.

The sudden need to have her all to himself rushed though him and took him by surprise. He hauled Peaches to her feet, lowered himself into her chair, and pulled her onto his lap. Her full round breasts hovered inches from his hungry mouth. Drawing one puckered nub between his lips, he gripped her hips and rubbed the tip of his dick over her clit.

Air rushed from her lungs and she began moving against him, demanding more. He held her back, teasing her, prohibiting her from impaling herself on him.

When Peaches reached out for Brad, Brad quickly joined in the action. Her small fingers wrapped around Brad's cock, and together, both Brad and Jennifer began stroking his engorged shaft. Jack sucked in a tight breath and watched the way Peaches undulated against his cock, rubbing her wet, swollen clit all over him as she serviced Brad's cock.

"Please . . . Jack," she begged, her eyes burning with lust.

Jack pitched his voice low. "Please what?" he asked.

"Please fuck me."

Desperately needing to do just that, Jack guided her onto his cock. The second he breached her opening, she jerked her hips forward, impaling herself on him.

"Holy fuck," he growled when her heat closed around him. He caught Brad's glance and watched his friend's nostrils flare. Juices pearled on the tip of his cock and Jack knew the action had pushed Brad over the edge. Brad's hands picked up tempo as they raced over his erection. A moment later he threw his head back and ejaculated.

Moaning out loud Peaches milked Brad dry and then turned her full attention to Jack. She gripped the back of the chair and began riding him. Dark eyes met his and locked in a heated embrace, captivating him and bringing them to an even deeper level of intimacy.

It occurred to Jack that there were three people here, all involved in the physical act of sex, but there were only two people here who were connecting on a different level. Peaches leaned forward and pressed her lips to his. Everything inside him softened.

"Hey, baby," he whispered into her mouth, powering upward to fill her with his cock, needing in some unfathomable way to give her what he'd never given another. Because the truth was, no woman had ever felt so good or so right in his arms before.

He deepened the kiss, claiming her, branding her with his heat as everything in him screamed possession.

A whimper escaped her lips. "Jack . . . ," she murmured low in her throat.

That one word drummed in his head as her strong sex muscles tightened around his cock, the sweet friction shattering all his composure. She began bucking against him, making him wild, stirring things deep inside him. With need consuming them both, he increased the intensity and began pounding into her, driving them both to the edge of sanity.

When a shiver wracked her body, her eyes widened.

"That's a girl," he whispered. "Come all over my cock." Jack slipped a hand between their bodies and caressed her clit, knowing just what she needed to take her over. Her breath caught and then suddenly she shattered all over him. Warm heat poured down his shaft. As she gave herself over to her orgasm, Jack drove himself as deep as he could and stilled his movements. Enclosed in the circle of his arms, she threw her head back and cried out his name. Watching her come quickly brought on his own climax.

"Oh, fuck, yes!" he growled. His cock pulsed and throbbed as he released high inside her.

A moment later she collapsed against him, resting her head on his shoulder as they both took a long moment to regain control.

When she finally pulled back and met his glance, Jack gave her a tender smile and traced her lips with his fingers. A soft moan escaped her mouth and in that instant something blossomed inside him. Jesus, he really hadn't anticipated that Jennifer could be the one. The one he wanted to keep all to himself.

"Let's get out of here," he whispered, needing to get her alone so he could explore the feelings she aroused in him.

"I'll follow you," Brad said as he gathered their clothes.

Jack smoothed Jennifer's hair from her forehead and helped her off his lap. With Jennifer pulling her cheerleading outfit back on, Jack turned his attention to his friend. Jack slapped Brad on the shoulder and said, "Not this time."

Brad angled his head, assessing him. "What's gotten into you, pal?"

Jack shrugged. "I don't know, but when I figure it out I'll let you know." What he did know was that there was something undeniably soft and sweet about Jennifer and he no longer wanted to share her with anyone, not even his best friend.

"Oh, fuck, you've got it bad."

Ignoring his friend's sudden epiphany, Jack pulled on his clothes and then wrapped his arm around Jennifer's waist, anchoring her body to his.

Just then Miranda stepped up to Brad, slipped her arm though his and said, "Come on, Brad. Let's get a drink."

Knowing his friend was in good hands, Jack turned his attention to Jennifer. Grin wicked, he said, "My place or yours."

*My place or yours.*

Standing there radiating contentment after the most incredible sex of her life, Jennifer rolled her eyes. "That has to be the worst pickup line ever."

Jack gave her a sexy, lopsided smile and lowered his voice. "I think we're past pickup lines, don't you?"

She smiled, astonished at the tenderness in his tone. "Yes, I believe we are," she admitted honestly.

As Jennifer let her glance linger on his handsome face, it occurred to her that Sam was right. Jack really was one of the good guys—a man she wasn't quite ready to walk away from. He'd put her needs and desires first tonight, taking his time to pleasure her and allowing her to live out a few of her wild fantasies. What girl in her right mind would walk away from that?

Knowing she was far from ready to let this night end, she coiled her fingers through his and said, "Let's go to my place." She wanted to invite him into her condo, her life, to learn more about him and see if there could be more between them.

A short while later they made their way to her complex. Once inside she slipped out of her cheerleading outfit and into a soft robe, then she went to work on pouring them each a glass of wine.

"Let's get comfortable," she said, giving him a wink. "And then I want to hear firsthand all about these libido research projects you're involved in." With a nod of her head, she gestured for Jack to follow her into her small living room, where books and articles were strewn across her sofa. Jack picked up the books to clear a spot. When he read the title of her textbook he glanced at her.

"So you really are studying psychology, then?"

She nodded.

"When I Googled you I only found links to Peaches."

Jennifer laughed. "I was wondering if you would Google me."

"Of course I Googled you." He cocked his head and studied her. After a long thoughtful moment he said, "But you knew I would, didn't you?"

She gave a casual shrug. "I guess so."

Jack stepped closer, crowding her, overwhelming her with his enticing scent. "And you knew what I'd find, didn't you?"

She nodded, and gave him a sheepish look.

"You're not really Peaches, are you?"

She shook her head. "No."

"I didn't think so. So what's going on, Jennifer? Why the act? Not that I didn't appreciate it, mind you," he said, a sexy grin curling up his lips and warming her all over.

Feeling very close to him and wanting to share another side of herself, a side that she'd never shared with anyone before, she went on to explain, "You see, I wanted to explore one of my fantasies, and the second I set eyes on you, I knew you were the guy I wanted to explore them with. I wanted to step into the role of Peaches, and just let my inhibitions go."

"Lucky me." He took the wine from her hand and placed both their glasses on the side table. Wrapping his arms around her waist, he pulled her in tight. "Because I do love Peaches."

Jennifer ran her thumb over his sensuous mouth, remembering the way those lips felt on her body. "And then not only did you fulfill one of my fantasies, you fulfilled two," she said, thinking about how delicious it was to bring a second guy into the mix.

A low chuckle rumbled in his throat. "I do what I

can." Taking her by surprise, his mood changed quickly. He furrowed his brow, his eyes turned serious. "Only problem is I don't want to share you with anyone. I want you all to myself."

Her heart did a little flip and her pulse leaped with excitement. "You do?"

He tucked a strand of hair behind her ear, drew a deep breath, and let it out slowly. "Yeah, I've never been exclusive before, but sweetheart, you have me doing all kinds of things I've never done before."

Her grin widened. "And you have me doing all kinds of things I've never done before."

That brought a huge smile to his face. "So tell me. Have you fulfilled all your fantasies, or do you have any more that I should know about."

She stood, grabbed his hand and guided him to her bedroom. "Maybe instead of telling you, I'd rather show you."

His glance went from her to her queen-sized bed. He arched a brow. "Oh yeah?"

She pushed him backward until his knees hit the bed. Another little push had him sprawled out before her. "Yeah," she said, reaching into her nightstand to pull out a flogger. A sexy little toy she'd purchased at a Pleasure Party, but had yet to try out. She slapped it against her palm.

Jack's eyes widened. "What the hell do you plan on doing with that, Jennifer?"

She gave him a devious grin, stepped into her roll, and said, "Jennifer? Who the hell is Jennifer? My name is Peaches."

CATHRYN FOX graduated from university with a Bachelor of Business degree, majoring in accounting and economics. Shortly into her career Cathryn quickly figured out that the corporate life wasn't for her. Needing an outlet for her creative energy, Cathryn turned in her briefcase and calculator and began writing erotic romance full-time. Cathryn enjoys writing dark paranormals and light contemporaries.

# Indecent Exposure

## Delilah Devlin

# One

*Twelve years earlier . . .*

*Dalton McDonough, you don't know it yet—hell, you don't even know me—but one day your fine ass is gonna be mine!*

A blush heated Harmony Wilkins's cheeks at the crudeness of the thought, but there you had it. When it came to Dalton, all the rules she'd been taught about being a good girl flew out the window.

Lord, he was a temptation—an obsession she couldn't shake. That she wasn't alone in mooning over the handsome high school senior didn't help one bit. There was something special about the strong curve of his jaw, the jut of his high cheekbones, and the deep mysterious set of his brown eyes. Add those characteristics to the rest

of the package—tall, lean frame and wavy dark hair—
and every girl in a tri-county area between the age of five
and ninety-five couldn't help but sigh and wonder what it
would be like to be the center of his undivided attention.

Only most girls didn't do any more than that—sigh
and wonder. Harmony, however, wasn't the kind to leave
matters to fate. Somehow, someday, Dalton would be
hers. All she needed to move things along a little quicker
was information. Being a studious sort, she'd decided
that winning Dalton wasn't any different than any other
goal she'd achieved. She just needed to know more about
him. Figure out his likes and dislikes.

Find the one thing that might spark his interest . . .
in her.

And studying up on Dalton meant she had to take a
few risks, because what she needed to know couldn't be
found in any textbook or *Cosmo* magazine article. Which
was why she was sneaking through the dark, risking her
reputation and her parents' trust. Then again, her parents probably wouldn't care, they'd been shouting at each
other so much lately.

Careful not to let the gate slam shut behind her, she
crept silently into Dalton's backyard, skirting the flag-
stones surrounding the pool, keeping to the soft, mani-
cured lawn to muffle her footfalls until she reached the
French doors outside his bedroom.

Seeking the shadows hugging the side of his house,
she hid behind the tall winterberry bush and peered
inside. She brushed away the niggling guilt she felt for
spying on the object of her affections. Suppressed the

unease that any night now, someone would see her stealing out of her bedroom window. But a desperate longing filled Harmony with a sense of purpose that pretty much wiped out every lick o' sense she'd inherited from her schoolteacher dad.

During the past week of her stealth campaign, she'd learned some pretty interesting things about the quiet, intensely private boy.

Like Dalton slept in the nude.

She knew because Tuesday she'd peeked through the glass and seen a pale buttock exposed beneath the edge of the blue sheet tangled around his legs. She wasn't sure how useful that piece of information might be, but she'd learned how long she could go without breathing and not pass out.

She'd studied the odd items strewn around his room and discovered he was a Spurs fan. On Wednesday, she'd begged her mother to buy her a Spurs T-shirt, which she wore on Spirit Day at school. *Check*.

The numchucks hanging from a peg on the wall and the poster of Chuck Norris tacked to his closet door indicated an interest in martial arts. She'd enrolled in a karate class just yesterday afternoon. *Check*.

Yet, he'd passed her in the hall this morning, giving her bright silver and black tee and Aikido Academy sports bag barely a passing glance. That Dalton still didn't seem to know she existed didn't discourage her.

If Harmony was anything, she was persistent.

As she eased over to peek into his bedroom, she blinked, surprised to find light beaming from the hallway and his bed empty. She'd double-checked the driveway as she'd sneaked past to make sure his daddy's patrol car wasn't parked outside. Dalton was still awake, which was odd. All the football players had a curfew and followed Coach Hess's rules to a T. None more religiously than their starring quarterback.

After all, Friday night football was God in Satisfaction, Texas.

Then she heard the faint giggle coming from deep inside the house. A high-pitched whinny she'd recognize anywhere. Cindy Niedermeyer. A cheerleader whose coltish long legs and sprouting breasts made her the "the Girl Most Likely to Score."

Damn. With her stomach knotting, Harmony bit her lip and tried to stem her disappointment, reminding herself Cindy tended to string several boys along at the same time. Her being here didn't mean she'd set her sights for very long on Dalton.

Just when Harmony had decided to slip away, Cindy entered the bedroom, walking backward with Dalton pressed so close one leg slipped between hers, rubbing dangerously high. His hands clutched her jeans-clad bottom so hard, his knuckles whitened as they kneaded and rocked her hips against his.

Harmony froze, knowing what was going to happen next. She'd aced health class and read enough of her mama's romance novels to know exactly where this was heading. She might be the only eighteen-year-old virgin left in the state of Texas, but it wasn't because she wasn't curious or hadn't ever experienced desire.

Now, she had a choice to make. Do the decent thing and leave them to their play in private . . . or stay and possibly learn a little something more than she'd anticipated.

As she watched them grope each other's bodies, a twisting, desperate longing burned the back of her throat and tensed her belly. She didn't really understand what she was feeling, only knew she needed something only Dalton could provide. So there she stood, hiding in the darkness, watching him hold another girl in his arms.

When Cindy pushed away and began to tear at Dalton's clothes, any reluctance to stay and watch melted away. Harmony's gaze clung hungrily to Dalton's lean, muscled chest and ridged abdomen.

When Cindy's fingers walked south, Dalton's breath hissed out and Harmony's caught and held. Cindy's pink-tipped nails flicked the button at the waistband of his jeans then slowly slid down the zipper.

The expression on Dalton's face when her long slender fingers dipped inside his pants fascinated Harmony. The painful longing reflected there matched her feelings exactly.

Dalton muttered and pressed Cindy further into his room, and they turned toward the bed. That was when Harmony got a good look at exactly what Cindy held. Her fingers smoothed up and down a long column of satiny flesh.

Now, Harmony knew a man's private part expanded quite a bit as he grew excited. She'd read all about it, seen pictures of it, and had even seen Bobby Camacho's shorts tented when the girls' track team ran circles around the football field. Still, she wasn't prepared for the sight of what made Dalton most assuredly male.

Long enough that Cindy could have used both hands and still left an inch or two of tawny flesh exposed, Dalton's "manhood" was capped with a round blunt head that looked oddly soft and vulnerable. When Cindy laughed and sank slowly to her knees, Harmony's eyes widened.

"Yes. Oh God, yes," Dalton murmured. His fingers threaded through Cindy's long blond hair as he centered her between his legs and pulsed his hips forward then back, slipping his sex between her lips and thrusting so deep Harmony was sure the girl would choke.

Instead, Cindy only moaned and started to bob her head, her lips stretching around his shaft, shadows deepening the hollows of her cheeks as she used her mouth to pleasure him—oh, and pleasure him she did!

Dalton's eyes burned as he watched Cindy. His hard-edged cheeks reddened and his body tightened as he stroked in and out. The heat in his expression told Harmony just how incredibly wonderful he felt at that moment.

The beauty of his pleasure warmed her to her toes, and a tingling heat started in her breasts. She couldn't be jealous of Cindy at the moment, couldn't resent the slutty blonde's presence in Dalton's room, because, at last, Harmony had found the key to unlock Dalton's interest, if not his heart.

She wasn't sure how she'd do it, but she was going to

study up. Become the absolute best at giving Dalton that toe-curling pleasure.

In the meantime, Cindy drew off and shook her hair behind her, then sat back on her heels and tugged her shirt over her head.

Dalton's eyes narrowed as he stared at her breasts, and something a little frightening, and devastatingly more intense, entered his expression. He reached down, gripped Cindy beneath her arms and pulled her up. His kiss devoured her mouth and once again, he was walking her backward until her knees met the edge of his bed.

Harmony's breaths grew shallow and heat pooled between her legs.

Cindy broke the kiss, sat, and unbuttoned her jeans.

Dalton grabbed the bottom hem and stripped the jeans down her long legs. Then he pressed her to lie back. What he did next, shocked Harmony to her toes, and her body reacted with a flush of heat and a rush of moisture that taught her another lesson about what desire can do to a woman's body.

Lord, it was hot! Sweat beaded on her upper lip, and she sucked it into her mouth as she strained to get a better look at Dalton bent over the juncture of Cindy's thighs. She bit her lip and eased over a little more, lifting one leg to rest her foot on the water spigot beside the door for balance.

Suddenly, Dalton hauled himself up and over Cindy who welcomed him with an eager embrace. Harmony watched, enraptured by the play of muscle along Dalton's broad shoulders and back as he crawled over the other girl. Dalton rose on his arms and all the muscles from his back to his hips tensed.

Harmony couldn't breathe . . . had to get a better look. She leaned closer to the glass, not wanting to miss a thing, enthralled with the flex of his round buttocks exposed just above the edge of the jeans he hadn't bothered removing.

She stepped harder on the spigot to follow the couple's journey into a rapture she was quickly getting a glimmer of, when her foot slipped. The spigot spat water in a noisy, harsh gurgle.

Harmony froze as Dalton's head jerked back and his glance sliced to the French doors. She ducked to the side and silently cursed. In the distance, she heard something else—the low squalling whine of a siren.

Like a deer in the headlights, Harmony's eyes blinked wide while her heart thudded hard against her chest. He hadn't seen her. The siren couldn't have a thing to do with her.

Dalton cursed, hauled himself off a dazed Cindy, and zipped his pants as he stomped toward the door.

Harmony backed away, her mind racing. What would Dalton think about her now? If he found her peeping through his door, she'd definitely have his attention.

And holy hell, that siren seemed a lot closer now. Lord, how would she explain this to her parents? She'd be grounded for a month and her whole senior year would be tainted with the humiliation. Half her class would think she was a perv, the other—the female half—would probably get why she did what she did, but the whispers would never stop.

With a wild-eyed glance around the dark yard, Harmony did the only thing a girl about to be exposed as moon-eyed fool could do. She took her destiny in her hands and twisted it deftly in another direction.

She ripped her T-shirt over her head, dropped her shorts, and dove naked into the pool.

*Present day* . . .

Dalton cut his cruiser's lights as soon as he saw the little red Miata parked in the judge's driveway. He recognized it as the same sassy little car parked outside the court-house that morning.

After radioing to the dispatcher, he grabbed his flash-light and headed to the backyard. He had a good idea where their "burglar" would be. Sure enough, as soon as he rounded the corner of the house he found her, arms stretched in a lazy backstroke, her body nicely outlined by the recessed lighting rimming the bottom of the pool.

Flicking off the flashlight, he knelt beside the water and waited patiently for Harmony to finish her lap, en-joying the sight of her sleek, toned frame as she glided to the edge of the pool. Her body hadn't filled out all that much since high school, but her slender curves were still all woman. Dusky nipples drawn into tight little buds rode the crests of shapely little breasts. He forced his gaze away from the thatch of dark hair between her legs.

However much he enjoyed the sight, he had a job to do. Tonight was just one of the perks.

As her hand grabbed the edge of the pavement to stop her momentum, she stared up at him from upside down, a slight defiant smile curving her full lips.

He pointed to the steps. "I'll wait 'til you're dressed."

Harmony kept floating and set her lips into a pout. "Sheriff, you sure know how to suck the fun out of a little civil disobedience."

Dalton felt his mouth stretch into a grin as he shook his head. "Did you know the judge was out of town?"

One dark brow rose. "Why, of course. He mentioned it just as he was rendering his judgment against me. Said something like, 'Gotta fishing trip to make. Thanks for givin' me something to talk about, little girl.'" Her nose wrinkled. "I hate it when he calls me that."

"So, this was just for you? A little revenge?"

"No, Sheriff. It was for you," she said, and turned, giving him a flash of her pale bottom before pushing off the side of the pool for another lap.

Dalton grew still, his eyes narrowing on Harmony Wilkins. The last time he'd seen her naked and wet, his dad was wrapping a towel around her shivering body and leading her back to her home, all the while reading her the riot act. Dalton had been grateful for the few minutes of reprieve to hustle Cindy Niedermeyer into her clothes and out the back door, but he'd never forgotten the stubborn set of Harmony's shoulders or the pink blush that stained her cheeks and the tops of her tiny breasts as she'd been led away.

He'd have thought the humiliation of that first charge of indecent exposure would have been enough to teach her a lesson.

Apparently not. Nor the second or third.

Dalton lifted his cowboy hat and raked his fingers through his hair. Harmony had caused quite a stir in their high school all those years ago. Her arrest had only been the beginning of her high jinks. It seemed every time he turned around she was sitting outside the principal's office, her chin high, a smile pasted on her lips.

It had taken finding her stark-ass naked in his pool for him to finally remember her name, but she'd earned a new one that followed her into the pages of yearbook immortality—Trouble.

After graduation, she'd disappeared. Left for college, some said. Met a bad end, his father believed. Dalton had never forgotten her. Every time he looked at his dad's pool, he remembered that even after getting his satisfaction with Cindy, he'd wanted to slide right into Harmony's wet, sleek body.

Still did, if the tightening in his balls was any indication.

She had to be yanking his chain about being here for him. Testing him, maybe. Or just trying to get out of another arrest. He wondered how far she was willing to go.

Dalton didn't move from his spot beside the pool, deciding to wait until she turned into a prune. If she didn't mind him looking, he wouldn't pretend to be a gentleman and find somewhere else to pin his gaze.

The sight of Harmony's firm little ass drew him—all the way up the pool. He prepared for disappointment when she made the return trip, but she flipped over, letting him watch her breasts ride above the surface of the water, her nipples tight and dimpled. The sight of the dark hair between her legs had him gnashing his teeth by the time she stopped again, just below him.

Dalton tried to keep his gaze locked with hers, but her lips parted, her breaths panted slightly, which lifted her chest and drew his gaze down her length again. He cleared his throat. "I'm still waiting."

A dimple deepened in one cheek. "Why don't you come and get me?"

"You want me to haul you out of the water?"

"Ooh!" she said, shivering. "Then you'd have to touch me, but I'm all wet and wiggly. What do you think you'll grab first?"

Dalton stared and felt heat rising to stain his cheeks. No woman he barely knew ever talked to him like that. Most were a bit intimidated by the uniform. "I'm still gonna arrest you."

"Did I offend anyone? Did I damage anything?"

"You trespassed."

"You always follow the rules?"

"It's my job."

Her dark lashes swept down, and then she gave him another flirty glance. "Ever do anything naughty, just 'cause you couldn't resist the urge?"

"Of course."

"Then be naughty with me. Here."

Drawing a deep breath, he ground his teeth. "The judge has motion detectors set around the house. You set off a silent alarm. You must have been trying to get inside the house."

"I saw the Brinks sign and rattled a window. I knew you'd come."

"Now, I know you're playing me. I'm not the only officer on call."

"But I knew you'd make it your business to check out the judge's house. Personally."

"What if I hadn't been alone?"

A wicked smile stretched her lush lips. "Then this would be twice as interestin', don't you think?"

Dalton snorted. "You gonna add to your crimes, sweetheart? I'm sure there's a law on the books for that sort of thing—this is the Bible Belt."

Her eyelids dipped again and she sank in the water, coming up to rest her arms on the pavement and unfortunately cutting off his view of her most interesting parts. Her gaze slowly rose to meet his and Dalton felt his chest tighten. With her dark hair slicked back, her large brown eyes dominated her face. Gone was the defiance, and in its place was a vulnerability he'd never seen. She looked incredibly young . . . and sweet.

Had to be an act.

"Why'd you come back to this little town, Harmony?"

She wrinkled her nose, but her eyes glinted with added moisture. "For a little . . . satisfaction?"

"Cut the crap. Tell me straight, or I will haul you out of that pool and take your naked ass to jail."

She reached up and smoothed one hand over her hair, her gaze falling away. "I came back because I had a confession to make. To you."

"A confession, you say?" He took a deep breath and pretended an irritation he was far from feeling. Fact was, she amused him. "All right," he ground out. "I'm game."

Her gaze almost pleading when it met his, she whispered, "That night . . . at your daddy's house, when I was in the pool . . . remember it?"

"Think I could ever forget?" he said, his own voice softening.

"I wasn't there to skinny-dip."

"What were you doing, Harmony?" he asked, although he thought he might already know.

"I was spying on you. I saw you with Cindy and I couldn't stop," she said in a breathless rush. "I stepped on the spigot and had to do something. You're dad was pulling up, you had jumped out of bed—I couldn't think of anything else to do."

"So you caught me screwing Cindy. What were you doing outside my door in the first place?"

"I wanted you. So I got it in my head I needed to know everything about you."

"You do it more than once?"

Her cheeks glowed with a pretty blush. "I was pretty ashamed. More afraid of people finding out why I was there than the fact I jumped into your pool naked."

"So you've carried this guilt around inside you all this while and had to come back to 'fess up now?" he asked softly.

She nodded, her gaze growing just a little too watchful. "Bullshit."

Her eyes rolled and she drew an exasperated breath. "All right. I came back to check on my mom's old house. It's a rental now. I've been painting and cleaning. Decided to take a break and laid down outside on a towel."

Dalton lifted one eyebrow, telling her he was ready for the rest. "Now we're back to Miz Murtry."

"Yeah, the old biddy filed a damn police report. For indecent exposure! Can you believe that?"

"You were naked," he said, keeping his voice even and enjoying the outrage sparkling in her eyes.

"In my own backyard—with a six-foot privacy fence all around it!"

He couldn't help goading her just a bit more. "Miz Murtry can't be over five foot two."

Her scowl nearly drew her dark, finely arched eyebrows together. "The old biddy was spying on me through a knothole!"

"So, you were arrested again."

"What is it with this town and clothing? Couldn't I have been ticketed? Isn't it basically a misdemeanor, anyway?"

"This is a conservative little town, and you knew before you came here people would be waiting for you to step over the line. So what does this have to do with me?"

She blew out a breath and the scowl deepened. "I saw you today. At the courthouse. Wearing your shades and looking so damn smug when I walked into court."

"I didn't stay to gloat. Hardly even noticed you were there." *Liar, liar . . .*

"I know. But it got me to thinking. I made myself a promise all those years ago, when I was watching you get nasty with Cindy Niedermeyer."

At last, he thought she might be telling the truth. "What promise was that?"

She swallowed hard and lifted her chin higher. "That I'd have you—have some of what you gave Cindy Niedermeyer."

Dalton's trousers suddenly felt too tight, but he was damned if he'd adjust himself now with her wide eyes staring up at him and her teeth worrying her bottom lip. She'd surprised him. What she'd said took courage.

Still, he wasn't about to let her get hold of the reins just yet. "Damn. You couldn't have thought of any better way to ask a man out?"

"Oh, I don't want a date, Sheriff McDonough," she said, her voice sliding into a sexy drawl. "I wanna fuck you raw. Scratch an itch I've had since I was a teenager." She tilted her head to the side. "So, what do you say?"

*Damn.* He sucked in a slow breath, leaned close to her slowly curving lips, and whispered, "I'd say . . . you're under arrest. Now, get your ass out of that pool."

# Two

Harmony clamped her mouth shut and glared. *Sonof-abitch!* She thought she had him. Thought their sexy little exchange was his brand of foreplay. His body looked so hard he could have pounded nails with his thighs. Guess he needed all that muscle to substitute for his teeny-weeny brain!

She'd watched him watching her all the way up and down the pool, felt excitement tingling in her breasts and pussy. Thought she'd seen it building in him, too, the way his eyes glittered and his breath sucked and gusted at all the appropriate moments.

No way in hell he didn't feel the same damn way! All hot and bothered and so horny she thought she'd die if he didn't take her now.

Or had she just made a complete fool of herself? For

all she knew, he and Cindy BJ still played slap and tickle games every Friday night.

"Stop wastin' time. I'm gonna give you to the count of five—"

"I'm not a child."

"Then quit acting like you're still in high school. Get out of the water."

If she hadn't been bobbing, she would have flounced her way back to the steps, she was so angry—with herself for being a fool and thinking he might want a go at her after all these years—and at him for being such a serious prick.

The idea had come to her after she'd seen him in court. She thought for sure his gaze had followed her behind those dark sunglasses. Past history told her he only seemed to notice her when she misbehaved. All she wanted to do was scratch an ancient itch—one she thought she'd left behind when she brushed the dust of this hick town off her shoes after her parents' divorce.

Harmony walked quickly up the steps, excruciatingly conscious of the fact he could now closely examine every part of her body. Why she grew embarrassed now, she didn't know. She'd eagerly anticipated his attention when she'd slipped out of her clothes preparing for her swim, practically laid herself and her modesty on a silver platter for him to gobble up. Too bad he was too uptight to take a bite.

She'd have bet half a year's pay he could make a meal of a woman's pussy—lick her up and down 'til the only name she could recall started with an "O" and ended with "God."

Now, she hoped she could get dressed quickly before the pool water dried on her skin and left only the telltale trickle of excitement to slick her thighs. She gave him a blistering stare as she passed him and turned away to reach for the clothing she'd thrown over a lounge chair.

"Not so fast," he said, his voice coming from so close behind her she gasped because she hadn't realized he'd moved.

"I'm not makin' a run for it, Sheriff," she said, her breath coming faster as she noted the heat radiating from his body. "I'm just getting my clothes."

"Did I say you could get dressed?"

*Kinky much, Sheriff?* She froze, wondering if she'd won, after all. Without looking back, she squared her shoulders. "What do you want from me?" she asked, hoping he'd show her any minute now.

"I want your hands behind your back."

"What?"

His hand snagged one of hers, and something hard and cold slipped around her wrist. Before she could pull away, he'd clamped the second steel handcuff around her other wrist.

"Now, how am I supposed to get dressed?"

"You can figure that out in the back of my squad car."

"You sonofabitch!" She tried to jerk away from him, but he hauled her back against his body. Then a foot nudged one of her feet, shoving it to widen her stance, which put her off balance, and she leaned back to steady herself. Right against his rock-solid chest.

"Gonna frisk me?" she asked, suddenly breathless. "I don't mind."

"Easy now. I wouldn't want you to hurt yourself," he said softly, then with one hand pulling the chain between the cuffs, he reached around her and grabbed her clothing, his long, hard body sliding against her bottom and the backs of her thighs.

Harmony's wet skin clung to his clothing as he slid against her, scraping deliciously. Her nipples spiked impossibly longer.

When he straightened, he gave her a look completely wiped clean of any emotion or interest. "Now, let's get out of here—and behave yourself."

Dalton led her around the house and down the driveway to his squad car, opened the back door, and cupped the top of her head as she slid onto the warm backseat. After he wrestled the seat belt around her, his hands gliding impersonally over her naked flesh, he tossed her clothing in beside her.

"I can't believe this," she muttered, hunching low after he'd pulled onto the street.

"Me neither," Dalton said, seeming distant behind the wire cage separating them. "Been an interestin' night. Not the sort I'd expect around here."

"Glad I could provide the entertainment," she bit out.

They rode in silence for few moments, and Harmony sank back against the seat, wondering how she'd managed to make such a total screwup of this night.

"Were you tellin' me the truth?"

She shook her head to clear her thoughts. "Which part?"

"About comin' out here . . . for me."

Harmony closed her eyes, wishing she could drop through the floor of the car. *Yeah, I had to go and tell him that, didn't I?* "Just chalk it up to my bad judgment. What are you going to do? Put it in your report?" When he didn't answer, she shifted to look out the window. "I think you missed your turn."

The silence stretched and Harmony straightened. Dalton ignored the turnoff for the station as well as the road leading to her house. "What the hell?"

Maybe she'd put too much faith in the fact he was the town's sheriff. She was trussed like a turkey, completely defenseless. He could do anything he wanted.

Suddenly, she relaxed. Dalton didn't have a mean streak—he had a mile-wide wicked sense of humor. "You changed your mind."

His gaze locked with hers in the rearview mirror. "I'm thinkin' someone needs to teach you a lesson."

Warmth swept over her skin, calming the gooseflesh that had risen in the air-conditioned air. "You the man to do it?" she drawled.

"Guess we'll know come mornin'."

Her dejection melted away beneath the promise in his deepening voice. "These cuffs aren't very comfortable," she said softly.

"Tough. What were you thinking, anyway?"

"That you'd see me naked and not be able to resist me," she quipped, feeling happier by the second.

"You're not that cute."

"Ouch! That hurt," she said, scrunching her nose at him.

"Not Cindy-cute, anyway. She still is, by the way," he continued, so casually she started to fume again.

"No backpedaling now. So, I'm not your usual type, but you won't throw up?"

"You always this prickly?"

"Yeah."

"Must be hell on men."

She shrugged, not particularly caring whether he saw her response or not. *So he doesn't like the way I look?*

"You're different. I don't think a guy would get too bored looking at you."

"Gee thanks. I won't take that as a compliment." She sighed, some of her excitement fading. "So what's gonna happen?"

"Depends on you."

"You're still leaving me a choice?"

"Disappointed? You want me to choose?"

Well, she did have this list of wild-assed fantasies. . . "Maybe the first time, I'll let you choose."

"The first time?"

"Well, you're not just gonna do me and throw me out the door . . . are you?"

"Not wrapped too tight, are you?"

"You saying I'm nuts? Or stupid?"

He snorted.

"I'm really beginning to hate that sound." Only she really didn't. It was so masculine it had her squirming on her seat, wondering if she'd leave a wet spot on the hot vinyl beneath her bottom.

"How'd you manage to live this long?"

"I only act this way here. Satisfaction just makes me—"

"Itch?"

"Something like that. I never fit in."

"And you do . . . back in Houston?"

"You know where I'm living?"

"Your address was in the police report."

"Oh. Yeah, I live a boring life there, all right. No ex-quarterbacks tempting me out of my mind."

His head shook. "You always say exactly what you're thinking?"

"I'm not out to impress you."

"Baby, I'm mighty impressed." His gaze met hers in the mirror. His eyes wrinkled at the corners.

Harmony couldn't help but smile back. "Glad you finally noticed."

Dalton pulled into a driveway, coming to a halt in front of a white limestone house at the end of a cul-de-sac.

He cut the ignition and turned to give her a quizzical stare through the wire. "Whoever thought to name you Harmony, anyway? Must have been wishful thinkin'."

Harmony gave him a withering glance, but Dalton just grinned as he got out of the car and escorted her up the sidewalk and through his front door. Didn't the man know there'd be consequences for continually insulting her? If he thought for one minute she'd be obliging him with anything like what Cindy had given him—

"Quit thinking so hard," he said, as he turned the key in the lock. "Those wrinkles won't iron out."

"I don't know how I ever thought you were the nice, quiet type," she grumbled, as he opened the door and pushed her inside. "And aren't you just a little bit worried your neighbors might see you leading a naked woman into your house?"

"What would they do? Call the Sheriff?" He closed the door behind them and leaned against it, his hands sliding into his pants pockets. "Why are you so upset? Gettin' naked's your MO."

"Just 'cause I streaked the homecoming game—"

"And left your blinds open every night—"

Her lips slid into a sly smile. "You watched me undress?"

"I watched you do a whole lot more than just take off your clothes."

Her eyes rounded as she grinned. "So, who's the Peeping Tom now?"

"I didn't trespass," he said, one wicked brow rising, "and seems like you wanted me to watch or you wouldn't have kept the light on."

"So why didn't you take me up on my invitation?"

"Maybe I was scared?"

She snorted this time and realized she'd never had so much fun baiting a man. "You know, I'm still wearing these damn handcuffs . . ."

"Your shoulders startin' to ache?"

She nodded, stubbing her toe into his deep beige carpet.

"Come here." He brought a little key out of his pocket. When she started to turn away, he shook his head. "Just come closer. I'll reach around you."

Never a girl to miss a chance at grabbing the gold ring, she stepped forward, setting her feet down on the outside of his and leaned so close her nipples scraped his starched shirt. "Close enough now?"

His gaze never left hers as he smoothed his hands down her arms. The moment the cuffs fell away, she moaned.

"Feel better?" he asked, his lips an inch from hers, his hands gliding up and down her arms in a soothing massage.

"*Uh-huh,*" she murmured, waiting for him to close the distance between them.

His hands lowered and cupped her buttocks then one lifted and gave her a stinging slap.

"What was that for?" she gasped.

"I did promise punishment."

She grinned and settled heavier against him, then rose on her toes to bump his cowboy hat and lift it with her head to get closer. "Do it again. I've been a bad, bad girl."

"I bet you have." His mouth swooped down and covered hers, his lips opening, molding hers as his head circled. His hands squeezed her bottom, pulling her hips hard against him.

Harmony drowned in his kiss. His lips were warm and suctioned softly against hers, the circling motion drugging her. So dizzy she had to clutch his shoulders for balance, she followed him as he sank against the door, rubbing her nipples on the stiff fabric of his shirt. She wanted more of a taste and plunged her tongue between his lips, only to groan when he sucked it. God, she wanted that mouth suctioning her nipples with the same sweet diligence he paid her lips and tongue.

Not long on patience, she continued rubbing on him like a kitten and widened her stance, tilting to push her pussy against the thick ridge building at the front of his trousers. Then she tipped his hat off his head and thrust her fingers through his thick, wavy hair.

Dalton groaned and reached lower to wrap his fingers around her thighs and lift her against his body.

Harmony quickly twined her legs around his narrow waist, not letting him break the kiss as he headed deeper into the house. Each step scraped his cock against her pussy. She squeezed her legs around him, rolled her hips to tell him how excited she was, and sucked his tongue deep into her mouth.

By the time they fell onto his mattress, she was ready to explode.

He reared up and began to unbutton his shirt, but she pushed his hands away and tore at them. First the shirt, then the Kevlar vest. His T-shirt landed on the top of the stack beside the bed before he tried to pull her thighs down from his waist.

"No!"

"Let me get my pants off—"

"Too long," she panted, her fingers flying at his buckle. She had him unbuttoned, unzipped, and free before the next steamy breath.

His arms hooked under her thighs and shoved them against her chest. Then he nudged his cock against her, found her opening, and slammed home.

"Sweet Jesus!" she cried out, her back arching off the bed.

"Should have let me go slow," he rasped, leaning against her thighs to rest his forehead on hers.

"Are you kidding me?"

"Too fast. Should have let me get you ready."

"You're not feeling how ready I am? I'm so wet, so hot . . . *Dammit, Dalton, move!*"

A husky bark of laughter ended on a groan when she mashed her mouth against his.

Dalton didn't need a second reassurance. He lifted his hips and slammed deep inside her again, beginning a pounding that wasn't graceful or controlled. All Harmony could do was grab the covers at her sides and hold on for dear life, while the boy . . . *God no* . . . the man she'd dreamed of all these years fucked her like a wild thing.

Dalton's arms strained, veins riding the tops of his muscles. His face tightened into a frightening mask, reddening, his lips drawing away from his clenched teeth. His hard abdomen felt like a ridged oak plank banging the back of her legs—and his cock—*holy shit!*

"Sweet Jesus!" she cried out.

He shafted her, driving faster, harder, grunting with the effort, until at last his breath hissed between his teeth, followed by a low, guttural groan as his hips slowed, rocking her, bumping her clumsily while come bathed her channel and he rode the last wave of his orgasm.

When he finally stopped, his eyes opened and his expression relaxed into regret. He slumped against her. "Damn, Harmony. Sorry."

His arms released her legs, and she slid them down his body to rest alongside his. Her heart still raced, but her breaths were evening. "Don't worry about it. I'm proud as punch I got you so hot and bothered you decided to ride that bronc without me."

"Cut the cowboy talk," he mumbled. "You sound ridiculous."

"Sore because I didn't come?"

"No, mad at myself. Although I don't know why—it's your own damn fault."

"Turned you on, watching my ass in that pool?"

"And your tits and sweet little pussy."

She slapped his arm.

"What do you want me to call them?"

"Guess those names will do just fine," she grumbled, "so long as you're planning on getting to work on them sometime soon."

"Just let me catch my breath." His forehead snuggled into the corner of her neck. His sigh blew warm against her skin. "Nice."

"Glad you're all comfy."

His chest shook, and she rolled her eyes, staring at the ceiling. Not exactly what she'd imagined, but she thought maybe male pride would be incentive enough to rouse him in a minute. Thinking she might hurry him along, she smoothed her hands up and down his slick back then curved them to follow the swell of his flexing buttocks.

Dalton jolted back, pulling his cock out and rolling away. "Shit! I forgot a condom." He sat on the side of the bed and raked a hand through his hair.

"Hey, come back here," she said, gliding a hand up and down his back. She couldn't stop touching him. "Too late now, anyway. 'Sides, I'm on the pill."

The scowl he shot her could have curdled milk. "You should be asking me how many partners I've had and whether I've seen the doctor lately."

"Okay, how many and have you seen the doctor?"

When he closed his eyes, she thought he might be counting to ten. "None lately, and yeah."

"Well, same here. Aren't we lucky?" She sat up and wrapped her arms low around his waist and tried to pull him closer, but he resisted. "Come back inside. I'm feeling a bit of a chill."

His scowl faded and another look, one more speculative, narrowed his eyes. "None lately? How come? Don't the men in Houston go for skinny-dippers?"

"I'll have you know I'm the model of propriety there. I live a very boring life."

"Then that's a damn shame," he said, turning to climb back over her. "And about to change, right now."

"Oh?" She reached between their bodies and wrapped her fingers around his semierect flesh. "Is Litt-o Dalton going to wake up and pway?"

His eyes narrowed. "Better let go right now."

So the man didn't like baby talk. "That sounded kinda ominous."

"Now that the fog has lifted—"

"You admitting you've been a little dense?"

"I'm admitting I could have fucked that knothole Miz Murtry peeped through you had me so tied up. It's hard for a man to think straight when a pretty girl's seducing him."

"So you think I'm pretty now?"

"I'll let you know once I have a closer look."

"When am I gonna get a closer look?" she said, eyeing his sagging blue jeans.

Dalton shook his head as though she'd said something he didn't understand. Then he lifted one foot at a time and pulled off his boots, chunking them into a corner along with his socks. Next, he stood and shoved down his pants. "Satisfied?"

"You know better than that," she said, wishing she didn't sound quite so out of breath, but damn, the man was fine!

He climbed back onto the bed, looking like a cougar on the prowl. With his fists planted on either side of her shoulders, he swooped down to kiss her, robbing her of the rest of her breath. When her fingers sank into his thick curls, he pulled back.

"I promised a closer look." Without warning, he scooted down her body. He plumped up one breast and scraped a fingernail over the tip. "Pretty, all right. Same color as a hound dog I had once." He ignored her gasp of mock outrage and latched onto the nipple. "Been . . . wondering how sweet . . . these are," he said between licks.

Harmony lay grinning at the ceiling. Who'd have thought

Dalton McDonough could be so much fun in bed? She grabbed his ears and steered him to the other breast.

"Bossy!"

"Damn straight. Now quit talkin' and get to work."

"Yes'm." His lips closed around the nipple and he sucked it hard into his mouth, teasing the tip with his tongue then chewing it tenderly.

Small, sensual lightning bolts shot straight south, and Harmony clamped her thighs hard around his midriff, loving what he was doing, but eager for that mouth to head to new territory. She was ready for some of what Cindy Niedermeyer had.

Threading her fingers in his hair, she pushed on his head, trying to give him the hint he should change course.

He mouthed her breast and came up for air. "Don't like what I'm doing, you can take over any time."

"I like it fine, but I need more."

"'More' usually means a woman's ready to be fucked."

"Damn, how'd you get so smart?"

"You're still the biggest smartass I ever met. You don't seem to understand I'm not through punishing you."

"This is punishment?"

"Haven't gotten serious about it yet. Thought I'd break you in easy."

"Are you planning to torture me?"

He fluttered his tongue against her nipple then looked up. "I'm gonna inch you toward heaven 'til you're beggin'."

Damn, she liked the way that sounded, especially delivered in that gravelly, growling tone. "Oh my," she sighed.

"Still want to take over?"

She shook her head, too excited to speak. Not wanting to alter his plans for her. She had to know what wickedness she inspired.

His hands landed on the mattress on either side of her body and he shoved himself downward again. He paused over her hips and glanced back up. "I don't care if you pull my hair."

The way he looked at her, his expression growing taut with need and his eyes darkening, had her bones melting and cream moistening her folds. "Am I going to want to pull your hair?"

"It's guaranteed." His lips and tongue glided down her belly while his hands pressed her thighs wide and up.

Harmony's breaths shortened then caught when he rimmed her belly button and pressed his tongue against the center. "Do you think it's a damn ignition switch?"

He bit her skin playfully, then moved lower still until he planted his elbows between her legs, spread her labia with his fingers and stared at her pussy.

Harmony reached for a pillow and stuffed it behind her head. "You just gonna look?"

"I'm waiting."

"For what? The second coming? I'm telling you it ain't happening until you do something."

"You blasphemous little thing." He leaned close and blew a stream of warm breath over her.

She couldn't help the little squeeze she gave that tightened her opening.

"Liked that, did you?"

"I'd like something coming up it even better."

"Any preferences?"

"I want what you gave Cindy Niedermeyer."

"That's been so long ago, how am I supposed to remember that? You'll have to remind me."

Remind him? Then he'd know it was burnished in her memory. Oh hell, didn't he already know? She cleared her throat. "You licked her and put your fingers inside her," she said, surprised at the hoarseness of her voice.

Dalton kissed her belly just above her mons. "That wasn't so hard, was it? Asking for what you want. I'd have thought a girl like you, one who always says exactly what she thinks, wouldn't have any trouble askin' a man to go down on her."

"I can't believe you talk so much. Don't men lose the ability to speak, go primal, when they're having sex?"

"Already done that."

"Oh yeah. You got yours," she said snidely.

"Harmony?" he said, stretching out her name in warning.

"Yes, Dalton?"

"I don't want to hear anything but pretty little sighs and moans for the next few minutes. Deal?"

"Deal," she said shakily.

Dalton squeezed the hood of her clitoris between his thumb and forefinger, and Harmony had no problem at all going "primal." If she'd had the breath, she would have warbled like Tarzan when Dalton bent and sucked her clit, swirling his tongue over it again and again until her hips rocked up and down and her cries grew ragged.

When two thick calloused fingers plunged into her vagina, she thought for sure she was seconds from exploding, but Dalton released her clit and held his fingers still inside her until she got her breathing back under control.

"Not nice . . . you almost had it," she rasped.

He kissed her inner thigh. "I know."

"Oh yeah . . . torture." Knowing he wasn't taking her anywhere in a hurry, she settled back on the bed and stretched one leg alongside his torso, teasing what she could reach with her toe while she fought for an even breath. "They teach you that at the Police Academy?"

"Nothing to do with the law, sweetheart. Might have to check the books again. Think I'm gonna break a few ordinances here before I'm through."

She felt a smile tug at her lips. "Good to know you're not completely by the books."

"Feeling better now?"

She raised her head to skewer him with a sharp glare.

"Guess so." He pulled his fingers out and spread her folds wider. Then he bent and licked her in broad strokes, lapping at her outer lips, pausing to nibble them, and then slipping between to tease the more delicate inner set. Using the flat of his tongue he stroked over her center, capturing the cream spilling from inside her.

With his gaze locked with hers, he plunged into her, which had her toes curling and her teeth gritting it felt so delicious. The motions, repeated endlessly, were almost soothing . . . if not for the increasing tension coiling tightly in her womb.

"How 'bout raising your knees again?" he murmured against her thigh.

"All right," she said, all the starch gone from her tone. In fact, she wasn't the least embarrassed to admit she sounded like an eager puppy. She bent her knees and placed her heels wide on the bed, adjusting them outward again when he insisted with his hands.

His licks lengthened, becoming long rasping glides from the bottom of her pussy to her clit, each lap starting lower until she grew restless because he approached "virgin" country.

"You want me to cry uncle? Because it won't happen," she warned him.

When the tip of his tongue grazed her little hole, she stifled a gasp and her back arched. His thumbs glided down and pressed apart her entrance, ratcheting up her tension and causing her thighs to tremble. She was so tight, so primed, she feared she'd start howling, so she bit her lip.

His tongue rimmed her.

"God, Dalton," she groaned, no longer trying for control. Her hips undulated and she lifted her feet off the mattress, straining to raise her hips higher against his wicked mouth. She needed more, needed penetration, needed him to stop playing with her and *fuck* her.

He accepted her invitation to explore, rubbing his mouth over her opening, and then slid a thumb through the moisture he'd left there, pushing inward.

Harmony stretched her back, turning her face into the pillow to muffle her cries as he slid inside her. The pressure burned. Her opening contracted hard around him, trying to reject him.

Dalton didn't stop at the first sign of resistance. He flexed his thumb, circled it, then withdrew a fraction of an inch and pushed inside again. Slowly, he eased past the tight little ring, pressed deeper, then retreated and came deeper inside again.

Harmony panted shallowly; her belly jumped; her whole body quivered. Her breaths came so chopped and shallow now, she thought she might faint before she came.

She reached down between her legs, threaded her fingers through his hair and pulled hard. "Please, Dalton. Please, I need more."

Dalton withdrew his thumb, reached up and kissed her pussy then hauled himself up to kneel beside her. "Turn around," he said, his voice thick and harsh. He held out his hand to help her rise.

She didn't know she needed the help until she was on her knees and trembling. So overcome, she crossed her arms over her breasts and pleaded with her eyes for him to end the game.

"To hell with that," he said, pulling her straight into his arms and crushing her against his chest.

Harmony straddled his thighs, whimpering now that she sensed he meant to finish it. With his cock straining against her tummy, she stared into his eyes, wishing she knew what he was thinking behind his taut features and hungry gaze.

## Three

*O*nce again, Dalton felt tightness invade his chest as he held Harmony close. Her liquid brown eyes were huge in her face. A pretty rosy blush stained her cheeks and the tips of her ears. The way she quivered in his arms made him feel . . . powerful . . . and damn lucky.

Her gaze clung to his. Her bottom lip trembled as a small, ragged gasp escaped. Her excitement thudded inside the chest snuggled up close to his. Swept clean of any hint of defiance or pluck, her expression reflected trust and incredible need.

Dalton noticed every little change—something new for him. Where women were concerned, the play was just that—playful, strenuous, and satisfying. With Harmony, it was getting complicated pretty damn quick.

Not in what she demanded, which wasn't much, but in what he wanted to give her—and especially, what he wanted to keep.

He hugged her closer to his chest. If he didn't get hold of his own rising passion fast, he'd leave her wanting again. That hadn't happened since he was a teenager—until tonight. Damned if he'd embarrass himself like that again.

"Dalton," she said, her voice soft and trembling. Her lips skimmed his shoulder and then her tongue glided up his neck to his chin.

With his hands cupping her firm ass, he lifted her, nudged his cock along her slit until he found her opening, then slowly lowered her down the length of his cock, grinding his teeth as he fought his own burning need.

A low, kittenish moan accompanied the downward glide, and Harmony's thighs shook as she lifted herself to bounce in sharp, sexy little motions that churned the heated moisture spilling from deep inside her. The friction she built between his cock and her snug channel had him cursing under his breath, because his control unraveled a little more with each thrust.

Her inner muscles tightened around his dick, rippling along his shaft. Her fingers curved into his shoulders, digging harder into his skin the closer she drew to her release.

Dalton slid one hand up her side to scrape his thumb on one tightly sprung nipple and leaned close to nuzzle her neck. His body grew rigid as he fought the urge to take control.

"Dalton," she gasped.

"Yeah, baby?" he gritted out.

"Please, please, I can't . . ." She leaned down to capture his lips then lifted her mouth, panting, "Please . . . I need you . . . to fuck me. Hard."

Like a spring-loaded trigger, Dalton shot upward, lifting her off his cock. "On your knees."

Breathless gasps shaking her tiny breasts, Harmony turned, letting him push her down on her hands as he thrust an arm beneath her belly to raise her hips. Before she'd even braced her weight, he spread her with his fingers and guided his cock into her pulsing opening, watching as her cunt swallowed him in one greedy gulp.

Then all thought blew his mind as he gripped the notches of her hips and powered his cock in and out, tunneling hard with each stroke, grinding in as deep as he could reach. His groans ripped from deep inside his chest as he pounded her ass with the force of his hips, shoving her up the bed while he followed on his knees, not giving her a respite from his quickening strokes.

Harmony reached up to brace a hand against the wooden headboard and tilted up her hips, accepting everything he forced her to take, her body shaking then stiffening as her cries turned into mewling, breathy moans. Then she screamed, her back arching, her cunt clamping harder around his shaft.

Only then did Dalton let himself go, shouting his relief as his balls tightened and come pumped through his dick in a pulsating stream, easing his slowing thrusts.

When at last he'd emptied everything he had to give her, he slumped over her slick back, dragging in deep, harsh breaths as the heartbeat pounding at his temples slowed.

His arms wrapped around her quivering belly and he drew her up to her knees, hugging her close, his hands smoothing up her damp skin to gently cup her breasts. He nuzzled her neck and pressed kisses along her shoulder as he rocked against her bottom.

For the first time in his life, he wished he could stay locked in an embrace, his cock buried, his body fused with heat and sweat to one woman.

Trouble—that was what Harmony Wilkins was.

Harmony's head fell back, and her cheek rubbed against his like a cat. "That was incredible," she whispered.

"I wasn't too rough?" he said, his voice thick.

She glanced over her shoulder and gave him a look filled with mischief. "If I say yes, whatcha gonna do about it?"

"Guess I'll have to try to do better next time." He covered her grin with a kiss, sucking her bottom lip between his before letting it go. "Just give me a while to recover. I think I blew a gasket that time."

"Oh, is Litt-o Dalton sweepy?"

"Worn to a nub, woman."

She squeezed her inner muscles. "Doesn't feel like it to me."

Sighing, Dalton gripped her waist and lifted her off his lap, and then lay down on his back beside her. He couldn't resist reaching up to cup her breasts as she raised her arms to stretch. Velvet-soft nipples softly dragged across his palms.

Harmony slid her hands along the backs of his, pressing him closer. "*Mmmm* . . . I like that."

"Come lie down," he said, urging her over his body.

She slid a leg over his hip, paused to give him a saucy grin, then reached down to grip his semierect cock. As she scooted over him, she guided his dick back inside her.

"Now, that's wishful thinking," he said, smiling. When had he ever talked so much to a woman?

"I'm into making dreams come true."

He tucked his hands behind his head. "But whose dreams, *hmmm*?"

"Feeling a little smug, are you?"

"Shouldn't I have reason to be? I was incredible, remember?"

Harmony settled onto his chest, a finger lazily circling one of his nipples. "I don't think I like you very much."

"Liar," he drawled.

"You don't think this could all be about sex? That I was overcome with lust?"

"Nope. You already told me I'm the only one who makes you crazy."

"Me and my big damn mouth," she muttered, only she didn't sound too disgusted with herself. "Maybe it's just this place. Satisfaction makes me itch."

Dalton cupped her chin and turned her face toward his. "I make you itch."

She wrinkled her nose. "You're right. You've probably given me one nasty case of the—"

"Harmony?" he said softly.

"Yes?" she whispered, her expression as guileless as a puppy dog's.

"Why don't you just admit you like me?"

"Because it's not fair."

"Why isn't it?

"Well, you know . . ." She shrugged and moisture glittered in her eyes. "If a girl goes and says something like that a boy starts looking for the next challenge."

His thumb scraped absently over her lush lower lip. "I'm not a boy."

She blinked and the corners of her lips twitched. "I noticed. You grew some."

He slid a hand between their bodies and clasped a breast. "You didn't."

Her gasp was too outraged to be real. "And you want me to admit I like you?"

"I wasn't saying you lacked a thing, sweetheart. Fact is, I think I kinda like puny girls."

"I'm not a girl."

"I noticed."

They shared grins until Harmony blushed and laid her head back on his chest.

"So how long are you here for? Can I see you again?" As soon as the words were out of his mouth, he cringed. Could he sound more eager?

"I'm not sure," she said, her voice muffled against his skin. "I have a lot to do, what with getting Mom's house ready."

Dalton wondered what she was thinking. Was she

playing it loose because she thought he wanted that? Or was it possible she wasn't as interested? "Not going to stay awhile and spend some time with your dad?" he asked casually, trying not to let his irritation bleed into his voice.

"Of course. My daddy and I are still close."

"So why are you trying to brush me off?" *So much for casual.*

Her gaze shot upward. "Oh, don't get me wrong. This was good and all—"

"Just good?"

Her thick lashes swept down. "Well, it was very good, but contrary to whatever impression you may have gotten, I'm really not looking for a fling."

"So what was this?" he asked, feeling insulted by this point.

"Fulfillment of a fantasy?" she whispered, her lashes lifting to reveal her troubled gaze.

"I measure up to your imagination?" he bit out.

When she looked away, he wasn't having any of it. He cupped her chin and turned her back. "No hiding now. Is this all you think I'm good for?"

"I didn't mean to hurt your feelings."

"Maybe I'm ready for something more. Ever think about what I wanted?"

"Yeah, with me?" she scoffed. "Nineteen ninety-six's Miss Trouble with a capital *T*?"

"The logistics suck," he said, ignoring what she'd just said. If she didn't want him now, he'd have to wear her down. "You being in Houston, my being the sheriff here. It's hard for me to get away. Maybe you could come visit—say every other weekend?"

She lifted her head. "You'd expect me to drive here every other weekend?" she asked, her voice rising toward the end.

"Is that a lot?"

"What if it's not exactly convenient for me? What about my job? Don't you think it's as important as yours?"

"Can you quit?"

Her mouth opened, then clamped shut. Outrage burst in brilliant pink on her cheeks.

Had he pushed her too far?

"Tell me, Sheriff," she said, her eyes narrowing. "If I told you it might be possible for you to see me more than every other weekend, would that make you feel . . . trapped? Hunted?"

Dalton thought for a moment this time, before he spoke. Rather than answering her question, he posed another, knowing it would annoy the hell out of her when he hedged. "What kind of guys have you been dating?"

"Commitment-phobes," she said, her voice dead even, which meant she was really pissed.

"I see. Explains a lot," he said slowly.

"It doesn't explain a damn thing."

Her hips wriggled against his and before she could move off him, Dalton grabbed her bottom to keep her locked to his body.

"I'm through playing," she gritted out. "I want to go home."

"Do you really?" he asked, digging his fingers in deeper when she reached behind to push at his hands. "Because I'm not through. This has been all about what you wanted up to this point. My turn now, don't you think?"

"You got yours," she said, still squirming.

"I got off, but I'm not through here."

"So what do you want?" she asked, finally holding herself still, her eyes blinking rapidly.

"For you to cut the crap and talk to me, Harmony." Seeing the moisture welling in her eyes, he sighed. "I'm sorry I sounded a little . . ."

She sniffed. "Smug? Patronizing?"

"Yeah, both, but I'm trying to have a conversation with you and you're avoiding telling me anything I want to hear."

Both eyebrows shot upward. "Will you listen to yourself?"

"Okay, I'm not saying it right. Or at least not the way you would have me say it, but I'm not thinking straight."

"I think you're saying exactly what you mean."

"Of course, I am," he said, letting his frustration bleed into his voice. "I want you here. What's so wrong with that?"

"I have a life of my own. I want you to respect that."

"I do, I guess."

He knew he'd mangled that line as well when she bristled and her lips pressed into a thin line. "That part where I said I don't like you? I'm really meaning it now."

"No, you're not," he said, squeezing her bottom harder as she squirmed again.

"You can read my mind now?"

"I'm not doubting you're mad as hell, but you're wet and getting wetter by the minute. You want me more than you're mad at me."

"I'm not mad—I'm fucking furious!"

"Can we be fucking while you're furious?"

Her screech nearly pierced an eardrum. He'd have tossed her off, if she hadn't pushed off his chest to straddle his hips. His cock, recovering nicely now, crowded upward inside her sweet, hot channel.

"Anytime you're ready, sweetheart." Dalton watched her struggle with her anger and her desire. He eased his hold on her bottom, waiting.

Her mouth opened, then clamped closed. She shot him a glare and lifted off him . . . and then slid slowly back down.

Feeling sure her choices were narrowing to one, he continued to talk. "I'm not saying this is a forever kind of relationship I'm offering here. We're just getting reacquainted, but I'd like to try it. What do you say?"

She gulped and rose again, this time circling his hips. "You're looking at Satisfaction High's new geography teacher."

"A teacher?" he asked, trying to keep his mind focused, but drowning in sensation as she swirled. "You?"

"Don't look so shocked."

His hands clamped harder around her bottom and shoved her up and down a little faster. "Your latest little arrest cause you any problems?"

"My dad's the principal, remember?" she said, her

voice sounding more strained this time. "And he knows Miz Murtry pretty well, but if you add trespassing charges . . ."

"I already called in a false alarm." He punched his hips upward, spearing deep.

Her head fell back and her breasts shivered. "Before you cuffed me, Sheriff? Is that ethical?"

"Nope," he said, getting his second wind. He planted his feet in the mattress and pumped up in short, sharp bursts. "Expedient, though . . . knew who I'd find in that pool."

"I knew you wanted me back there in the courtroom." Her hands lifted to her breasts, and she squeezed as she countered his thrusts. "Did you want me in high school?"

"Nope," he lied, watching her face flush a pretty rose as she labored. "I was into the Cindys—big-breasted blondes. My tastes have matured—now, I'm into scrawny brunettes who can't seem to keep their clothes on when they're around me."

Harmony fell forward, grabbing his shoulders, her mouth only an inch from his. "Guess you'll have to keep me under surveillance."

"House arrest. Mine." He raised his head and slanted his mouth over hers, then lay back to hammer harder into her sweet body.

"I'm a schoolteacher . . . ," she gasped, "I can't shack up with the sheriff."

"Moving into your mom's house?" At her nod, he closed his eyes. "Guess I'll have to get that knothole filled." Reaching the end of his endurance, he rolled her to her back, hooked his arms under her legs and locking his gaze with hers, showed her exactly what his intentions were.

Harmony shivered as the cool winter air hit her moist skin. "Must be gettin' kinda serious, Sheriff." She grinned at Dalton and tightened her arms around his neck, sliding her front snug against his—for warmth, of course.

"Maybe," he said, with a lopsided smile that spelled mischief. "What do you think, deep enough?"

She lifted one brow. "You or the pool?"

"Baby, if you have to ask, I'm not doing this right," he growled, and pushed her back against the side of the pool.

She couldn't help the giggle—she did a lot of that lately, laughing a lot like Cindy Niedermeyer did all those years ago.

Dalton, however, knew exactly how to kill the humor. He shoved up hard inside her, robbing her of breath. "I am serious. Think I'd sink a pool in my backyard for just anyone?"

"Trying to make sure I don't get into any more trouble?"

"Making damn sure the only place you're swimming nekkid is right where I can watch." The water churned around them as he started to move.

Harmony reached out, spreading her arms along the edge of the pool and closed her eyes, enjoying the contrast of brisk air licking at the moisture beading on her exposed skin and the silky warmth churning below.

A heated pool—the man had spared no expense for her pleasure. She opened her eyes and stared at the colorful lights he'd strung beneath the eaves of the house.

She never would have imagined that one momentary lapse of judgment could lead to such an unexpected end. If she'd never leapt naked into his daddy's swimming pool, she might not be here, fucking him in his newest home improvement project.

An early Christmas present, he'd said, just for her.

"Are you trying to tell me something?" she asked, then gave him a look, all wide-eyed innocence while her heart thumped against her chest.

"Think you already know what it is?"

Remembering the last time she'd hedged, she decided to say exactly what she hoped was true. "You love me."

"Maybe." His mouth swooped down to capture hers for a fiery kiss as he thrust deep.

Harmony smiled against his mouth, not the least worried by his noncommittal answer. Dalton only teased when he was happy or when he was feeling ornery, but he was never cruel.

Dalton loved her!

"I've been thinking," she said, when he dragged his mouth from hers.

"About what?"

"About that thing you wanted to do?"

"That thing?" he whispered, his lips stretching wide.

He was going to make her say it. "You know, that thing . . . from behind."

Dalton's hips halted, and he grunted as he slid out of her.

Missing his warmth already, she said, "Hey wait, can't we do it here?"

"Need a bed for that."

"Maybe we should wait."

"No way. You're finally giving me the green light. I'm not givin' you a chance to change your mind. Out you go!" he said, grabbing her hand and heading toward the steps.

"But it's freezing out here," she complained, not really meaning it.

Dalton knew better than to believe her. Still, as soon as they stepped onto the cold pavement, he swept her into his arms.

"Does this mean I have to move in? Pack my things?" she teased. "So much to do, how ever will I cope?"

"Most of your things are already here. The rest I'll box up myself." He struggled to slide open the door, then closed it behind them. Blessedly warm air surrounded them.

Harmony traced the outer edge of his ear as he walked quickly down the hallway toward his bedroom. "Miz Murtry will miss seeing you."

"That old biddy will have to retire her drill and spy on someone else." He dropped her on the mattress, letting her bounce once, then came down beside her.

"Wonder why she never reported you."

"Maybe she liked looking at my ass better than yours?" Dalton rolled her over and shoved a pillow under her tummy. "Although why anyone wouldn't want to spend a lifetime looking at this ass . . . hell, need another," he said, reaching for a second pillow to lift her higher. "Better."

"I'm not so sure about this now," she muttered, burying her face into the mattress.

"I promise you'll like it. But if it's too much, you just say so. I'll stop," he said quickly, already reaching for the lube.

His eagerness carried her along, dispelling some of her doubts. His mouth, trailing kisses over her bottom, went even further to reassure her. His tongue dipping into her pussy had her dripping cream and promising him the moon if he'd just hurry it up.

Dalton knelt directly behind her and smoothed his hands over her bottom, massaging the globes, spreading them. His mouth dragged along her tender skin. He thrust two fingers into her vagina at the same time his lips sucked on her hooded clit.

Harmony wiggled, trying to force him deeper, all the while biting her lower lip as she withheld her cries. No sense letting him know just how close to the edge she was—the man could be downright mean when he teased.

When his lips slid upward, her breath hitched. Still twisting his fingers inside her, he licked a path from her pussy, skipping briefly over her asshole and continuing along the crease that divided her bottom. When he lifted his tongue, she waited in an agony of suspense as he shifted behind her, withdrawing his fingers, only to prod her back entrance, rubbing in lubricant he squeezed from a tube. When the metal tip entered her, she sank her face into the coverlet while cool gel filled her.

The sound of something tearing had her peeking over her shoulder to watch him roll a condom down his thick, ridged dick. Holding her gaze, he squirted more gel in his palm and slicked the outside of the smooth latex, rubbing up and down his shaft, squeezing the head of his cock when he reached the tip.

"Damn, Harmony. Wish I wasn't so hard."

"You really want this?"

His snort held no humor. His features sharpened, honing to a dark intensity, which never failed to thrill her. When a hand smoothed over her ass, the calloused palm chafed. His fingers curved into a bruising grip.

Harmony was ready. Looking straight ahead, she spread her knees wide and let her back sink to tilt her bottom right at his cock.

A finger slid into her ass, gliding into the gel, circling to ease the muscles clamping tight around it. "Relax, baby. Breathe. It's gonna be all right."

A second finger slipped inside her and Harmony sucked in a breath, reminding herself, she'd been here before. Dalton often teased her ass while he fucked her. He'd been preparing her for this moment while giving her mind-blowing orgasms. The sensation was pleasant still, only a slight burning as her tissues stretched.

This wasn't any different than before.

A third finger slid inside and her ass puckered up, gripping hard. The burning wasn't so pleasant now, but the pressure she felt caused little pulses all along her vagina.

Dalton's breath grew unsteady. "The muscles are so strong. You're gonna chew my dick right up."

"Is that a good thing?"

"Baby, I can't take any more. I have to fuck you. This may be over quick, so don't move when I come inside."

When his fingers pulled out, Harmony braced, clutching the bedding. A moment later the thick, round head of his cock pushed against her opening.

The muscles surrounding her entrance resisted, stretching as he pushed the blunt knob harder against her opening.

Harmony whimpered. "God, Dalton, I don't think . . ."

"Don't think. Relax, baby. Let me in." His thumbs pressed on either side of her opening as he continued to prod her. When the tip slipped between the constricting muscles, he halted.

Her ass burned with the pressure. It was almost too much. She would have said so, except her cunt leaked a steady stream of excitement, making little moist noises as it clasped air.

She needed him inside her. She closed her eyes, rolled her face on the mattress and forced herself to relax. The pressure eased and suddenly he thrust the rest of the way through.

She echoed his deep, agonized groan as he slid deep inside her ass.

When he halted his thrust, he leaned over her, kissing her between her shoulder blades. "You okay?"

"Just don't move for a minute," she mumbled.

His body shook against hers.

"Laugh and I think I'll kill you."

"Not laughing . . . swear it."

"Liar." Her smile was tight. She wasn't sure she could take more, but she didn't want to disappoint him. She felt incredibly stretched and filled.

One hand smoothed over her belly, gliding down between her legs. A finger slid between her folds, raking her swollen clit as it sank inside her pussy. It was just enough to send her over the edge. "Now," she sobbed, "move now!"

Dalton pulled out an inch or two and thrust forward again, tunneling deeper into her ass.

"Faster, bastard. Don't tease me now. *I'm commmmminnnng!*"

Dalton hammered her ass, stroking in and out, his taut, hard belly slapping her bottom with his harsh thrusts, slamming faster, harder.

Harmony curved her back, tilting her ass high to meet his strokes. Her entrance burned like fire, but the tension wound tighter in her core, and tighter still as he pummeled her until at last she screamed at the moment she hurtled over the precipice.

When his hips slowed, jerking against her as he shot come, Harmony sobbed softly, her body slumping on the pillows, her legs trembling and weak, and her whole body shuddering in the aftermath.

Dalton withdrew gently and climbed off the bed. The sound of water running in the bathroom didn't stir her. The warmth of a cloth sliding between her legs to cleanse her couldn't rouse her. Dalton tugged the pillows from beneath her hips and pulled her into his arms, spooning her back against his belly.

Her head resting on his arm, she didn't move even as he intertwined his fingers with hers and brought her palm up to press a kiss to the center. "Thank you," he whispered.

She snorted softly. "I'm nearly dead from an orgasm and you're thanking me?"

She felt his lips stretch into a smile against her hand. "That good, was it?"

"I love you."

"Damn, I must be a god."

"Don't suppose you're hard enough to slip him back inside me?" she whispered shakily.

"Feeling lonely?"

"Feeling weepy . . . scared?"

Dalton gently lifted her thigh and slipped his cock between her legs.

Harmony reached down and guided his softening flesh inside her and sighed. "That's better."

He brushed her hair from her neck and kissed her. "You're going to marry me, right?"

"You asking me when I'm weak as a kitten?" she mumbled.

"Figure you wouldn't have the strength to argue."

He said it so cheerfully, she wanted to hit him, but she

was just too damn spent to make the effort. "You think I would? Argue, I mean?"

A long indrawn breath pressed his chest against her back. "I think you don't believe me half the time when I tell you I want you here."

"You're making me a believer," she whispered.

"Harmony, just say yes."

Harmony couldn't help the tear that slipped down her cheek to track across Dalton's arm. "Yes, Dalton, I'll marry you. Can I go to sleep now?"

His arms tightened around her. "I think I like you weak as a kitten."

"I like you even when you're an asshole," she said, her voice breaking.

His lips glided along her shoulder, then left a tender kiss behind her ear. "Baby, I'm glad you chose my pool."

DELILAH DEVLIN has lived in Saudi Arabia, Germany, and Ireland, but calls Texas home for now. Always a risk taker, she lived in the Saudi Peninsula during the Gulf War, thwarted an attempted abduction, and survived her children's juvenile delinquency. Creating alter egos for herself in the pages of her books enables her to live new adventures—and chronicle a few of her own. (You get to guess which!)

# Forbidden Fruit

## Lisa Renee Jones

# *One*

*L*ust.

That was what she had felt for Blake Alexander so many years ago. It had been lust, and nothing more.

She refused to believe that it had been something bigger, more meaningful. Biting her bottom lip, she fought the disbelieving laugh that threatened to erupt, directed at her own stupidity. Why, if it had been nothing more than lust, did hearing he was in town and coming to her brother's Super Bowl party make her heart race and her palms sweat? Not only was he back in town, he was here to stay, throwing down roots and opening a skydiving business with some of his army buddies.

Sitting on her brother's sofa, Laura Cameron took on the tedious task of peeling the label from her beer bottle; desperation was spurring the need to do *something* with all the nervous energy pouring through her body. Any minute now, Blake would walk through the front door.

She would be face-to-face with the man who had inspired pretty much every nighttime fantasy she had ever conceived as a teen. Back then, she had easily conjured hot, wet, steamy images involving her and Blake naked. Compliments of a wild imagination—and good dream recall—she had done all kinds of naughty things with that man.

Reality made her sink her teeth into her bottom lip, almost drawing blood. Okay, so her little fantasies about Blake had lasted well into her college years. She just didn't like to admit as much, even to herself. Years after he had joined the army her sophomore year, leaving her behind—and angry—she would wake wet with need. The times she had woken up, a near-orgasmic ache between her legs, were too many to count.

Perhaps that's why she moved away herself to complete her last two years of college. But there was no escaping her fantasies. In fact, they seemed to grow more explicit. The more she evolved into womanhood, the more she played out sensual, tempting scenarios in her sleep. And sometimes even in her waking hours. But that was then and this was now.

Still, it was hard to forget that Blake Alexander, her brother's best friend, the man who was about to be in the same room with her, had been the star of those fantasies. It had been the move to Manhattan that had seemed to appease her need for him. Her new life had brought with it a refuge of sorts. She had been freed from her "Blake haunting." She almost laughed at the thought. That's how hot she had been for Blake. She had dubbed her obsession a "haunting."

Shoving the thought away, she reminded herself that things were different now. She was twenty-five and a grown woman with life experiences under her belt. Now back at home in San Francisco, she'd landed a job as a buyer for Macy's corporate offices and life was good. The past was the past. Blake would probably be nothing like she remembered. His impact on her would be a big whopping zero.

She frowned and tossed a piece of the beer label onto the coffee table. It was just so damned ironic that Blake had left the army and returned home only weeks before her arrival. When her brother had told her Blake had bought a skydiving school with several army buddies, she had been floored.

*"Boo!"*

Startled by the sudden voice behind her, Laura jumped so hard that her beer splattered out of the top of the bottle. Her brother Matt, now sitting next to her, laughed. "You are too easy to scare, little sis."

She made a face and wiped at the dampness now on her jeans. "And you are just as childish as I remember, Matt Cameron."

Linebacker big and teddy-bear cute, Matt had blond hair and blue eyes, and a quirky sense of humor to complete the package. He winked at his sister. "But you love me, and you know it."

That was the truth. She did love him, and had missed

him immensely. "Yes, you big lug, I love you." She gave him a nudge that bordered on a shove.

He wrapped a big arm around her shoulder. "It wasn't the same, having football parties without a girl here."

"Mom would have filled in for me if you'd asked her. She loves football." They both knew why he didn't want Mom present—football made her a little crazy.

"Yeah, well, Mom gets a little too rowdy for the guys," Matt said with a grimace, and that was saying a lot because several of them were firemen like Matt. He laughed but without humor. "It's no wonder Dad took a dislike to the game. I've never seen a woman act like that over football. Back in my days on the field, the referees knew her by name. She was lucky she wasn't banned."

Laura laughed. "I remember Dad taking something he called 'nerve' pills before your college games, afraid she would embarrass you."

Matt grunted. "Me?" he said in disbelief. "He was afraid she would embarrass *him*."

Around them, the room was already bustling, full of young men eating, drinking, and talking junk to each other. The doorbell rang, and someone yelled for Matt. He kissed Laura's forehead. "Good to have you home."

He was up and gone, but not without showing a contented smile on his handsome face. It was good to be home. For a long moment, she savored the thought.

"Laura?"

She looked up to see the very man she had been fretting over just minutes earlier.

Blake.

He stood before her, looking every bit the sinfully handsome male she had been remembering. But better. Experience and age had given him a mature quality that clung to him like a second skin, made him seem like he knew things. She could almost bet he knew plenty about pleasing a woman. Laura inwardly cringed. He was already making her have naughty thoughts.

"Blake." She said his name as if confirming he wasn't a part of one of her dreams.

Try as she might, her eyes wouldn't stay fixed on his face. They traveled the length of what had become a delicious display of pure male power. Blake had always looked good, but now . . . now he was like a work of art.

His powerful legs rippled with muscles beneath his faded Levis. And then there was the snug black T-shirt. She had a new appreciation for the basic tee as of now—at least this particular one. It did a mighty fine job of hugging a chest so broad and hard, it made her mouth water.

On his six-foot-two frame, his physical presence could easily be considered intimidating. To Laura, it was like being injected with an instant dose of desire. With lightning speed, she became aware of the prickling in her nipples. Her arms crossed in front of her body, reacting to the tiny ache. She prayed her aroused state couldn't be seen through her thin pink tee.

Only Blake did this to her. It was crazy.

Forcing herself to meet his gaze, Laura found his sea-blue eyes darker, and far more intense, than she remembered. "It's been a long time," he said, in that deep, baritone voice of his that she had always loved so much.

Simple words, but they evoked much more than a simple response.

Her body quaked with the potency of her attraction to him—so long in the making, so alive despite the interval of time apart. All the while, her heart raced with the emotional intensity that seeing him evoked.

She set her beer on the coffee table, forcing herself to unlock her arms from their defensive posture and praying her hands didn't shake. "Yes, yes, it has."

He was staring at her with an indecipherable look in his eyes. She resisted the urge to cross her arms again, feeling self-conscious under his scrutiny. What did he see?

Little girl . . . or woman?

"You've changed," he finally said in a hushed tone.

Her knees were pressed primly together, a reflex reaction to the dull ache that had traveled with excruciating accuracy from her breasts straight to her core.

She barely found her voice. "Have I?"

A slight smile played on his lips as he stepped forward. Anticipation rushed across her nerve endings. Would he hug her?

"Yes," he said as he sat down next to her. Close. He sat really, really close. She could smell him. She'd always found his scent to be arousing. To touch him would take nothing more than a raised hand.

It was tempting. Her fingers twitched with the need.

Instead, he reached for her.

Her breath caught in her throat as his hand gently touched her hair. Basking in the moment, her lashes fluttered shut as his fingers traced a long strand of red. "You changed your hair."

Nervously, she forced her eyes open and a smile to her lips. He'd only seen her hair short. In her youth, she'd wanted to fit in with everyone else. The bright auburn color had seemed too bold, so she had kept it short to downplay its existence. She would have colored it had her mother allowed it.

Now, as a grown woman, she felt the freedom of being unique and loved it. Her hair was now long, below her shoulders, and she liked it that way. Remembering his old comments about how her fire-red temper matched her hair, she wondered if he was thinking the same thing now.

Her voice was soft as she replied: "It's been like this for years."

His eyes seemed to go to her lips. It took effort to resist the urge to wet them. But she wet them; she couldn't help it. His eyes followed the action, lingering, and then lifted to her eyes. What passed between them in that moment made her breath catch in her chest. Hot, primal passion burned in Blake's eyes, and she forgot everything but him. Their attraction danced between them, alive and charged with heat.

It couldn't be real. Could it?

*Blake.* His name was a question. Did he want her like she had always wanted him?

Memories seemed to walk from her mind to his and his to hers. All the times they had spent together over the years. . .

Late-night talks when her brother was asleep on the couch . . . those had been her favorite times. She and Blake would sit on the floor talking for hours. Then there were the nights when she, Blake, and Matt would make popcorn and watch scary movies.

Sometimes Blake would force her to watch the same old movies over and over. Her brother would bail time after time, saying he couldn't watch the same movie again. But even then Laura had loved Blake. They had been friends, and so much more.

Watching a movie ten times with him was fun.

Yes, there had always been something between them. They simply hadn't allowed it to bloom. No. *He* hadn't let it. Suddenly, she understood why she had never been able to dismiss Blake as a crush. He had been so much more. But he hadn't let it evolve, holding her at arm's length. She had been forbidden, and he had known it.

She had been his best friend's sister. That made her untouchable.

But that was then, and this was now.

And there was no question they wanted each other. It was like a low, hot simmer that threatened to go up in flames.

"Hey, Blake, Laura, come check out the pregame show. That damn quarterback from Utah is in a monkey suit, acting like he knows football when he can't even complete a pass."

Matt, as usual, had crummy timing, appearing beside them just then. He had successfully ruined the moment. Blake looked away. Laura scowled in Matt's direction, fighting the urge to throw her beer on him.

Matt looked at Laura, and then at Blake. "I can't believe you're both here. It's just like old times. We guys can cut up, drink beer, and listen to my kid sister tell us we don't know what we're talking about." He made a cheering motion with his beer bottle. "Life is good."

Blake looked at Matt, then eyed Laura with a cool look, several notches of warmth below his prior one. "Yeah," he said. "I guess it is just like old times." His gaze switched back to Matt, with finality. Laura was shut out. "I need a beer."

As Blake walked away, Laura tried to calm the explosion of thoughts erupting in her brain. He had just dismissed her like a bad habit. No matter what had just passed between them, she was just Matt's kid sister. Always was and always would be. But Blake was wrong. Everything wasn't just like old times. She was older and wiser. In the past, she had dismissed their attraction as schoolgirl fantasies.

Not anymore.

She had seen what was in his eyes. He wanted her. And damn it, she had wanted him a long time.

All she had to do was prove just how womanly she was, and the "kid sister" would be forgotten. And why wait? She'd start today.

## Two

The main group of Super Bowl watchers had gathered in Matt's living room. Among the group there were seven rowdy guys, all with beers in their hands, eyes on the television, and smart-ass comments blurting from their mouths. Laura sat among them, shocked that she wasn't the only female for once. One of Blake's partners, Bobby, had brought his wife, Jennifer.

"We need a beer run," Matt yelled from the kitchen.

Laura had almost forgotten. "I have a couple cases in my car."

"Way to go, Laura," Joey, another guest said, and then winked. He pushed to his feet. "I'll carry it in for you."

To Laura's surprise, Blake stood. "That's okay, I got it, man." He exchanged a look with Joey, who quickly sat back down, bowing out of his offer to help.

Her eyes narrowed as they met Blake's, noting his silent intimidation of the other man. But she didn't say anything. *Interesting.* She wanted to see where this was going. Turning on her heels, she let Blake follow her outside. With every step she took, she felt him behind her, watching her, moving with her. She hit the clicker to her car and popped the trunk open. When they were both standing behind the raised lid of the trunk, he turned and faced her.

He stared at her pointedly for a moment, but his expression was unreadable. Damn him for having a good poker face. His tone was equally hard to read. "Joey's a dog. Stay away from him."

She laughed. He had to be kidding. "I'm a grown woman, Blake. I hardly need you to tell me who I should stay away from. Besides," she added, purposely dismissing his warning, "he seems nice enough to me."

His hand came out and touched her shoulder. She looked down at it, and then up at him. "He's not just a dog, he's a junkyard dog," he stated flatly.

She let out a breath. "How do you suppose I survived without your warnings all those years while you were gone?" She screwed up her face. "I can decide who I date—or don't date, for that matter—very well on my own, thank you."

She started to turn, but his hand gently closed around her arm. "You're considering dating him?"

She wasn't. "Maybe."

His eyes darkened. "That's crazy. Matt will have a fit."

Her eyes narrowed. "Matt, huh? So you are doing this for Matt?"

"Not for Matt." He spoke the words softly, with a hint of discomfort ringing in his tone. "You're like a sister to me as well, and you know it."

That made her angry. No way was she letting him get away with this. "Funny," Laura challenged, "that look you gave me in the living room didn't look too brotherly."

She stepped forward, bringing them so close together that their thighs were almost touching. Her hand flattened on his chest. She was so nervous her insides were shaking, but Blake had avoided what was between them for far too long.

Her voice was a soft, seductive purr, and she inwardly complimented herself on her exterior facade of composure. "You looked at me like a man looks at a woman, Blake."

His eyes were half veiled as his gaze slid down to where her hand rested on his chest. For a long moment he stared at it before once again making eye contact. She could smell his spicy cologne—a temptation to bury her nose in his neck.

His eyes found hers.

He didn't move, nor did he deny her words. "Your brother is my best friend."

She ignored his words. "Does that mean you know how you looked at me?" The muscles in his chest flexed under her fingers.

His voice was low. "Seeing you again took me off guard."

She took his statement as a small admission. "You took me off guard, too."

"Meaning?"

She had to go for it. "Meaning, I had hoped my schoolgirl crush was gone."

His eyes flashed with surprise. "What crush?"

"We both know there has always been something between us."

"We were kids."

"We're not anymore."

His hand went to her hair as it had earlier. "I love your hair like this."

The touch of his hand made her insides flip-flop. "And I want you to like it."

His eyes went to hers. "Your brother—"

She finished his sentence for him. "Knows I'm a grown woman."

"Would kill me."

"No," she insisted, and if he did, she'd kill him. "He won't."

"He will."

"Kiss me."

He stared down at her, and then to her complete, utter shock, he did as she asked. Not only was he kissing her, his arms had slid around her waist. He pulled her tight against that hard body of his, and she got a taste of heaven on earth.

Instantly, she melted into him, molding her softness against those delicious muscles. Her hands slid around his neck. The action pressed her aching nipples against his chest, and she moaned softly into his mouth.

Divine, soft caresses of his tongue played sensual

havoc with her entire body. It was just a kiss, but it was also so much more. Years of pent-up desire had been set free in both of them. Wetness dampened her panties as if there had been twenty minutes of foreplay instead of simply this one tease of a moment.

God, how she wanted him. Her leg went up and wrapped around his calf, pulling his hips against hers. Feeling the evidence of his arousal press against her stomach was fuel to the fire. She wanted to be alone with him, naked and intimately joined.

He nipped at her lips. "We shouldn't be doing this."

"Why not?" she asked breathlessly.

He raised his head just enough to look into her eyes. "You know why."

"I want you, Blake. Is that wrong?"

He made a low sound, much like a growl, and then kissed her again. This time, his kiss was different. He seemed more primal in his need, taking her mouth with more hunger, his tongue sliding along hers with long, sensual strokes. The potency of their shared desire was consuming. Hot. On fire.

A door slammed somewhere in the distance, but it hardly registered. Her mind and body were both completely focused on Blake.

"Hey, where's that beer?"

The voice—Matt's—was a jolt of reality.

They froze, lips pressed together, eyes flying open. Then, at the same moment, they moved away from each other like two bad children caught with their hands in the cookie jar.

Blake ran his hand through his hair and muttered a curse. "This stays between us," he warned.

"I never intended it any other way," she whispered, a second before Matt appeared in front of them.

"What's taking so long?" Matt's gaze traveled from Laura to Blake. "She giving you smack about your team again?"

"Of course," Laura agreed. "We've never agreed on a football game in our lives. Why start now?"

Matt grinned. "I know. I love it. Makes things interesting." Matt eyed the trunk, reaching for a case of beer. "Game's about to start. Let's go get the battle started."

Blake grabbed the second case and slammed the trunk shut, his eyes catching Laura's. "I think you pick the opposite team just to be difficult."

Laura leaned against the bumper. That wasn't true. Blake always picked the underdog. Maybe because in some way he thought he had been, at one point, and come out on top. "I tell it how I see it." An idea hit her. "How about a bet for old times?"

"Oh yeah," Matt said, rubbing his hands together. "Our team against Blake's."

Blake scrubbed his jaw and laughed. "All right. What's the bet? All the beer for the next game?"

"Higher stakes," Laura said. "If we win, you have to participate in the charity bachelor auction sponsored by the fire department next Saturday night."

Matt laughed. "Oh yeah. I already tried to rope him into doing that and he said no. This is perfect." He rubbed his hands together. "I don't have to be a victim alone."

"You're not alone," Blake said, shaking his head, resting the case of beer on his hip. "All the single firemen are doing it and from what you said, plenty of others. You don't need me."

"You're just afraid some old lady will bid on you and win," Matt goaded.

Blake eyed Laura, his expression guarded, but she knew he was well aware that she intended to win him in that auction. His gaze held hers, "I'll buy beer or no bet."

"You really don't believe in your team, that's what you're saying," Laura commented. "I see why, of course. The quarterback—"

"Is one of the best in the league," Blake countered.

"At throwing interceptions," Laura replied in rebuttal. Matt chuckled.

Blake eyed them both with irritation. "I know the two of you. I am not going to get out of this auction thing without beating you in this damn bet. But if I win, the auction is closed to discussion." He started walking, ending the conversation with the declaration. Laura and Matt laughed, following him.

*It really is like old times,* Laura thought. The old chemistry between the three of them was alive and well. Just like the attraction between her and Blake.

"Yes," Laura said, smiling, falling into step with Matt as they exchanged an amused look. "Let's go watch the game."

Long after Matt stopped grinning ear to ear, Laura smiled inwardly. That party would be the perfect venue for seduction. Her mind raced with endless possibilities. A sexy costume, an escape from reality into a sensual fantasy.

This was the bet of a lifetime.

Blake leaned against a wall, one booted foot over the other, a beer in his hand, feigning interest in a game that would normally hold his full attention. Not even the bet kept him focused on the television. No. It was the woman who'd just goaded him into a bet meant to lead him farther into the land of temptation. The woman who, only minutes before, he'd kissed, tasting just how sweet that temptation could be. He could still taste her on his lips, still feel her soft curves pressed to his body.

He shoved aside the bittersweet fantasy with a forceful push. What the hell had he been thinking kissing Laura like that? For God's sake, he knew how protective Matt was of his sister. To take his relationship with Laura beyond the safe zone of friendship would risk losing Laura completely, not to mention her highly protective family—his second family.

So why was he standing here with a freaking hard-on, his mind conjuring wicked images of her naked and in his arms? Not that he really had to ask that question. He knew why. Laura had always been in his head. They'd had something special, even in their youth, sharing a connection he'd never re-created or ever managed to dismiss as a youthful infatuation.

Years in the Rangers had certainly presented him with his share of women willing to spread their legs. But there had been only one who drove him to distraction, one who wouldn't get the hell out of his head. And that one was Laura. The woman who sat in the center of a group of guys talking trash about the quarterback whom he happened to like. The woman whose lips tasted so addictively sweet. He thought time would have extinguished this fire between them. If anything, time had done nothing but heighten the burn.

She laughed at something someone said, the soft sound erotic in its impact, sending a rush of molten heat through his veins. He watched as she pushed to her feet, her eyes seeking his, as aware of him as he was her. She held his gaze, sashaying to his side. "Can I get you something from the kitchen?" she asked, the look in her eyes clearly offering more than another beer.

"No thanks. I know my limits. I've had enough." He wasn't talking about beer any more than she was.

She shrugged. "And here I thought Army Rangers had stamina. Maybe I was wrong." Boos filled the room as her team scored again. "*Ouch.* Looking more and more like you'll be auctioned off to the highest bidder. It really is daunting, isn't it? Wondering who will win the bid? What she'll want to do to you once she gets you alone." She started to walk away, then hesitated: "Did you know it's a masked ball with silent bids? It's meant to encourage more activity. Nice and discreet." Her eyes sparkled with mischief. "No telling who might win." A hint of a smile played on her full lips before she walked away, those tight jeans exposing everything and nothing, his mind filling in the blanks. The message was clear. She'd offered herself up as a perfect, one-night fantasy. No one would know but the two of them.

Holy shit! His cock twitched with the obvious promise of pleasure she'd delivered. *Down boy. She is so not within reach. Morning will come and then what?* But there was no holding back the places his thoughts were taking him, the intimate possibilities he imagined taking place if she won that auction. He was treading in dangerous waters, but suddenly, losing this bet didn't seem quite so bad.

One night. Maybe it would be enough to put out this raging fire between them. It was a dangerous proposition, but he didn't see many options. They couldn't go on like this for very long without Matt noticing, anyway. It appeared that Laura was the bittersweet temptation that just might be the demise of his good intentions. But damn, if he was going down, he was going to enjoy every last minute of it.

masks and fancy face painting offered by the women—looking for the focus of a week's worth of fantasies. Okay, more like a lifetime of fantasies, but this past week, the idea of finally finding his way inside Laura had him in one big ball of lust and desire. Could she really pull off bidding on him without Matt knowing? Could this secret seduction really happen?

God, he hoped so.

A sizzle of awareness raced through his body, drawing his attention to the front entrance, a magnetic pull of sorts. A dark-haired woman in a sexy red dress entered. Amazingly, he felt the punch of desire in his gut normally reserved for Laura; the kind of punch that rocketed through his blood and landed in his groin.

He studied the woman, intrigued, analyzing why he was so drawn to her among so many. Her stockings were black, the dress hitting midthigh, her legs long and alluring. Waist tapered, hips slim but curvy. That her body was hot wasn't in question. It was his reaction to her that begged for explanation. There were plenty of gorgeous women here tonight. Why did this one garner his attention despite his distraction with Laura? She started walking, or rather sashaying, with a sexy sway to those curvy hips. A rush of familiar heat washed over him this time. So very familiar. His eyes rocketed to her face, to the black and silver mask, and fancy paint, hiding her identity. As if she sensed being watched, her gaze slid to his, latching onto his. The connection, the impact, was intense, instant. Awareness turned to understanding. Laura. Of course. Even in disguise, with her hair dark and her face covered, she rocketed pure lust through his body.

Suddenly, Matt appeared by his side. "You aren't going to believe this," he said, and then turned his attention to the bartender. "A Bud Light."

Blake watched Laura weave through the crowd. "What am I not going to believe?"

Matt accepted his beer, and turned to lean his elbows on the bar as Blake was doing. "My sister is freaking sick. Says she's been throwing up."

Blake's attention shot to Matt. "Really?"

"Yeah, and since I know she'd *never* miss you up on that stage tonight, she must be pretty bad off. I guess I'd better check on her after the party."

Inwardly, Blake smiled, his gaze seeking Laura again, but finding her missing. Ah, but not for long. Laura had planned this all perfectly, a shared gift. A night no one would know about. A night that didn't require him driving to her house and working through his guilt. She would bid on him and win. Then, he'd have no choice but to be hers for more than the auction dinner date—hers for a passionate night that would be their little secret. A fantasy come to life.

An announcement sounded over the loudspeaker: "Bachelors, please take your place on the stage."

Matt sucked down another slug of beer. "Please, Lord, let me get a hot woman."

Blake laughed at Matt, who had been fretting over the possible horror stories the dinner date could create with the wrong winning bidder. But Blake wasn't worried; he was anxious to get down to business. Pushing off the bar, his adrenaline pumping, his blood thick with desire.

Let the auction begin.

An hour later, Blake stood on the stage, Matt by his side, among twenty other men. It was finally time to announce the winners of the auction, which would include one supervised night out with the bachelor. Silent auction meant no one knew who won the bachelors until the winner's assigned number was called for each date. Upon announcement of the winning bidder, the anonymity began to be shed as each woman stepped forward to claim her man for a dance. But she still had her mask and nameless identity to play with for this one night. No one but her, her bachelor, and the charity heads would know she had indulged in buying a date that night, if she so pleased.

As Blake listened to the matchups being announced, the edge of nerves kicked in. What if Laura didn't win? All this anticipation would be down the drain.

The announcer called out Matt's name. "Wish me luck," he murmured a second before the bidder's number was called out. A gorgeous blonde who stood at the front of the stage waved her number and rushed forward. Matt looked skyward. "Thank you."

Blake would have laughed under other circumstances, but instead, he said his own silent "thank you." Matt was gone and well distracted before Laura was within his reach.

Two more names and numbers were called before

Blake's. Finally when he heard the winner announced, he held his breath, waiting to see who would emerge from the crowd. And then he saw her, his woman in red, his lifelong fantasy. He wasted no time crossing the stage to meet her at the bottom of the stairs, waiting as she offered her number to the person logging the wins.

When she was ready, he offered her his arm. A seductive smile played on her painted red lips. Their eyes held for several seconds, a silent message of shared desire sizzling its way into existence. She reached for his arm, never looking away from him. The instant she touched his elbow, the air crackled with newfound electricity, their stare heating up a good ten notches. Blake's entire body lit up like the Fourth of July. His skin warmed, his cock pulsed—anticipation was a powerful aphrodisiac. He'd wanted Laura forever it seemed, but had resolved he'd never have her. Until now. Blake led her toward the dance floor, now full of couples, but when he would have pulled her into his arms, she took his hand. Silently, she backed up, urging him to follow, a second before she turned and started walking. Excitement flared in his gut, his groin, his limbs. He had no idea where they were going, nor did he care. Preferably someplace they could be alone. Someplace nice and private where he could ravish her until she could take no more.

She led him through a back door, exiting the ballroom, down a hallway and then to their right. Without ever looking back at him, she started up the darkened stairwell, her confident steps telling of her clear destination, as if she'd explored her path before now. They were treading in dangerous waters, risking being caught, but he didn't care.

At the top of the stairs they walked down a hallway, passing several doors before Laura opened one. A second later, he found himself inside a conference room, the moonlight streaming through a massive window the length of the room. He didn't give himself time to think, to reconsider. He shut the door, settling her back against the wooden surface, and kissed her. Kissed her with a possessive fierceness he could do nothing to contain, the desire he felt unleashed now, potent and demanding. Laura met his demands with her own, her tongue tangling and teasing his, her body arching into his, hands moving over his back and shoulders.

Something inside him screamed with the rightness of this moment, with a rightness that extended beyond a hot encounter in a secret place. He tore his lips from hers, hands framing her face. "God, I missed you. I don't want to lose you over this."

Her eyes softened, a mixture of tenderness and passion. "You will never lose me. Never. There is no pressure, Blake. Tonight is for us. We don't have to think about tomorrow. We don't even have to acknowledge this tomorrow. You have my promise."

His eyes narrowed, perhaps because he didn't want this to be so easily dismissed, even if he knew it should be. "Don't make a promise you can't keep."

Her hands covered his. "I realized something tonight, watching you up on that stage. I love you, Blake. I always have. I'd never do anything to take my family from you.

Never. We can walk away from this and never look back. I won't ever tell Matt, if you don't want him to know. "

Her words blew him away, warming him while also scaring the hell out of him. But she didn't give him time to consider their content or to his reply. Her lips pressed against his, her hands traveling, exploring, finding their way to the front of his zipper and outlining the ridge of his rock-hard erection. A second later, her hand broke the clothing barriers, soft skin touching his cock. And he was gone, lost to the moment, lost to passion.

Somewhere in a far corner of his mind, her words replayed. She loved him. Deep down, he'd always loved her. He'd simply feared the repercussions of admitting such a thing. And damn it, he didn't want Matt to know about them. He'd always wanted to claim her. Hell, he'd come back here to claim her. What that meant, he didn't know; he couldn't think about it, not now, not in the heat of passion.

Not when he barely knew what he was doing.

Acting on pure adrenaline and fire, one hand laced into her hair, the other cupping her firm, high breast, thumb stroking her nipple taut. His tongue thrust deeper and harder into her mouth, his desire responding to the way her velvety soft fingers teased him. Damn, she felt good, so good; he could barely breathe just thinking about what it would feel like to be inside her. Somehow, one of her legs was at his hip. He might have lifted it, maybe she did. He didn't care. He used the access it offered, his hand sliding up her thigh, and beneath a tiny strip of panties. Relentless in his quest, he shoved them aside and caressed her sensitive flesh—so wet for him, so ready.

A soft whimper escaped Laura's lips, molten heat rushing through his veins at the sexy sound. He pulled back and looked at her, drinking in the heavy-lidded, passion-laden expression on her face, the passion he'd put there, the passion he wanted to claim—forever. And all he could think was "more" pleasure—not for himself— but for her. He wanted *her* pleasure. He wanted her memory of this night to be focused on her satisfaction, not his greed. Not that he didn't feel greedy. His shaft was engorged, painfully so, aching for what he'd lusted for a million times over—Laura wrapped around him, a tight glove of warmth and sensation. But they had all night, and he would endure, wait, make this last.

He held her gaze and said, "I have to know what you taste like." She shivered in response, the only encouragement he needed. He ripped her panties away, drawing a gasp from Laura. "I'm going to make you come now, Laura. The first of many times tonight."

He tossed aside the panties and dropped to his knees, keeping that one leg over his shoulder, staring up at her as he shoved her skirt up those gorgeous hips of her. She was breathing heavily, her chest rising and falling. He wished she were naked so he could see her breasts, see her nipples, hard and taut with arousal. He vowed he would soon.

The sprinkle of red hair in the vee of her body drew his attention, neatly groomed and dainty, just like the woman. He sunk farther back on his heels, eyes lifted to hers again as he lapped at her clit. She moaned softly, hands pressed against the door, fingers spread wide. Slow caresses of his tongue followed, one finger aiding his efforts, teasing the slick folds of her core. She moaned louder as he suckled her clit, teasing it with his lips and tongue. Her hips arched against his mouth, hands sliding into his hair, her need to find release making her wetter, more desperate, little sobs escaping into the air. He licked her more fervently now, up and down, all around, thrusting his tongue into the wet heat of her body, mimicking sex. His fingers worked where his lips did not until she cried out and stiffened. Blake slid two fingers deep inside her, suckling her clit and pushing her over the edge. Tight muscles locked onto his fingers and then spasmed. When she'd ridden out the waves, he gently eased her leg back to the ground, sliding her skirt back into place. His eyes locked with hers and he realized she was blushing.

"I think I—"

"You're beautiful when you come," he whispered, brushing his knuckle over her cheek. "Take me home with you where I can make love to you properly." But he didn't give her a chance to move; his emotions were suffocating. He pressed his forehead to hers. "I came home for you, Laura. I didn't want to admit it, not even to myself." He eased back to look at her. "I love you, Laura. But I need to know I'm still a man you can love. The army changed me. I need to know before—"

This time she interrupted him, her hands framing his face as she compelled him to look at her. "Before Matt knows."

# *Four*

*A*n array of places that she and Blake might make love washed through her mind, as Laura turned to the mirror. She quickly used a washcloth to dissolve the glue around her hairline, her hand shaking with the excitement coursing through her body. About to remove the wig, she froze. Blake appeared in the mirror. Naked. Hard. For her. Her hands gripped the sink for support. Good Lord, the man was gloriously male. A work of finely crafted art, his muscles defined in ways only hard effort created.

She watched him approach, her eyes riveted to the mouth-watering vision he made. He enclosed her in his strong arms, his erection pressed between her legs. "I couldn't wait," he said, lifting the wig from her head and tossing it onto the counter.

Pins held her hair in place and he removed them, her mass of red hair falling free around her shoulders. He ran his fingers through it. Their eyes locked in the mirror, everything inside her quivering at the intensity of the connection.

Holding her gaze, he caressed her hair. "I like you this way, without the wig." His palms continued downward, over her shoulders, leaving goose bumps in their wake.

"I like you the way you are right now as well." She liked that he made her comfortable enough to joke around even in the midst of passion.

A hint of a smile played on his lips as he started to slide her dress upward. "You'll like it better when you take this off," he promised, sliding the material farther up her hips.

Laura responded without hesitation, letting go of the counter, Blake anchoring her with his pelvis quite nicely. She slipped the dress over her head and tossed it aside. The dress had included a built-in bra, so she was now completely bare for Blake's view. And though she was confident on the outside, insecurity overtook her. This was a man she loved so much, who was seeing her naked for the very first time. What if she wasn't all he expected?

Taking comfort in the long, hard length of his erection between her legs as a sign of his desire for her, she studied herself in the mirror, trying to see what he would see. Her pale skin was without freckles, a gift from above she had always been thankful for. The paleness contrasted with her rich auburn hair. Her rather ample breasts were high, now aching for his touch, her rose-colored nipples tingling with arousal, tightening under his inspection.

Her gaze dared to lift to his face in the mirror, to validate what the growing hardness between her thighs confirmed. One look in his eyes in the mirror, at the pure unadulterated lust burning in their depths, put her fears to rest.

"You're beautiful," he said, filling his hands with her breasts and rolling her nipples with his thumbs.

Her nipples were highly sensitive, and she felt the attention to them all over her body. She moaned, her head falling back on his chest, eyes fluttering. Furthering the impact of his touch, Blake tugged on the peaks, applying pressure. Laura squeezed her thighs together, rubbing against his cock, thankful for the high heels she still wore when she realized they allowed him to fit perfectly in the vee of her body.

Blake continued kneading her breasts but he bent to find her mouth. Laura lifted her lips to his, hand on his cheek; his taste, his scent, heady and addictive. She wanted to turn to him, to touch Blake more fully, and she tried to move. Stopping her, he said, "I want you to see us together, to watch our first time together."

Her stomach fluttered with the words, heat licking at her limbs. She'd never watched herself with a man before, but the idea aroused her beyond belief. "Okay," she whispered, tilting her face up to his, offering her lips again, her voice simply not fully attainable.

Blake stared down at her with a look so tender it stole her breath, his finger sliding tenderly over her bottom lip a second before his mouth brushed hers.

Too soon, the kiss ended, and Laura saw Blake reach for a condom on the counter. She didn't remember him putting it there. But then, she'd been distracted by his . . . well, his everything. She shivered when he backed away from her to put it on, wishing him back, but stimulated by the view he now offered. She watched him in the mirror as he rolled the condom over the head of his engorged cock. He was a big man, his body thick with muscle, his cock appropriately large. She swallowed hard, feeling the core of her body respond. She was so wet; it was almost embarrassing.

As Blake slid the condom down his length, she watched every moment with pleasure. When he finished she felt both aroused and relieved, relieved that he was moving back to her. His hand slid over her backside, admiration in his touch—the best kind she realized. His finger brushed the crevice of her cheeks, and then slid into the wet center of her body. Laura moaned, so ready for him, she could barely stand it. The intimacy of his fingers caressed and teased, driving her insane. "Blake! Please."

He responded without question. Suddenly his shaft was between her legs, teasing her the way his fingers had, gliding back and forth, teasing her yet again. "Blake, please!" she repeated. "I thought you couldn't wait?"

A low laugh, deep and sexy, filled the air a second before he filled her. His cock entered her body and sunk deep. She gasped with pleasure, then gave a sigh of relief at finally having him where she wanted him—inside her. Buried to the hilt, he lingered in that position, his hands covering her breasts, his chest deliciously pressed to her back, his head tilted to kiss her neck in teasing butterfly caresses.

His eyes lifted to hers. "This is where I want to stay forever."

Everything inside her warmed with those words, as if that were possible, considering she was burning up with nothing shy of pure lust. She leaned into him, her hips rotating, pushing against his pelvis. She needed him to move, needed it so damn badly she could barely endure the burn.

Blake pumped into her, still molded close, as if he couldn't bring himself to pull away. His hand settled on her upper stomach, anchoring her, as he pumped hard, deep. She couldn't breathe for the sharp jolt of pleasure it delivered. He did it again. She cried out.

"Open your eyes," he ordered.

With effort, she complied. He immediately thrust again. Her breasts bounced with the action, his eyes fixed on the movement, and man, oh, man, it turned her on in a big way. Her core spasmed slightly, almost as if she might come right then.

His gaze lifted to her, as if he'd felt what she did. The connection held and then seemed to spur the rage of heat. He released her upper body, hands going to her hips, as he thrust, pumped. Her breasts were swaying, her body arching into each action. *Need. More.* That was all she could think. *Need. More.* She reached behind her, trying to grab his ass to pull him deeper but couldn't reach him. Her hands braced on the counter again as she pushed against his movement. "I . . . harder," she said, she couldn't help herself. She couldn't get enough of him, "More, Blake."

A primal look flashed in his face, and he thrust harder, faster, driving into her with so much force it should have hurt. But it felt good. So. Damn. Good. "Yes. More." She was murmuring the words over and over. Laura barely recognized her own voice. She'd never verbalized her wants during sex before. Never. In a far corner of her mind, she recognized how comfortable she was with herself and her needs around Blake. A thought that disappeared as the rise of orgasm came over her. Her limbs tingled a second before she stiffened and tumbled into delicious release. Her muscles grabbed his cock in hard waves that shook her entire body. Blake worked his shaft in and out of her, sliding through the spasms until he arched that gorgeous chest and shivered right there with her, spilling himself inside her. When they stilled, he leaned forward, holding her, touching her. Seconds passed before he gently eased from their connection long enough to turn her into his arms. He kissed her then, a long, soft kiss that said more than words. When she thought the moment could get no better, he once again picked her up and started walking. Carrying her to the bed where she was certain they would be doing everything but sleeping. At least for a long while.

Blake was home and so was she.

Life was certainly taking a delicious turn.

Blake woke as the sun peaked through the window shade. He opened his eyes and sucked in a deep breath. He still smelled the floral scent of Laura's favorite bubble bath that lingered after savoring a long, sensual bath with her. His nostrils flared, the memory vivid, and he smiled. She was pressed to his side, hair spread across his chest. Brazen and bold during waking hours, she was soft and delicate in sleep. A male fantasy, his fantasy. With an eye of appreciation, he studied her face. Her dark lashes rested against her pale skin, skin as perfect and creamy as new snow from head to toe.

Shutting his eyes again, he soaked in the moment, reveling at the sweetness of waking up with Laura by his side. Next to him, Laura made a soft, sleepy sound and snuggled closer.

*"Hmmm,"* she moaned. "What time is it?"

His fingers lightly brushed hair from her eyes before glancing at the clock. "Nine. Why? Do you have to be somewhere?" They'd talked about spending the weekend together.

"Not without you," she murmured. "Just curious."

"We could rent some scary videos this evening, like we used to," he commented. "This old house would make them fun."

She stretched and slid between his legs, resting her hands on his stomach and her chin on his hands, a smile on her lips. "I'd like that. Can we stay in bed and make love all day?"

He grabbed her and pulled her more fully on top of him. "How about we make love now, and then I take you to brunch before grabbing the movies. Then we come back—"

"And make love again," she whispered huskily as her lips brushed his. "Yes to the making love. We'll talk about brunch after." Her tongue darted against his, and Blake forgot brunch, consumed by only one hunger—the hunger for Laura.

It hadn't taken long for him to realize that what he'd been missing, and hunting for every place from bars to deserts, had been right here at home.

And when the time was right, when he was sure that an old army hound dog like him could make her happy, he'd make it official. He'd marry her if she'd have him.

# Five

Sunday morning, in the midst of a wonderful weekend with Blake, Laura stood in the kitchen, sipping her coffee and feeling on top of the world. Any second now, Blake would come walking out of her bedroom, freshly showered and now a part of her life.

She poured another cup of coffee. The weekend had seemed to pass in seconds, not hours; this attraction baffled her. Somehow, she doubted a lifetime in bed with Blake would sate her desire. But she'd certainly enjoy trying.

Setting her cup on the counter, she was reaching for the sugar when the front door opened. Turning toward the sound, Laura wondered absently if Blake had sneaked past her. Her brows dipped. But why would he want to?

"Hey, Sis. What's cooking?"

It was Matt looking rumpled, athletic, and younger than his age in a baseball cap, jeans, and a 49ers T-shirt. Setting her spoon on the counter, she tried to calm the racing of her heart, which had kicked into marathon speed. This was so not how she and Blake wanted Matt to find out about their relationship.

Once again, Matt proved he had the worst timing of anyone she had ever known. Always had, always would. He had managed to interrupt her and Blake all of the two times they had been together since her return home.

She had to warn Blake and give him a chance to decide how to handle this. She discarded option after option, her mind racing with possibilities. And what about Matt? Hearing his sister was dating Blake was one thing. Finding Blake in her bed, with no idea he even wanted to be there, was another.

Taking a deep, calming breath, she braced her hands on the counter behind her for stability. She plastered a smile on her face and tried to sound nonchalant. "What are you doing here?" But delivering the words through gritted teeth didn't help her cause much. Realizing her error in judgment, she gave up on the fake smile. Matt wouldn't be fooled. He knew her too well.

He gave her a mock wounded look. "Well now, from that tone I'd have to think you aren't glad to see me. How could that be?" He walked straight to her cabinet, pulled out a coffee mug, and reached for the pot.

"I'm truly wounded at the less than tender reception," he jibed. "After all, I came to check on you and see if you felt better. You don't return phone calls." He poured his coffee and sat the pot back on the burner. "I don't remember that being sick made you quite this cranky in the past."

Crap. It was nice to know her brother would check on her. Where was her cell phone? In the car, maybe? Now she felt bad. And she didn't want to lie to him. So she didn't. "Sorry. It was a long night. I didn't get much rest." All true statements. She was sorry for being cranky. The night was long, though not long enough. And she hadn't rested. Not that she had wanted to.

She took the spoon he was holding and had a thought. Did he see Blake's truck? Where had he parked? Out back. Yes. Okay. Breathe, Laura. Breathe. "I might be contagious," she offered, trying to get rid of him before this turned into a real disaster. "You'd better run, so you don't miss work. All those smoke fumes and now maybe a stuffy nose wouldn't be good. "

He grabbed the spoon from her hand with a quick, irritated motion. "Give me that."

Same ole Matt. Always taking her stuff. "I was using it." As she had been when he'd walked in the door. The door he needed to immediately walk back out of. Besides, about now, she needed that damn extra cup of caffeine with a huge spoonful of sugar more than ever. "You could get sick for using it, too," she added, responding as the sibling she was, determined to get her way.

Laura reached for the spoon again.

He pulled it out of her reach and shifted his weight to look at her more fully.

He gave her a disbelieving look. "What is your deal?"

"I just want my spoon," she said through tight lips, "to dip the sugar into my cup of coffee—the coffee that is now getting cold." She looked at the cup and then at him.

"Go home, Matt." Her hands went to her hips. As soon as she finished speaking she knew she had been bad. She just didn't want this thing with Blake to blow up and turn bad. Pressing two fingers to the bridge of her nose, she sighed heavily and then looked at him.

Tone much softer now, she said, "I'm sorry. It's a bad morning. I appreciate your thoughtfulness, but—"

He cut her off with a roar of a laugh. A knowing, brotherly tease of a smile appeared on his face. "You have company, don't you, little sis?"

Oh no. The truck. Had he seen the truck? Either way, all hopes of negotiation or a smooth cover-up were gone. Begging was her natural response when her brother turned into a hard-ass tease. "Matt, please go home."

"Do I smell coffee?"

It was Blake. Both Matt and Laura froze, eyes locked. The smile slipped off Matt's face as he slowly turned. "Blake?"

Laura watched Blake turn pale on the count of two. "Matt." The name was delivered in a flat tone. Somehow, Blake managed a friendly nod of his head, though Laura knew his mind was racing. To his credit, after the initial shock, it didn't show.

Fixing Laura in a steady gaze, he walked toward her and took her coffee from her, taking a sip. Laura was shocked at the intimate act done in front of her brother, and at his nearness, with their shoulders touching. "How'd Friday night go for you?"

Matt stared a moment. At Blake. At Laura. Then, abruptly, he burst out laughing and, to Laura's shock, exclaimed: "Finally! I thought you two would never get a room!"

Laura looked at Blake; his expression was as stunned as hers must be. "You knew we were attracted to each other?"

"The whole world knows!" Matt declared, and then eyed Blake. "But you still know that if you hurt her, I'll kick your ass." His gaze shifted to Laura. "Same goes for you. You hurt him, and it will be my extra pleasure to kick yours."

Matt couldn't have said anything more right. He'd declared them equals in a way, his desire to protect them both clear, but so was his approval of them together.

Despite Laura's pleasure about how Matt had handled the situation, she felt he took an hour too long to go home. "Thank goodness!" she declared, shutting the door behind him and falling against the wooden surface. "Alone again."

Blake pulled her into his arms. "Now, where were we?" He smiled. "That's right. Making love."

Laura smiled and slid her arms around his neck. "Yes," she whispered. "Making love."

LISA RENEE JONES owned and operated a temporary staffing agency for over ten years, earning numerous industry awards. The corporate world offered only limited opportunity to explore her creative side, so she began writing romantic suspense. Since starting her career, she has placed in numerous contests, including winning the Romantic Times Aspiring Writers contest for her romantic suspense, *Hidden Instincts*.

# Billboard Babe

## Myla Jackson

# One

*N*ormally calm, cool, and professional, Angie Jordan—more generically known in the office as A.J.—stared out the wide expanse of plate-glass window to the woman staring back at her. Her heart raced in her chest and she rubbed sweat-dampened hands across her smoky gray suit skirt. What had she been thinking? Though she had to admit, no one would ever guess the woman stretched out on the snow-white billboard wearing sizzling-hot red satin was advertising executive yours truly. No one saw behind the subtle gray suits and sensible plastic-framed glasses to the desirable woman beneath the wool-blend fabric.

Hell, A.J. hadn't seen herself beneath the layers of dull clothing until Bryce, her best friend and a miracle-working artist-photographer, convinced her to pull this stunt.

Sure she and Daniel had been tasked—no, *threatened* was the correct term—to come up with an ad for the agency to bring in more business during the most critical of holiday seasons, Christmas. As Rob Davison, vice president of Tate and Westerfield Advertising, had so bluntly put it, "Get more business or I'll get new staff."

But to put herself on the billboard? A.J. grimaced at the five-foot-by-six-foot face staring back at her through the window. She glanced down to the street four stories below, where people stopped to stare and point at her picture.

She should be overjoyed the billboard was getting all the attention, but she just wasn't sure what Daniel's reaction would be when he came in. Bryce and his makeup artists had certainly made a silk purse out of this sow's ear. A.J. barely recognized herself in the gorgeous red gown, exposing more skin than she'd ever dared without being in a swimsuit on a beach.

Bryce sailed through Daniel's door and grabbed A.J.'s arm. "Here he comes. You sure I can't stay and see his reaction? I'd give my favorite lens to be here."

"You can't," A.J. said, her voice squeaking like a teenager's. "He'll suspect something. I'm not even going to be here."

Bryce tsked. "I'd love to see his face when he sees your . . . *ahem* . . . assets." With a smirk, Bryce left. A minute later, Bryce could be heard halfway down the hall saying, "Oh, hello, Daniel. Fabulous day, isn't it? Almost feels like Christmas."

Fear fluttered in A.J.'s belly like a swarm of honeybees. What would he think? Would he know? Wasn't that the point? Didn't she want him to see her, not just the suit?

At the last minute, A.J. got cold feet and closed the blinds. Better to break it to him gently. Or better yet, not at all. Too late, she was trapped in Daniel's office. One way or another, the cat would escape the bag.

"Bryce," Daniel nodded to the photographer, in passing. Fabulous day? He'd yet to come up with a decent campaign to pull Tate and Westerfield Advertising out of the red. He and A.J. were supposed to talk this morning about an idea she'd had. Maybe she'd come through and both their butts would be saved from starting the New Year with pink slips.

Vince Mueller stepped out of his office two doors down from Daniel's. "Dan, my man. I see you and A.J. have been hard at work. I love the new campaign. It's freakin' fantastic." He clapped his hand against Daniel's back, grinning ear to ear. "Old Westerfield will be giving you two a raise by the end of the week." He pulled Daniel close. "What I want to know is where'd you find her? I want her full statistics and a phone number to go with it. Better yet, can you fit her in my Christmas stocking?"

Daniel sniffed his friend's breath. "Did you pull another all-nighter? Are you still high? What the hell are you talking about?"

"Don't play dumb with me. You and A.J. struck gold on this one. Mark my words. I'm just jealous I didn't find her first."

"Find who?" Daniel continued on to his office and tossed his briefcase onto his desk.

With a frown, Vince followed Daniel into the dark office and spotted A.J. standing in the corner by the windows. "Oh, there you are. Daniel's been playing dumb with me. What's the scoop?"

A.J. blinked, her gaze shooting from Daniel back to Vince like a shiny orb in a pinball machine.

Daniel's eyes narrowed. "What's Vince talking about?" Had she done something without running it by him first?

Her rosy cheeks screamed guilt and she reached up to push her glasses back up her nose. That was the thing Daniel liked most about A.J. She was a terrible liar, and she knew it. Okay, so that wasn't all he liked about A.J. The trim curve of her hips encased in pencil straight skirts, the full swell of her breasts beneath her business suit jackets and the long smooth line of her neck had him panting in sales meetings.

But he'd made a rule a long time ago never to mix business with pleasure. Although, on more than one occasion in the past two years, he'd been very tempted to break a few rules with A.J. "Did you need me?" Okay, so that didn't quite come out right.

"I see you and Vince have things to discuss. What I had to say can wait." She ducked and scurried out of the room. If Daniel wasn't mistaken, A.J. was hiding something. Something big enough to make the self-determined young account executive leave the room as if her tail were on fire.

Vince whistled. "Damn she's got great legs."

"Leave A.J.'s legs alone," Daniel muttered, his attention on those firm, fabulous calves peeking from beneath her skirt, the incredibly tiny ankles and the arch of her feet in the low-heeled pumps. "What do you want, Vince?"

For a moment Vince didn't answer, his head tipping thoughtfully to one side. "You've got a thing for her, don't you?" His focus shifted from the doorway back to Daniel.

"No, we just work together." His rule. He lived by it.

"You know if she was to lose the ugly glasses and let her hair down, I bet she'd be a knockout."

Daniel had no doubt about it. He'd wondered himself and had dreams about removing the glasses, business jacket, and skirt. Fantasy. Pure fantasy. They lived and worked in the reality of this office. He dragged his gaze away from A.J.'s disappearing skirt to his friend. "What were you talking about when we came into my office?"

"Don't tell me she didn't tell you." Vince pounded Daniel's back. "Does our A.J. have a devilish side hidden beneath that prim and proper business act?"

"What the hell are you talking about?"

Vince marched straight to the window and tugged at the cord on the blinds, lifting them all the way up. The cool winter sun shone into Daniel's office. "Her." Vince poked his finger toward the glass. "I want her number."

Daniel moved around Vince and stared at a woman staring back at him from a billboard—a billboard three times the size of a tour bus, stretching a full city block on the side of the huge warehouse building directly across from the Tate and Westerfield Advertising building. Her slinky red dress displayed more skin than it covered, the front dipping almost to her belly button, showing enough cleavage to cause a wreck.

Five stories below, tires shrieked and metal slammed against metal.

"Damn, did you see that?" Vince stared down at the street. "That car just stopped in the middle of the road and the one behind him rear-ended him."

Daniel hadn't seen it. He'd been too busy staring at her. Despite the cleavage, it was the eyes that had captured Daniel's interest. Eyes as fathomless as the galaxy stared back at him, a misty hazel with flecks of gold, green, and blue lending mystery to her overwhelming beauty. Auburn hair hung over one shoulder in shiny sleek waves, brushing the sides of her breast. She was every man's wet dream.

"You feel it, too, don't you?" Vince said, his voice barely above a whisper. "She makes me hard just looking at her. And I couldn't have come up with a better slogan."

For the first time since he'd seen her gazing back at him, Daniel focused on the words below the beautiful reclining figure: GOT YOUR ATTENTION?

Boy did she, and then some. Not only did she have his attention, she had his cock very nearly standing at attention. He moved around his desk before his friend had a chance to notice and rib him about it.

Vince cleared his throat and blatantly adjusted his package. "I'm all over her. I just need her number." He turned a pointed gaze at Daniel. "So, who is she?"

He sat behind his desk and raised his eyebrows at his friend. "Guess you'll have to wait and find out like everyone else." *Including me.*

A frown formed on Vince's brow before his usual good

humor resurfaced. "Oh, I get it. It's all part of the radio and television campaign. Brilliant tactic. Brilliant." He shook his head as he headed for the door. "Wish I'd have thought of it myself." His laughter followed him down the hallway.

Radio and television? From his desk, Daniel pulled the tiny portable radio he kept for the rare times he got down to the corporate workout center. He plugged an earpiece into his ear and adjusted the dial to a local station.

"Tate and Westerfield Advertising have outdone themselves this time. The entire downtown Dallas area is crammed with traffic stopping to stare at the billboard babe plastered across a full city block. Thanks Tate and Westerfield for helping to beautify the city, and put us in the holiday mood, one old warehouse at a time. We've had calls from our viewers demanding to know who she is. If you're listening, Tate and Westerfield Advertising, we'll give you season tickets to the concert hall of your choice if you'll just tell us who she is."

Daniel yanked the earbud from his ear, wincing at the sudden pain. What the fuck? What had A.J. done without telling him?

With another lingering glance at the babe on the billboard, he left his office, pausing long enough to adjust his straining cock before stepping through A.J.'s office door.

She felt him enter the room before she actually heard him. The man moved like a cat, all grace and stealth. Every hair on the back of A.J.'s neck and across her arms sprang to attention.

"What the hell's going on, A.J.? I thought we were working this project together."

*Breathe in, breathe out.* A.J. turned, with what she hoped was an innocent, questioning look. "What do you mean?" She stood with her back to the closed blinds, wishing the floor would open and swallow her. Her heart beat so fast, oxygen didn't have a chance to make it into her lungs and feed her gasping brain cells. She fought for calm before the gray cloud threatening to steal away consciousness made her pass out on the speckled cream Berber carpet covering the floor of her office.

As her vision cleared, she stood straighter, adjusting her glasses on the end of her nose. The hard plastic frames giving her a sense of security, a place to hide, in the face of Daniel's obvious anger.

"You know perfectly well what I'm talking about." He marched across the room and stood toe-to-toe with her.

When he reached out his arm, A.J. all but sagged against him, catching herself before she drooled all over the man she'd lusted after for the past two years.

But he only reached out to open the blinds and jab a finger at the window. "Why didn't you consult me?"

*Oh, her.* "Call it an experiment. I d-didn't know whether or not it would work. Besides, it was your idea."

"Mine? I don't recall mentioning plastering a forty-foot-long—" his gaze panned the figure lying across the sign "—Billboard Babe on the side of a warehouse. I think I'd recall such a conversation."

He hadn't backed a step since opening the blinds. A.J. swayed, the scent of Daniel's aftershave and the raw musky maleness of him practically sent her into orgasm. Man, she was pathetic. And the longer she worked with him, the worse it got. Thus her complete departure from her normal sensible decisions.

"But you *did* mention it. I give you all the credit. You said, and I quote, "In order to get noticed, we'd have to do something so wild and exciting that it captures and holds the city's attention. Something bigger than life." With him standing directly in front of her, her voice rose a little higher and her breathing came in rapid, shallow breaths. "So . . . 'Got your attention?'"

He stared at the sign without saying a word for several long seconds. "Oh yeah. You got my attention. What I want to know, along with every other male in downtown Dallas, is who is she?"

A thrill of conquest ripped through her veins and gave A.J. the backbone to reach for her glasses and the pins securing her hair in a neat French twist at the back of her head. Now was the time to reveal, to show him that not only was she a brilliant advertiser, but she could be an equally brilliant and desirable woman, just like the babe on the billboard.

"I came here seeking the answer to that question myself, but I find that I want it to remain a mystery a little longer." The booming voice from the doorway startled A.J., and her glasses remained on her nose, the pins in her hair untouched.

Daniel spun toward the door, stepping away from A.J. "Mr. Westerfield."

"Daniel, A.J., I usually get the final approval on major

projects, especially ones aimed at promoting the agency."
He directed a stern look from Daniel to A.J. and back to
Daniel.

Flashes of pink slips blasted through A.J.'s senses.
One for her and one for Daniel. Damn! Would her stunt
result in Daniel's firing? Great way to get noticed by the
man you've been obsessed with for so long. She stepped
forward, swallowing past the knot in her throat. "Sir, it's
not—"

Mr. Westerfield held up his hand. "I'm not calling you
two on the carpet . . . yet. That billboard is generating a lot of buzz on the radio and now on television. I'm
going to let it ride a couple days and see where it goes."
He nodded. "But next time, make sure you get my approval before you go live." Without giving either one of
them a chance to respond, he left A.J.'s office.

Deafening silence reigned in the boss man's ab-
sence . . . for all of five seconds.

Then Daniel turned and glared at A.J.

She backed away until her butt pressed against the
open blinds. "I tried to tell him it wasn't your fault."

"Don't bother. It looks like we're in this deal together,
like it or not." Daniel inhaled and let out a long breath. "I
just want to know who the hell she is?" His gaze drifted
from A.J.'s face to the window. "And where has she been
hiding?"

For all he cared, A.J. didn't exist. Her hand went up to
her glasses and paused. A moment ago, she'd been ready
to reveal the identity of the woman on the billboard with
the great expectation of surprising Daniel into recogniz-

ing her as the model. But now her hand froze and she couldn't take off her glasses. Couldn't expose herself to his potential ridicule.

All she'd wanted was to get his attention. Well she had it. Only she didn't. Billboard Babe had it, from his mesmerized gaze down to the rising bulge in his trousers.

And damn it, she was jealous! Of herself! Of all the pathetic cases in the world, she was the worst. And the sad part was that she still wanted Daniel Adams more than ever. She'd come this far, she couldn't go back now. No matter what the outcome of her experiment, she'd already decided to leave Tate and Westerfield soon or go stark raving mad. How much temptation can a woman take, working side-by-side with a man who didn't even see her?

So be it. On to plan B.

# Two

"*I* can do this. I know I can." A.J. adjusted the neckline of the go-to-hell red dress for the hundredth time, her hands cool and damp, her nerves bouncing around her insides like a Ping-Pong ball.

"I think I've created a monster." Bryce applied a light dusting of rouge to her cheekbones. "You'd be better off just telling him how you feel. Guys don't like it when you play them for fools."

"I have to get him out of my system once and for all."

"And seducing him is the answer?" With a roll of his eyes, he leaned back. "Not that you'll have a problem in that department. Not with my magic."

"This is the only way I can do it and maintain our working relationship until I turn in my resignation. Once I leave Tate and Westerfield, our paths will likely never cross again."

Bryce sighed. "I'm going to miss you around here. You're the only one who really understands me. Will you look for a position for me where you're going?" When she didn't answer, his dark brows rose into the carefully coiffed spiked blond hair with black tips. "You do have another job lined up, don't you?"

A.J. frowned. "Well, not really. I've been thinking about painting full-time. It's been one of my dreams since I was a little girl."

"And give up the corporate life?" Bryce snorted delicately. "I can't imagine the play-things-safe A.J. plunging into the world of starving artists." He tipped his head to the side. "But then I never expected you to go along with my idea to pose for the billboard shot."

A.J.'s chin tipped upward. "It's part of the new me."

"I like the old you." Bryce grabbed both of her hands. "If I weren't gay, you'd be the girl for me." He leaned back and studied her. "If this doesn't give him a stiffie, I don't know what will. You look absolutely fabulous."

"Thanks, Bryce." She hugged him tight. "I couldn't have done it without your help."

"Damn right, you couldn't!" He gathered tubes of lipstick, mascara, and foundation, laying them neatly in a hot pink tackle box. "Now, go knock him dead. And if you aren't laid by morning, he'll have me to contend with. Hell, if you don't sack him, maybe *I* will. The man has to be gay to pass this up." Bryce laughed as he shoved her out the door of the dressing room located in the basement level of the corporate offices of Tate and Westerfield Advertising.

Alone in the elevator, A.J. had more time than she

could handle to get cold feet. Several times, her hand darted out to punch the stop button only to halt in mid-poke. She couldn't give up now. She'd wanted Daniel Adams ever since Westerfield hired him and gave him the office next to hers two years ago.

Every day that he walked by in his tailored Armani suits was more than any warm-blooded woman could stomach without exploding into a million unfulfilled orgasms. Tonight, she'd either have her wicked way with the man or die trying.

Or die of embarrassment if he found out who she was. A quick glance at the reflection in the polished brass walls of the elevator convinced her that Daniel would never guess the babe from the billboard was even remotely related to A.J. Jordan, his plain-Jane coworker.

A ding sounded as the elevator neared the fourth floor. A.J.'s heart leaped into her throat and her knees shook with the weight of her bold plan. At the same time, her pussy creamed in anticipation of Daniel Adams finally taking her, thrusting deep inside her and fulfilling her wildest, most erotic dreams.

When the door slid open, A.J. stood rooted to the floor. Not until the door started closing did she move. She hopped through the opening onto the fourth floor.

A.J. inhaled and let it out, willing her heartbeat to slow its erratic pace. How cool and sophisticated would she look if she arrived at Daniel's door breathing like a marathon runner on her twenty-sixth mile?

Silence made the click of her heels on the cold, hard marble tiles deafening. So much for sneaking up on her prey. And wasn't that exactly what she was doing? Mild-mannered corporate executive turned vamp. Ha! Her footsteps faltered. Really . . . Who was she kidding? She couldn't do it.

She paused in front of her open office door and stared in at the neatly stacked papers in her in-box, the meticulously clean desktop and the homogeneous prints decorating her walls. Was this all there was to life? Go to work, go home, eat TV dinners, and go to bed? Alone? She didn't even have Christmas decorations out yet.

How long had it been since she'd had sex? Two and a half years? She really couldn't count Sam in Receiving. His extent of foreplay was "Get in bed." That was it. No buildup. Just *wham, bam* with no-thank-you Sam. And afterward he'd turned on the sports channel. No, Sam hadn't been the answer to her cravings.

After replacing her vibrator batteries five times in the past year alone, A.J. had vowed to find relief. She wanted more. She wanted hot, sweaty sex that lasted longer than a television commercial break. More so, she wanted it with the man she'd been lusting after since he'd come to work at Tate and Westerfield. She wanted Daniel Adams. Now, on his desk, in his chair, against the wall. Her body ached with her desire, her nipples puckering in anticipation.

Her shoulders straightened, and she ran her hands over her hips, letting the satin of her red dress remind her how sexy she looked. Wearing contacts and with her hair hanging down around her shoulders, Daniel would never recognize her as his teammate from the firm. A.J. would have her wicked way with him and he'd never know it was her.

A shiver of excitement slithered across her skin, nudging her forward. Everyone but Daniel had gone home for the night. As was his habit, he stayed late more often than not. A.J. had stayed late on many occasions, just to have him to herself . . . sort of. He'd stuck to his office and she'd been too afraid to venture out of hers.

But not today. With the courage of what her mirror had shown her, she was hell-bent on being hell-bent over his desk. She turned the knob and stepped through the door.

The surprise on Daniel's face and the slow burn of his gaze rising up the split skirt to the top of her thighs and beyond was worth the risk of total humiliation.

Let the game begin.

The woman in the smokin'-hot red dress leaned her shoulder against the door, her hip swayed out to the side, the slit in her dress revealing long, luscious legs that went on forever.

It was her. The woman he'd stared at all day. The bigger-than-life sexual fantasy pasted on the side of a warehouse directly across from his office. He hadn't been able to finish a sentence, much less do any work all day long for staring out at the woman in red. Had he been staring so long, he'd gone to sleep? Was she part of a wishful erotic dream?

He dragged a hand down his face and blinked. No, she couldn't be a figment of his imagination. Daniel stared for how long, he wasn't sure, before his tongue reengaged. "You're her." He jerked his head toward the windows. Earlier that day he'd pulled the blinds all the way up. Darkness had settled around the city to be replaced by the lights shining up at the woman lounged across a city block.

Her deep-red sexy lips quirked up on the corners, her eyelids, drooping at half-mast over soulful eyes a startling combination of brown, green, and gray. The vee of her neckline plunged low between her breasts, almost to her belly button, just like in the picture. "Looking for me?"

"*Uh*, yes. I mean no." Daniel stood and almost sat back behind his desk. Flying at half-mast all day because of the billboard babe, his cock responded to the real thing by jerking to full sail and hardening to steel. What was he thinking? He jammed his hand into his pocket flaring his trousers out in hopes of hiding his condition.

"Is it yes, or is it no?" The hint of a grin on the woman's face graduated into a full, sultry smile, her gaze dropping to his crotch.

If his penis had a voice, it would say a resounding, "Yes! Yes! Yes!" Daniel reined in his leaping libido and eased toward the woman and the doorway. What was the catch? "Did A.J. put you up to coming here?"

When he moved around her to poke his head out the door, she leaned into him, the scent of her hair and perfume clogging his neuropathways with sensory overload.

She didn't make it easy for him to get through the door. He had to press against her to make it out. The electric shock pinged his inch-thick antenna, making it even harder. "A.J.!" He ducked into her office and back out. "Where is she?"

"Maybe she left for the evening." Her voice called out from inside his office.

"Was it Vince? Did he find you and set you up to this?" Daniel searched a few more doors down before he returned to find the siren lying across his desk, her likeness mirroring her perfection through the window behind her.

Jeezus, the long red slashes of material draped over her breasts weren't doing a very good job of covering anything. One perky nipple peeked out the side, tempting him past redemption.

Daniel swallowed the lump in his throat, willing his dick to go limp. Like that would happen as long as she was in the same room. "That's it, where's Vince? Is this his idea of a practical joke?"

"No, I'm all yours." She slid off the desk to her feet and stalked him, one lovely, arched step at a time, her high heels cleaving the carpet, bringing her closer.

"Okay, I'll bite." He heaved a sigh, then asked, "What do you want?"

She stopped in front of him, her breasts a breath away from his chest. Long, slim fingers walked up his shirt-front and circled his neck, then reached past him to close the office door, shutting them in and anyone who might wander by out. She stood up on her tiptoes and breathed in his ear, "I want you."

Plastered to him like a second skin, she hooked his calf with one of her own, her leg sliding up his until her crotch skimmed the top of his thigh.

Blood hammered through his veins, pushing up into his head and down to swell his penis to painful proportions. Without thinking, he raised his hand to the middle of her back.

Big mistake. The second his fingertips collided with the naked expanse of skin, all reasoning flew from his mind.

He wanted to rut with her like a stag in season. In a smooth turn, he had her back against the door, her arms pushed high over her head. "No, really, what do you want?" he said through clenched teeth. His cock pushed against her belly, hard and throbbing.

"No, really," she mocked, "I want you." Her legs rose and wrapped around his waist, the dress pushed to the side.

Holy Mary, the woman wasn't even wearing panties. Daniel groaned and dropped his hold on her wrists. "Do you know what you're doing?" All day long, he'd stared out the window at the sultry sexpot lounged across the warehouse. All day long he'd fought a hard-on so rock solid he could barely rise from his office chair. All fuckin' day long he'd fantasized about driving his cock deep inside that forty-foot likeness of the woman standing in front of him in flesh, blood, and that ruby red dress.

Now he had to taste her, touch her, feel her sexy body naked against his. Leaning forward, his lips descended to her neck, pressing against a pulse beating as fast and furious as his own. She wasn't lying; she was as hot for him as he was for her.

Those long, slim fingers insinuated themselves between her chest and his and she pushed him away. "Ever had sex against the wall, Daniel?"

Her bold question made him push her higher against the door. "No, but I'm willing to try anything once." Where had that come from?

"Then try this." Her lips descended to his, their luscious fullness more than he'd dreamed when looking out at her picture.

With his head telling him to put the brakes on, this wanton stranger and his pecker shouting "Go for it!" Daniel chose the fast lane. The hell with thinking! He let go of her hands and buried his fingers in her hair, crushing her mouth, thrusting between her lips to taste her tongue. Warm, wet, and sexy as hell, her pussy pressed down over the ridge of his fly.

He pulled back enough to whisper. "Are you a dream?"

Light laughter filled the air around him and she threw her head back, exposing her long neck to his lips. She unclasped her legs from around his waist and let them slide down the sides of his thighs. "Can a dream do this?" She moved lower, her fingers grasping his belt. With a quick tug, she had the buckle loose and the belt snaking out of his belt loops. Next, she slid his zipper all the way down, the wool-blend trousers falling away from Daniel's hips when she let go. His cock pressed against black, silky bikini underwear.

She arched her brows upward. "Who'd have thought the great Daniel Adams wore sexy underwear?"

"I don't usually, but the cleaning lady didn't make it to my apartment this week." His breath rasped in as with a slow, sensuous drag of one of her long, tapered fingers, the underwear followed the trousers to the floor, the side of her smooth cheek brushing against his penis on her way down.

"What are you do—"

Her face turned, her lips breathing a kiss against the heated, exposed length of his distended dick. "Seems kind of obvious." Cool fingers wrapped around steaming flesh.

Daniel swore he heard the sizzle.

"I'm seducing you." The tip of her tongue snaked out and tapped against the smooth rounded head of his penis, igniting flames in his bloodstream and sending heat throughout his body.

"This isn't right." He reached for her shoulders with every intention of stopping her assault.

But when her lips circled his swollen head and sucked him into the warm moist interior of her mouth, his hands didn't drag her up. Instead, his fingers threaded through the sheet of silky auburn hair and dragged her closer until her mouth consumed him all the way to the base of his cock.

One of her hands cupped his balls, the other slid around the back of his buttocks and rocked him into her and back out.

A groan sounded long and low, warring with the drumming beat of his blood pounding against his eardrums. Was that him?

If this was a joke, the joke was on whoever pulled it. Daniel stilled for a moment and looked around the room, expecting the punch line any moment. What? No cameras? No hidden mikes? Just him and Babe. And oh what Babe could do to a man. Tension built to a ragged peak. Daniel jerked out of her mouth before he came. He wanted more than her mouth. He wanted to fuck her against the wall, to act on every sexual fantasy he'd ever had. He wanted Babe, hard, fast, and now.

Anger clashed with sexual desire and he stopped, standing perfectly still. Damn it! He had to know if this was a trick.

# Three

A.J. glanced up from her kneeling position. "Don't you like that?" She spoke low and sultry, as different from A.J.'s no-nonsense tone as she could be without sounding fake.

"Too much." He dragged her to her feet and pinned her wrists high above her head. "Who put you up to this?" His voice was gravelly, forceful, not the normal smooth modulated tones that made her melt like butter. This Daniel was more of an animal. Turning melted butter into bubbling hot lava.

And A.J. liked it. Wanted more of it. Wanted him to take her there in the office, with the exhilarating potential of getting caught the added bonus. Gone was the corporate A.J. who followed all the rules and hid behind plastic-framed glasses. In her place stood the sexy Babe that Bryce had so skillfully created and whose identity she had assumed as soon as she slipped into the red dress. "I put myself up to this." How much more truthful could she be? "Now, are you going to talk or are you going to fuck me like you mean it?" Wow, she'd even used the F-bomb. A thrill of excitement tingled in her belly.

Daniel breathed in and out, his eyes wild, his hair mussed. His enormous cock peeked through the tails of his crisp white dress shirt, hard and shiny from the moisture of her mouth.

A.J. ran her tongue over her lips, staring down at what she wanted. If only he'd just stick it in her and scratch her two-year-long itch, she'd be able to walk away with no regrets. "Just do it, damn it." She hated the pleading quality of her voice but couldn't help it. "Fuck me." *Please*.

His brows rose. "Why?"

"Why?" Her mouth dropped open and her gaze riveted on his deep green eyes. "Do you have any clue the effect you have on women?" She rolled her eyes to the ceiling. "And you have to ask why? Let me go. You're obviously gay."

He leaned closer, his cock pressing against her belly, the rigid length proof he wasn't immune to her. "Not gay. Just curious."

Oh, buddy, no, he was more than curious. That poker-hard rod could drive nails into a wall. With her hands immobilized, A.J. couldn't reach down and touch it like she longed to. "Let me go."

"Not until you tell me your name." His chest pressed

to hers and his lips skimmed along her jawline. "Two can play this game, you know." He gripped both her wrists in one broad palm. His free hand, roaming downward, slid inside the red satin to cup her breast.

"Babe," she exhaled, crazy with lust for this man, but not crazy enough to tell him she was his partner. He'd laugh all the way to the boss with that discovery. "Call me Babe. Now let me go." She wanted to run her hands over every inch of Daniel's body. If this was her one shot at sex with the man, she didn't want to waste a minute of their time together.

A frown creased his tanned forehead, adding more depth to his wickedly handsome features. "Babe?" His forehead smoothed, his eyes narrowing. "Okay, have it your way."

He let go of her wrists. With one hand on her breast the other ran over her shoulder and down her arm to her hip. The trail didn't stop at her hip, but continued on to the slit over her thigh. There, he slipped beneath her dress and cupped her ass, pulling her hips against his, trapping his penis between them. "How do you want it? Slow and tender?" Fingers massaged her right butt cheek, easing around to the center crease. The hand at her breast tipped the thick red strap of her dress down over one shoulder and then moved to drop the other strap. The dress slithered to the floor, leaving her completely naked except for her red high heels.

Instead of feeling exposed and shy, a startlingly uninhibited rush of freedom ripped through her veins. This sexpot thing was much easier than she'd thought.

With the right guy. And that guy was Daniel Adams. She stepped free of the puddle of red satin and ducked beneath his arms, walking away from him, putting just enough twitch in her bare hips, she hoped, to make him want to follow.

Not until she reached his desk did she turn back to him. He stood rooted to the spot by the door, his eyes glazed, his hands fumbling with the buttons on his shirt.

A.J. eased her rump up on the edge of his desk and planted one of her red heels on the sleek mahogany beside her, giving him a clear view of the mark. What more did she have to do? Draw a bull's-eye down there to get him to take her?

For a long, painful moment, Daniel didn't move.

Heat rose in A.J.'s cheeks and she was just about to curl up into a ball and run for her pride. Her eyes stung with ready tears and she squeezed them shut, tipping her head back. Of all the stupid things she'd ever done in her life, this one topped them in spades. He didn't like what he saw. She wasn't desirable.

The ping of something small and hard bouncing off wood made her look up.

Buttons popped, zinging in every direction as he tore the shirt off his back and flung it to the floor. Daniel, in all his naked, hunky glory stalked across the Berber carpet, a predatory gleam in his forest green eyes.

A.J. drank him in, memorizing every ripple of his muscles, his tight-as-a-stretched-drum abs and thickly muscled thighs. This was the moment she'd been waiting for, the one she'd remember for the rest of the lonely days ahead of her after she left Tate and Westerfield.

A rush of fear filled her and she reached up to push her glasses up her nose, before she remembered she'd worn contacts.

Blood rushed south in a flood, filling his dick to painful proportions.

The woman had come to his office and pretty much thrown herself at him. What man in his right mind could resist? From the moment she'd stepped through the door, Daniel wanted more. He wanted to know who she was. A hint of recognition gnawed at his insides, that something familiar about her voice and face making him crazy, like something he'd forgotten poised on the edge of his memory.

With her ass perched on the corner of his desk and her cunt, wet and shining up at him, he couldn't think with his brain anymore. All his brain cells shifted south. She was like a magnet, drawing him closer.

He had to have her. Had to know her. And yet, he felt he did. But who was she?

When Babe touched her finger to the bridge of her nose, Daniel stumbled. He'd seen someone do that recently—very recently—and in that same way. But for the brief second he tried to remember, he couldn't. He abandoned thinking altogether. Perhaps in the morning he'd reengage the gray matter in his head. Tonight he'd had a gift delivered to him, and he intended to take full advantage of the offering.

His hands reached for her legs, wrapping them around

his waist. He pulled her to the edge of the desk and touched his throbbing penis to her slick opening. "Are you sure about this? You don't even know me."

"I've known you a long time and I've never been surer of anything in my life." Her legs squeezed around his back, her heels digging into his buttocks, forcing him to make that connection.

He drove into her, hard and fast, her tight channel encasing him like a warm, wet glove.

Babe leaned back on her hands, her full, rosy-tipped breasts pointed at the ceiling, her back arched, a moan rising from her throat.

Daniel slowed. "Did I hurt you?"

Her head jerked up. "If you did, please hurt me again." She sat up, pressing her lips to his chest. Capturing one of his hard brown nipples between her teeth, she bit him gently.

"*Ouch!*" He jerked back and out of her, flipping her over the desk on her stomach, the better to fuck her. Ramming in and out of her like a machine gun on automatic, he held tight to her hips when he shot over the edge, his world quaking around him, his juices spilling into her. For a few blissful moments, he throbbed inside her, then he leaned over her back, kissing first one then the other shoulder blade. His hand sought her breasts pressed to his desk calendar and he cupped each globe. "Who are you?"

"Does it matter?" She moved, straightening.

Daniel slipped from inside her and let her up from the desk, turning her into his arms. A kiss to her throat, another to the line of her jaw. "Yes, it does matter."

"You'll know soon enough." Her hands slid down to his ass. "Let's not waste the night on questions. There are many better things to do than talk." She guided him backward until the backs of his calves bumped into the leather couch, and he sat.

He drew her between his legs and buried his face in the furry mound of her sex. "You're right. There are many better things to do." Parting her folds, he tongued her clit, inching lower to the opening of her cunt, lapping at their combined juices.

Babe's hands threaded into his hair tugging him closer. "*Ummm.* I never knew it could feel that good."

"Babe, you haven't felt anything yet." He laid her on the couch beside him, spreading her knees wide, his hands skimming her inner thighs.

"You've got my full attention."

"That's good because you've had mine all day." With the precision of a classical guitarist, he stroked her clit with his tongue, while his fingers pressed into her pussy.

A.J.'s back lifted off the leather, her hips rising toward his mouth and the magic he made with his incredible tongue. Just as she thought her body couldn't get any tighter, the sensations any stronger, Daniel sucked her clit into his mouth, tugging and flicking until she burst into a million fragments of colored sparkles, tingling throughout her system.

Daniel climbed up her body and sank into her, filling her to full, pumping her with long slow strokes.

Her channel stretched to absorb him, her red heels digging into the cushions, pressing her up to meet him. When he came, she clasped her ankles around his buttocks and held him close.

When his cock stopped throbbing against the walls of her pussy, he pulled free and collapsed on the couch beside her. He gathered her close, spooning her back against his chest, her bottom pressed against his flaccid, damp cock.

Exhaustion settled in, making her boneless. She couldn't budge even if the building caught on fire.

Daniel's chest moved against her back in a slow steady rhythm. He'd fallen asleep, one hand cupping a breast, the other draped over her hip.

Spent and satiated after the best sex of her life, a tear leaked from the corner of A.J.'s eye. She'd come with the intention of fucking Daniel to get him out of her system. She'd been a fool to think once would be enough with the man. When she left Tate and Westerfield, which she knew now she had to, she'd leave a gaping hole in her life and her heart.

More tears followed until A.J. drifted into a troubled sleep.

## Four

The gray light of dawn filled the floor-to-ceiling windows, nudging A.J. awake. A glance at the clock on the wall struck terror in her heart and she stifled a gasp. Six o'clock? She went from lazily drowsy to wide awake in two seconds when she realized exactly where she was and whose hand was tucked between her legs, pressed to her pussy. For a brief moment, she considered a quick fuck before rushing from the building, but she knew the cleaning lady came in bright and early at . . . holy crap! Six o'clock!

The hum of a vacuum cleaner shot adrenaline through A.J.'s blood and she flew off the couch, lunging for the clothing scattered across the floor.

"What?" Daniel sat up, his hair spiked and his face creased with the lines of the couch. "Where are you going?"

"It's morning." She tossed his trousers at him. "Get dressed." With the fear of being caught spurring her on, she had her red dress on and her shoes buckled before Daniel rose from the couch.

He stood with his trousers in his hands, his cock visibly swelling.

Smoothing her hair with her fingers, she struck out for the door.

Daniel moved to block her exit. "You can't go until you tell me how I can find you."

"You'll know soon enough."

"Not good enough." He dropped his trousers and grabbed both of her arms, his cock pressing into her belly. "I want to know who you are. How can I get in touch with you?"

A.J. leaned into him and inhaled the scent of his aftershave and the musky aroma of their sex. She was tempted to say to hell with everything and mount him like a prized stud. Her heart pounded against her chest, urging her to act on impulse and fuck the man until he couldn't remember what day it was.

The vacuum cleaner bumped against the wall outside Daniel's office, dragging A.J. back to reality. "I have to go." She pulled free. "I can't tell you what you already know."

The door handle jiggled, the lock keeping the cleaning woman from barging in.

"What's that supposed to mean?"

"You'll know soon enough." She glanced away from him, afraid to meet his eyes with tears filling her own. "Please, let me go."

A knock sounded on the door to the office. "Mr. Adams? Are you in there?"

He pulled her into his arms and kissed her, sliding his tongue across her tongue in a sensuous dance like the one they'd performed the night before. Another knock rattled the door and Daniel broke away. "I'll find you."

A.J. ducked past him and yanked the door open, tripping over the cleaning woman in her hurry to get away.

Daniel stood in numb silence watching as Babe raced down the hallway and disappeared into the bank of elevators.

Not until the cleaning lady emitted a long low whistle did he realize he was still naked. He slammed the door and scrambled for his clothing. Maybe if he followed her, he'd find out who she was.

He jerked his trousers on, almost scraping his cock with the metal teeth of the zipper. Slipping his bare feet into his shoes, he tossed his shirt over his shoulders and dove for the door.

By the time he reached the elevator, the digital display indicated she'd made it to the parking level. She'd be long gone before he got there. Damn!

Cursing his slow-witted response to Babe's departure, he trudged down the hallway, attempting to button his shirt, until he realized there were no buttons to button.

The cleaning lady had moved into his office with the vacuum. No respite there. Daniel eased around the woman and her noisy machine, snatching his socks out of range of the beast she wielded with such a heavy hand.

As she pushed the vacuum back and forth, she muttered, the sound drowned out by the whine of the beast.

Daniel wished the hell she'd get out so that he could think. He dug into his desk drawer for his spare shirt, shaking the wrinkles out of it.

The vacuum cleaner spun to a stop, the noise dying out on a final squeal of the belt. "That's her." The cleaning lady pointed out the window. "That's the lady that just left your office."

Daniel didn't have to turn to know who she was talking about. With fatalistic slowness, he did anyway and stared across the street at the woman of his dreams. Only she hadn't been a dream. She'd been real. His hands and dick still tingled from touching her all over her gorgeous body.

The woman wound the vacuum cord and paused at the door. "My son wants to know who she is. What's her name?"

He sighed. "If only I knew." A.J. knew who she was and as soon as she came into the office, he'd get his answer.

A.J. made it to the basement at the garage level and slipped into Bryce's miracle shop, where she'd left the clothes she'd worn the day before. Crap. She didn't have time to drive home and change into something different. She'd just have to hope no one noticed that she was wearing the same clothes as the previous day. Hell, who would? All her suits looked pretty much the same.

She held her gray suit out to the side and glanced at her reflection in the mirror. Even crumpled, the red dress did a much better job of showing off the figure A.J. never realized she'd had. Exactly when was it that she'd crawled into the gray suit rut? And why was it that the corporate ad executive that wasn't afraid to stand up in front of a bunch of men, lead meetings, and make decisions was afraid to tell the man she loved that she was a real woman beneath the business suit?

Bryce's cat clock, whose eyes tilted back and forth with each swing of the pendulum, meowed the half hour. Westerfield had called a meeting for seven o'clock. If she didn't hurry, she'd be late.

A.J. slipped out of the red dress, pulled the gray suit on like armor, and sighed as the truth hit her. She hid behind her glasses and the plain suits to keep from being hurt. No man had made advances toward her, including the one she'd seduced the night before. But then she'd seduced him as Babe, not A.J.

With a sigh, she tucked the red dress in her briefcase and brushed her hair away from her face, sweeping it upward into the French twist she wore like her suits . . . every day.

Her hairpins weren't where she'd left them, and Bryce didn't have any stashed in his makeup or hair supplies. With the hands on the clock inching closer to seven, A.J. didn't have time to worry about them. She shed the contacts she'd slept in, plunked her glasses on her nose, and went to work. *Glamourless.*

When she reached her office, she slipped in and quietly closed the door, locking it behind her. She'd have to give a full two weeks' notice or forget any chance of ever finding another job in the advertising business. Her resignation letter flew from her fingertips. The whole time she keyed it into the computer, she wished that she didn't have to wait two weeks to leave.

Now that she knew Daniel the way she did, how could she work by his side and not think of the intimacies they'd shared on his office desk and couch? Intimacies hell! Make that hot, sweaty sex. Her fingers paused on the word *sincerely* as her body rocked anew with the sensations she'd experienced in Daniel's arms. Just the thought of the stroke of his tongue on her clit had her orgasmic, sitting behind her desk. She groaned and let her forehead fall to the keyboard.

Without a doubt, she couldn't work with Daniel. She'd have to figure out another way. She lifted her head, squared her shoulders, and printed the letter. A quick phone call to one of her clients and she had her plan in place. For the next two weeks, she'd be on the road. She'd leave the resignation letter on the boss's desk right before she boarded the plane to Los Angeles.

At two minutes until seven, she ducked her head out the door. The coast was clear. No Daniel in sight. A.J. slipped from her office and dashed for the conference room.

"A.J.!" Daniel's voice called out behind her.

She pretended not to hear and made it to the conference room, where a dozen other ad execs claimed their seats around the polished mahogany of the table. A.J. chose a chair between Vince and Terri, purposely avoiding any chance that Daniel might sit next to her.

Last to enter, Daniel dropped into the seat directly opposite A.J., his brows drawn sharply together. "I need to talk to you."

Terri leaned close. "I like your hair down. You should wear it like that always. Makes you look like the woman on the billboard." Terri wasn't known for talking softly. Her words created a buzz around the room, everyone talking about the stir Billboard Babe had caused.

Not until Mr. Westerfield entered the conference room did A.J. dare look across the table at Daniel.

He stared at her so hard, she could feel the pressure of his gaze burning through her skin.

She pushed her glasses up her nose and looked away. Had he guessed? Had Terri's comment alerted him to her ruse? Could he see right through her plastic-framed glasses to Babe? She reached for the pitcher of water in front of her and poured a glass, her mouth suddenly as dry as Tucson in July.

Mr. Westerfield cleared his throat and everyone in the room quieted at once, all eyes turning toward the boss. "Ladies and gentlemen, I thought I was bringing you together today to discuss the deplorable condition of our sales. But . . ." He paused, staring around the table.

A few murmurs challenged the quiet.

"But that's not the case. Thanks to Mr. Adams and Ms. Jordan, for their innovative solution to our flagging sales, we might still manage to have Christmas."

Applause and cheers filled the confined space.

"We've had more calls in the past twenty-four hours than during the entire first quarter. The billboard was featured on last night's news on all the local channels here in the Dallas–Fort Worth Metroplex. It even made the morning edition of CNN. Not to mention it's caused five fender benders." A grin lit Westerfield's face. "All because of a little mystery and the perfect model to carry it all off."

More clapping and cheers rose. Terri and Vince both clapped A.J. on the back and others were giving Daniel the same treatment, only he wasn't happy about it.

"Sir, I'd like to make one clarification. I wasn't the one responsible for the billboard. It was all A.J.'s idea."

The clapping ceased and all gazes swiveled to A.J.

She laughed shakily. "Oh, Daniel's just being modest. It was his inspiration."

"Which brings me to the next matter," Westerfield cut in. "Now that we have the city's attention, we have to maintain it. I'd like to capitalize on the mystery woman. So far no one knows who she is. We've had more modeling firms call for her number than I can shake a stick at. It's the talk of the town and the advertising industry." He clapped his hands together. "So, what's next?"

A.J. sipped on her water and sucked it down the wrong pipe. A coughing fit ensued, giving her the perfect opportunity to escape the room and Daniel. "Excuse me." Out in the hallway, she raced to the water cooler and downed a cup of cold liquid, before staring around in a panic. She had to get out of there.

Before she made it back to her office, the conference room doors opened and the staff spilled out.

A.J. ducked into her office and flung her portfolio open,

slamming the nearly finished ad proposals inside for the client she'd see in L.A. If she played her cards right, she could get out of there without another confrontation with the man she'd slept with the night before.

Her traitorous body should have gotten its fill and let her go back to life as usual. Damn it to hell, but it hadn't. Escape was the only answer.

Daniel barged into her office, a scowl marring his handsome forehead. "Why didn't you tell the truth?"

A.J.'s gaze shot to his. "The truth?" Had he come to force her confession about who had done it with him into the wee hours of the morning?

"Westerfield needs to know that it was your idea, not mine to put that billboard up." His anger melted into a soft smile. He crossed the room and took her hands. "For such a hard-hitting ad exec, you can be a marshmallow sometimes."

The soft tone of his voice and the electric currents igniting where their hands met made A.J.'s knees weak. If she wasn't careful, she'd be throwing herself into his arms, confessing all her sins. And that she couldn't do. She jerked her hands free. "If you don't mind, I have a plane to catch." Not that she'd made reservations or packed a bag yet.

She turned to shove files into her briefcase, only then noticing that the red dress was on top, in plain sight.

Her heart leaped into her throat and her gaze shot to Daniel as she slammed the case shut.

He stood at the window, his full attention on Billboard Babe.

*Whew!* For a moment, A.J. thought she'd been caught.

"She's beautiful, you know," he said as if to himself. "I'd give my eye teeth to tell her she doesn't have to pose for a billboard to make a point. She's perfect just as she is."

A blast of green-eyed envy ricocheted through her veins. "She's just a poster, she's not real." If her voice was a little sharper than usual, so what. The man admired the hell out of Babe, but he couldn't even see A.J. standing in the same room with him.

"She's more real than you think," he turned to stare into A.J.'s eyes.

She looked away. Playing the role of Babe wasn't being true to herself. If Daniel couldn't love her as A.J., there was no future for them. It was time for her to leave.

"I have to go. Good-bye, Daniel." A.J. gathered her portfolio and briefcase and the envelope with her resignation letter and left.

## Five

A.J. had muted her cell phone for her entire stay in L.A., choosing to answer only calls from Mr. Westerfield. The first being an ear-blasting rampage when he'd discovered her resignation the day after she'd left for L.A.

"What do you mean you're leaving Tate and Westerfield? You're one of our top execs. I can't have you running to another firm. What are they offering you? I'll match it." He waited for her response. When there wasn't one, he added, "And raise them another thousand."

"I'm not interested in the money. Actually, I'm thinking of going back to painting."

"And waste all your talents starving on a street corner?" The conversation went on for another half hour before Mr. Westerfield slammed the phone down, ending the call.

A.J. made her business contact with the L.A. client

and sealed the deal on another large advertising account. A fitting way to end her career with the agency. During her two weeks in L.A. she found an art supply shop and bought paintbrushes, oils, and canvas. When she touched colors to canvas back in her suite at the hotel, the painting evolved into a portrait of Daniel, his green eyes laughing up at her.

"You're pathetic." She slammed her brushes down and walked out of the room.

Two days before Christmas, she was back in Dallas, entering her office with a box to pack all her personal items before leaving once and for all. She hadn't had the heart to look at the billboard that had been the catalyst for her change. She couldn't bear to see the woman Daniel loved. Despite her having posed for the picture, that wasn't the *real* A.J. Jordan up there. Thankfully, her blinds were closed and she'd parked on the opposite side of the building. A woman could only take so many reminders of the competition. She snorted a strangled laugh.

"A.J." The object of her misery stuck his head in the door, his face deadpan straight. "Westerfield's office. ASAP."

That was it. No *I missed you while you were gone* or *glad you're back*. It was business as usual. Without grabbing her pen and notepad, A.J. walked empty-handed to the other end of the long hallway to Mr. Westerfield's office for the last time.

When she knocked, her boss barked, "Enter."

"Sir, you wanted to see me?"

"Yes. Close the door, will you?" He had his back to her, staring out the window, probably at Billboard Babe. He had to look at an angle to get a clear view.

A.J. had chosen the warehouse because it was directly across from Daniel's office. From where A.J. stood, she couldn't see the billboard, which was just as well.

"I can't accept your resignation, Ms. Jordan." Mr. Westerfield turned to face her. "Your work is entirely too valuable to me. The Billboard Babe campaign netted more sales in two weeks than in all of last year. I wish you'd reconsider."

Even before he finished, A.J. shook her head. "I can't."

"Why? Is it something I said or did?" Her boss moved a step closer and stopped.

"Or was it something I said or didn't say?" Another voice sounded from the shadowy corner of the cavernous office.

A.J.'s heart flipped into her stomach and she spun to face Daniel. She swallowed several times before she could answer. "No, no. You've done nothing." *Therein lies the problem.*

"All I know is that the two of you make a great team and I'd hate to lose you both." Mr. Westerfield turned back to the window. "Especially considering the public reaction to the newest sensation you two have come up with."

A.J. hadn't been able to tear her gaze from Daniel.

"Don't you have anything to say about the billboard you inspired, *Babe*?" The corners of Daniel's mouth turned up in a sexy grin.

"My billboard? I've seen it." She shook her head. Why

had he called her Babe? The blood drained from her head and she leaned against a nearby wing-backed chair. "You knew?"

Daniel nodded. "You still haven't told me what you think of the latest billboard changes?"

"Changes?" All the blood rushed back into her head, making her face hot and her hands clammy. "What changes?"

"Look and see." Daniel gripped her elbow and guided her to the window.

Sparks of awareness erupted from the point where his fingers touched her elbow, rippling across her skin in electrical currents.

"It's damned impressive if you ask me." Westerfield stared out at the warehouse.

A.J. couldn't believe Daniel was touching her. Her knees threatened to buckle as he gently pushed her across the carpeted floor. Then she saw him.

Stretched out on the side of the warehouse was a gorgeous hunk of a man, wearing nothing but red and green satin boxer shorts, a smile, and sunglasses. His coal black hair hung rakishly down over his forehead, making every female in the downtown Dallas vicinity want to brush it away, no doubt.

A.J. gasped. The heat in her face shooting south. She knew who the model was. She'd seen every inch of that fabulous body up close and personal. The sunglasses did nothing to hide the fact that Daniel Adams had posed in nothing more than his underwear for a billboard ad.

After staring at his near nakedness for a full minute,

tears burned behind her eyelids. The two weeks she'd been gone hadn't put a dent in forgetting him. She still wanted him so badly, she could cry. Her pussy creamed in memory of the way he'd stroked her with his tongue, aching for more of the same.

The squeal of tires on the road below shook her gaze loose from the magnificence of Daniel's likeness, and she glanced down just in time to see one car crash into the back end of another.

A woman climbed out of the first car and pointed up at the billboard. Yeah, Daniel Adams was one huge car wreck to A.J.

He stood beside her, his breath stirring the loose hairs on A.J.'s neck. "Did you read the sign?"

For the first time since she'd seen the billboard, she focused on the wording in bold black letters. YOU'VE GOT MY ATTENTION, NOW DO I HAVE YOURS?

Boy did he, and then some!

"A.J., I have another meeting I can't miss, but I want you to reconsider my offer. The Tate and Westerfield Agency wants you to stay. Hell, I want you to stay." Mr. Westerfield gripped her hands briefly and then left the room, with a parting comment. "See what you can do to convince her, will you, Daniel?"

Daniel's gaze hadn't left A.J.'s. "You can count on it."

A.J. panicked. "I have to go." She didn't know why, she just knew she had to get away. Before the door closed behind Mr. Westerfield, she bolted through the opening and raced down the hallway to her office.

A murmur of voices followed as Daniel chased her

down, bursting through the door before she could lock it. He did the closing, shutting them in and the rest of the staff out.

A.J. stood with her back to Daniel, breathing hard enough to hyperventilate. "How long have you known?"

"Since the day you ducked out of town." The sound of his footsteps was swallowed by the carpet, but A.J. could sense when he moved closer. Every sensory preceptor sprang to attention and her body heated to an incendiary furnace.

"Why the disguise?" His voice caressed her ears, making her bones melt like marshmallows in a campfire. How did he do that? And how did she battle her reaction?

Anger bubbled up inside and she spun to face him. "Because you never noticed me as A.J. I'd had enough of being invisible. I wanted to do something that would get your attention, damn it!" What had started as anger fizzled to a pathetic sniffle. "But I'm not Babe. I'm just A.J." If he liked Babe, he couldn't possibly fall for someone like A.J.

"No." He captured her face between his palms. "You're both. And I think I could love Babe almost as much as I love A.J." He leaned forward and kissed the tip of her nose.

"But Babe doesn't exist." She blinked when his words slipped through her fog of misery. "What did you say?"

"That you're both."

"No, the other part." She pointed her finger to the right. "After the part about being both."

He chuckled, gathering her into his arms. "The part where I kissed the tip of your nose?"

She smacked her palm to his chest. "Don't tease me." This was too important.

"Don't leave, Babe." He nuzzled her neck and nipped at her earlobe.

A.J. groaned, her head tipping back to give him better access. "I'm not Babe."

"Don't leave, A.J." His lips seared a path to the valley between her breasts.

Her pulse pounded against her eardrums, blood rushing south where his knee pushed between her legs. "Give me one good reason."

"I'll give you two good reasons." His fingers slipped under the hem of her very proper business skirt. "You've given Babe a chance for me to love, but you haven't let A.J. have equal time."

When his hand slipped inside her panties, she gasped, a flood of juices slicking her pussy. "That's one reason."

"Reason number two . . ." He maneuvered her backward toward the closed door until her shoulder blades bumped against the wooden panels. "We never did do it against the wall." His finger stroked her clit, igniting flames that burned through her bloodstream.

"Oh." She lifted her legs, wrapping them around his waist at the same time as she fumbled for the door lock. "So we didn't. Maybe I'll stay long enough for the wall."

He growled against her throat as he freed his cock and pressed home, filling her with his steely length. "Don't forget there are more walls than just this one."

"So there are." Then she lost herself in his kiss and the giddy anticipation of many more walls to come.

MYLA JACKSON began writing in third grade, when she penciled a story about a princess in a castle in a magical land. She's been telling stories ever since. She enjoys writing fast, fun, and sexy stories that elicit laughter as well as tears from her readers.

# Wish upon a Star

## Sasha White

# One

*W*here have all the good men gone? Seriously.

Women often say it as a joke, but it's a very valid question, Sarah Williams thought as she glanced around Diamonds, the exclusive club where she was to meet her next client.

"Your drink, Miss Sarah."

"Thank you, Lisa," she said as she took the glass of wine from the topless waitress. "Is Mr. Redmond here yet?"

"Not yet, ma'am."

Sarah watched as Lisa sauntered away, breasts jiggling, ass wrapped in the red velvet and fur of half a Santa's helper costume. She was an attractive girl, and Sarah briefly entertained the thought of what it would be like to play her. Except, despite the holidays, Sarah wasn't at Diamonds for personal pleasure, she was there to work.

It was a nice club, but standing on the upstairs balcony looking over the railing she realized she was tired of the whole scene. It was always the same; full of people who were so completely wrapped up in their own fantasies that they couldn't see the reality right in front of them.

Then again, that was how she made her very lucrative living. Somehow, she'd managed to go from being a woman who enjoyed dominating others to a woman who got paid to do it.

At first, getting paid to do something she loved was a thrill, but then it became work. It became work because being the best at something drew people willing to pay for the best. Now, she had an extensive list of clients of who paid whatever she asked for her to spank their bottom—because it was a fad.

She cringed. When had BDSM become a fad?

When had she stopped looking for a good man, a good submissive, in order to cater to the many?

Men who wanted her were everywhere, but where were the *good* men?

Sarah spun on her heel and headed for the rooftop patio. While she couldn't pinpoint the exact date when her train had gone off the tracks, she knew *why* it had.

She'd drifted from the close-knit community where she'd trained as a Domme because they'd let her. No one had called her to see why she'd stopped attending the play parties or why she didn't show up at any of the events. No one had missed her.

The cold air hit her skin as she stepped onto the roof and she shivered. She'd drifted because she had no anchor.

Tugging her little leather jacket closed, Sarah walked to the edge of the building, leaned over the metal railing, and looked down at the ground three stories below her. People hustled along the sidewalk two by two, or four by four. Cars drove past, full of people out to have a good time. It was two days until Christmas and the people of San Francisco were rushing about, getting ready for family and celebration.

Heart heavy, Sarah tore her gaze away from the beautiful happy people below and looked up at the star-studded sky. It wasn't often she could see even one star up in that sky. One of the pitfalls to living in the middle of a large city; the lights of all the high rises and skyscrapers often obliterated the night sky. But not that night. For whatever reason, the sky was blacker, and the stars brighter, than normal.

She stood there for a moment, wineglass in hand, and wondered if she'd always be alone.

A yellow streak blazed its way across the sky and the childhood chant leapt to Sarah's lips automatically. "Star light, Star bright, I wish I may, I wish I might, have the wish I wish tonight . . ." Her pause was less than a second, "And tonight I wish to find one good man to be my other half. I wish to find my soul mate."

The falling star disappeared and Sarah bit her lip. It was silly to hope, especially when she knew that in–she glanced at the watch on her wrist–fifteen minutes she'd be entering one of Diamonds private rooms and going to work. It seemed like all she had these days was work.

Just as she turned to walk back into the club, a blind-

ing flash went off. When the spots cleared from her eyes
and she could see again, a giant had appeared directly in
front of her.

And he didn't look happy as he glanced down at his
clothes, then around the rooftop.

Sarah gave her head a shake and took a step back.
"Where the hell did you come from?"

"Earth?" He ignored her and shouted at the sky. "Gods
be damned, not now! Couldn't you have sent someone
else?"

She peeked around him at the door to the roof. It was a
good twenty feet away, and still closed. She took another
look at the guy in front of her and knew he hadn't come
from inside the club. Denim jeans, biker boots, and tight
white T-shirts were *not* the standard mode of dress for
Diamonds clientele.

Unease stiffened her spine. "Excuse me," she said
as she started to step around him to go back inside the
club.

That got his attention. His gaze snapped to hers and
her heart stuttered. Lord, he was fierce.

Pure emerald green eyes gazed at her from beneath
thick dark brows, one of which was dissected by a scar
that ran to his hairline. Taut skin covered sharp features
softened only by full sensual lips.

Excitement rippled through her. *"Yum."*

"Here we go," he muttered, and held out his arms, as
if for her inspection.

Blood heated and began to pound through her veins,
everything else forgotten except the man in front of her.

Tearing her gaze away from his mouth, Sarah took a better look at the rest of him.

He wasn't exactly good-looking, but there was something about him, an energy that was undeniable and totally hot. Maybe it was the dangerous thing he had going on? Big, tough, and rough were certainly words that fit. At least six and a half feet tall, and thick with muscle, he looked like a warrior from Sparta. Broad shoulders, contoured chest, flat stomach, trim hips, and long strong legs. He would be a wet dream in nothing but a crimson cape and a loincloth.

*Ohh,* and the passion that shone in those eyes. He would be a wicked ride, for sure.

"Do I meet with your approval?" he rumbled.

The sarcasm in his tone woke her up. It wasn't passion in his eyes. It was anger.

Giving her head a shake, Sarah straightened her spine and met his forceful gaze. "It takes more than a good body to earn my approval."

"Whatever." His muscled shoulders rolled, as if he were shaking off his own thoughts, and she wondered why he wasn't shivering in the December air without a jacket on. "Let's get this over with already. What can I do for you?"

"Excuse me?"

Large hands lifted, gesturing at her. "You called, and I came. I see no immediate danger, but your call got through for some reason, so you'll have to tell me . . . What can I do for you?"

She pursed her lips and tried not to think about what she'd *like* to do with him.

*Jesus, Sarah. Get a grip!* Part of her realized she should be scared, a big bad biker dude just appeared out of thin air in front of her, but she wasn't. Scared that is. A bit worried about her own sanity, yes. But not scared.

"Go back to wherever it is you came from," she finally replied.

If someone else stepped out onto the roof, would they see him, or would they see her talking to herself?

Impervious to her thoughts, he stepped toward her, a frown pulling his brows down in a harsh vee. "You called me. I can't go home until I fulfill the mission."

He looked solid enough. Very real and slightly angry. "I think you're mistaking me for someone else. I didn't call you, I don't even know you."

His eyes narrowed and he studied her for a second before throwing up his hands and shouting at the sky again. "A virgin! You sent me to a virgin?"

"I am *not* a virgin." Not that being a virgin was a bad thing, but—whatever. She'd had enough. Sexy or not, real or not, she had work to do. "Excuse me, I have to leave now."

"Oh no." He shifted to block her path and she bounced off his chest. "You called, I came, so just tell me what the problem is, and I'll solve it."

Shock hit first, her brain shutting down. He was real! Until that moment, she'd half expected him to be a figment of her imagination. Like the imaginary friends she'd played with as a child.

Sarah reached out and poked him in the stomach with a finger. Rock hard.

His words sunk in and panic hit. *Be strong,* she told herself, inching away from him.

Tossing aside the still half full wineglass she fisted her hands on her hips and glared. "You're the problem. I did *not* call you. Now get out of my way before I get really pissed."

He laughed at her. Laughed!

"Get the fuck out of my way," she shouted and shoved him with both hands.

The creep didn't budge; he just grabbed her hands and tugged her against his body. Sarah froze. "If you don't let me go, I'm going to make sure you sing soprano for the rest of your life."

"Relax, little one." He gazed into her eyes as he spoke, and the fear and panic in Sarah disappeared. "I'm not going to hurt you."

Neither of them moved as they stared at each other. His arms firm around her waist, her hands trapped between their bodies as the air between them heated. His head dipped and her eyes went to his mouth, her lips parting in anticipation.

"I am Commander Nealon Graves," he whispered. "And I'm here to fulfill your wish. You did call, it just appears that you weren't aware you did."

*Huh?* Sarah blinked, bringing herself back to earth. "You're not making sense. I didn't call you."

He was starting to freak her out a bit. Commander? Commander of what?

"No, you didn't call me. You called *for* me." His gaze gentled. "What did you wish for?"

"What?"

"When you stood under the night sky and spoke to the stars, what did you wish for?"

"None of your business."

He grimaced. "Yes, it *is* my business. I'm what you wished for, sent by my king to serve you."

Sarah's heart stopped, then kick-started against her ribs. "Oh God."

Those luscious lips smiled as he set her away from him. "I'm not a God, merely a soldier. Now, what do you need? Are you in danger? Do you need me to guard you, or do I get to hunt?"

She gazed at him with new eyes. "My soul mate," she whispered.

He frowned. "What?"

"I'm not in any danger. I wished for my soul mate."

## Two

Stunned, Nealon stared at the female in front of him. What sort of crazy-ass mission had he been sent on? A soul mate? Since when did he take on Cupid's duties? He was a soldier, a commander in King Uriel's Army, not some matchmaker of love.

The door behind him opened and he spun around, blocking the newcomer's view of his female.

Another female stuck her head out the door and looked around, her gaze stilling when it landed on him. "Miss Sarah?"

"Here, Lisa." His female tried to step from behind him. "Behind the giant. Get out of my way!"

He let her get as far as beside him, but a solid grip on her arm kept her from going to the blonde at the door. He was not letting her out of his sight until he figured this mission out. He couldn't go home unless he fulfilled the mission, and he didn't have time to fuck around. He needed to get back to Arista as soon as possible.

"Mr. Redmond is here. He's waiting in the Red Room for you."

"Thank you, Lisa. I'm coming right now."

The blond female nodded and withdrew back behind the door, her worried gaze never leaving Nealon.

When they were alone once again, the one at his side tugged at her arm, and he freed her regretfully. "You're not going anywhere yet, Miss Sarah," he stated.

She glared up at him. "I am, and you're not going to stop me."

He stepped in front of her. "You need to tell me what you were really thinking when you wished on that star because I don't do matchmaking, so that can't be the reason I'm here."

"I don't have time for this. Just get out of my way."

"No." He didn't move. "I don't have a lot of time to mess around either. Until we figure out exactly what my mission is, you're not going anywhere without me, so get used to it." He was implacable on that point.

Nealon watched as her delicate brow puckered, her mouth firmed, and a familiar light entered her eyes. One that made his pulse thrum.

It was the light of battle.

The little female thought to fight him?

He was almost disappointed when she didn't take a swing at him. Instead, she stepped back and stared at him thoughtfully. Her head tilted and she spoke softly. "You said you were sent here to serve me?"

"Yeah."

"So you take orders from me, while you're here, of course."

He bit back a groan. For a virgin, she caught on quick. He could see where her words were leading, and the tone of voice, that silky almost seductive tone, stroked something deep inside him.

"Yes," he answered. "I take commands from you. Unless I feel you are in danger. Then my rule supersedes yours."

"Then let me pass."

Nealon sighed and stepped aside, following a close step behind when she headed for the door.

"What are you doing?" she asked when she stopped at the door.

"Following you."

"Well, stop it."

"No."

"I'm telling you to stop it."

He didn't bother to hide his grin. "Sorry, this is one of those times when my rule supersedes yours. Until we figure out what you're in danger from, you are not allowed out of my sight."

Miss Sarah shook her head as she stared at him. "Suit yourself," she said. "But you do exactly what I say, and don't say a word."

# Three

Miss Sarah strode down the stairs and through the club with purpose, and Nealon couldn't help but notice the swing of her leather-clad hips as she went. God, how he loved a woman in leather.

When they reached the first landing, he peered over the railing to the pit below, and at once the reason for the booming music became clear. A nightclub. He'd been in nightclubs on previous missions to Earth and thought them nothing special.

Miss Sarah didn't even pause; she stepped past a male guarding the entrance to a dark hallway, and kept on moving. Nealon followed silently, committing the building layout to memory as he went.

The little female paused with her hand on a door and looked up at him. "If you follow me in here, you have to be silent, and obedient. *I'm* the Commander, not you."

His annoyance at being pulled away from home at a bad time was fast being replaced by curiosity about the lush little female who'd wished so hard for her soul mate that King Uriel had heard her. He wondered what he was walking into, but he didn't balk. "Call me Nealon."

She searched his gaze, then nodded once, pushed the door open, and strode into the private room. Nealon immediately saw that the Red Room was indeed red. The only relief from the red of the walls and the floor was the black leather padded furniture spread throughout. A table, a bench, and padded leather cuffs hanging from steel mounts in the far wall.

And in the middle of the room, kneeling on the floor with his head down was a naked man.

"Hello, Robert," Sarah said, and let the leather jacket slide down her arms as she sauntered over to the man. She set aside the jacket and ran her fingers through the male's dark hair.

"Hello, Mistress."

Nealon stood by the door, silent, watching with attentive eyes.

Miss Sarah stood in front of the kneeling man with her eyes closed and her fingers stroking through his hair. Her chest was rising and falling as she breathed in deep and steady. Meditating almost. Then she stepped back and spoke clearly. "Stand up, Robert."

The naked man stood, feet shoulder width apart, hands clasped behind his back, and head up. Miss Sarah walked around him slowly, running her hands over his body.

"You look good. You've been working out, staying nice and tight for me. I like that, Robert."

She stroked a hand down his back, and then smacked him on the ass. Pulling her hand back, she hit him three times in rapid succession, and a red handprint appeared on the man's white skin. "Yes, your color is very nice tonight, too. Over to the wall, Robert."

Miss Sarah turned away from the man and strode toward Nealon. She met his gaze and he saw her eyes widen at the interest that he didn't bother to hide. When she'd looked up at him earlier, filling his arms so lushly, she'd tempted him as a woman tempts any man. But the strength he saw in her now was utterly seductive.

She rummaged through a bag on the floor just inside the door, and Nealon couldn't tear his gaze from her. She removed a small leather sack, a couple of leather floggers, and a paddle from her bag before going back to Robert, who was waiting against the wall with the chains, without looking Nealon's way again.

The room was silent, except for Robert's excited breathing. Miss Sarah secured his wrists in the chains and had him face the wall. "Hands on the wall, feet spread, and arch that back, Robert."

Setting the other instruments aside, Sarah held onto the paddle. She started off gentle, smacking first one cheek, then the other. But within minutes she was hitting him harder, and faster. The male's ass cheeks were turning a bright red, the color spreading as his sounds of pleasure echoed through the room.

Nealon kept his lips pinched shut, breathing in deep,

and releasing it slowly in an effort to control his own rising excitement.

He'd been surprised when he'd felt the warning tingle that signaled a planetary transfer. While a Commander was always on duty, Nealon hadn't been on a mission in months, due to a near death injury from his last one. At first he'd been thrilled to be back on active duty, until he'd realized he was on Earth.

Earth was not his favorite planet.

Then to find out his principle was a virgin . . . and looking for a soul mate. No, he had not been thrilled for long.

But the soldier in him was strong. Even if he could go back to his planet without finishing the mission, he wouldn't. It wasn't in him to leave a principle unfulfilled.

Now, as he watched her work over the man in chains, he realized why *he* was the soldier sent on that particular mission.

Nealon's pulse jumped when Miss Sarah put down the paddle and ran her hands over the man's rump, her words carrying easily to him. "You blush so pretty for me, Robert. Your ass is the color of the walls, and this pleases me."

"Thank you, Mistress."

She set down the paddle and reached for the small leather sack. Nealon's dick jumped behind his zipper as he watched her spread lubricant over a neon green phallic object. She stepped forward and slid her hand between the man's cheeks. "I know you like it when I stuff your ass, Robert, but you are not to come until I say. Understood."

"Yes, Mistress."

She slid the object into the chained man easily, and Nealon bit back a groan. He could almost feel the thing enter him—the feel of his female's hand on his backside as she gently filled him. He closed his eyes for a moment, struggling for control.

"Stand up straight, now."

Sarah's command was followed by the unique sound of leather strands stroking naked flesh and Nealon could not watch.

She was good. Very good.

Sarah held one flogger at her side while swinging the other in a slow circle. The strands brushed her captives back on the upswing of every revolution. She shifted her weight and switched hands, the second flogger going in the opposite direction and hitting on the downswing while the first stayed at her side.

The speed increased, and so did the pressure. The captive's back changed color, and his moans echoed through Nealon's mind. The energy in the room kicked up a notch, and he caught his breath as Miss Sarah brought the other flogger back into play—also on a downswing this time.

She swung both at the same time, the slap of leather against flesh getting louder, filling the room better than any music ever could, as her skin glistened in the dim light.

Nealon watched, entranced, as she worked. Her small lush body rocked with her movements, her focus entirely on the man in front of her. He could almost see the energy exchange happening. She gave, Robert received and gave back.

"Turn," she ordered as she stepped back, both floggers still swinging. Her arms crisscrossed in front of her
with each revolution and she looked like a warrior.

Robert turned and pressed his back against the wall.
"Please, Mistress," he begged. "More."

Miss Sarah stepped forward again, the leather straps
whapping against the captive's chest immediately. She
didn't hesitate or slow her strokes, and Nealon saw the
man's cock jump as it strained against his belly.

Nealon's hands fisted, every muscle in his body tight
with the need to stride over there and take the captive's
place. He wanted to be the focus of his female's attention. He wanted to absorb her energy and serve her in
any and all needs she had.

Sarah's head swiveled and their eyes locked. Her
rhythm faltered for a second and Nealon started forward.
She shook her head once, and turned back to Robert.

Nealon couldn't stop the growl that rumbled out of
him, but he remained where he was.

Sarah bent at the knees, her strikes lowering to hit
Robert's bouncing cock and his upper thighs. "That's
it, Robert. Pump your hips, feel that rubber cock inside
your ass. Does it feel good?"

"Yes, Mistress." His voice was high with excitement.
"So good, Mistress."

"Good boy," she crooned.

She put her weight behind each strike with the flogger,
Robert's body jerked, and Nealon's tension rose

"Yes, please," the restrained male begged. "More
please, Mistress."

"More?"

"Please," he whimpered, his body straining forward, into her strikes.

"Of course, my good boy." Nealon could see the sweat drip down her neck as she put everything she had into the strikes. Faster and harder, it only took seconds until Robert was begging for release. "Mistress, please."

"Please what, Robert?"

"Can I come?"

"Can you?"

"May I?" He was almost crying as his body jerked beneath her dancing floggers. *"Please, may I come?"*

"Yes, you may."

Nealon expected her to stop the flogging, but she didn't. Instead, she concentrated her strokes on Roberts groin as the man's cock jerked, his groan of satisfaction filling the room.

Miss Sarah slowed her strokes to nothing, then dropped the floggers on the floor and stepped close to her captive. Nealon couldn't hear her words, but he didn't need to. The body language said it all as she cradled the man's head, and stroked her fingers through his hair once again.

Turning around, Nealon gave them some privacy as he fought for control of his own primal urges. He wanted to race across the room and snatch his female away from the other man. He wanted to pin her to the wall, spread her thighs and bury himself deep.

The sight of her working over the other man had been arousing almost to the point of hypnotizing. He'd been proud of her strength, of her command over the captive as well as over herself. But the gentleness she showed the captive now was too painful to watch.

Nealon hung his head and chewed on his bottom lip. There was no doubt why he was the one sent to fulfill Miss Sarah's wish. She was what he'd always dreamed about.

She was *his* soul mate.

# Four

They were silent as they left Diamonds through the back entrance. Sarah pulled her collar up against the cold and tossed her duffel bag into the waiting cab before climbing in . . . with Nealon right behind her.

The man had to have hot lava for blood because he still walked around in just jeans and a T-shirt, paying no attention to the crisp winter air. Lord knew it felt like lava was running through *her* veins at the moment.

She wasn't exactly sure what had happened between them in the Red Room, but it was disconcerting. And highly arousing. Sarah had played with an audience before, but never had it affected her the way Nealon's watching her had.

The heat of his gaze has stroked her as surely as her leather had stroked Robert. Yet, he hadn't pulled her focus from Robert; he'd fed it. Knowing Nealon was watching her had heightened the experience.

Erotic tension filled the backseat of the cab during the short ride to her apartment. Sarah wanted desperately to reach out and touch the man who sat still as stone beside her, but she knew the time wasn't right.

As soon as she touched him, they'd both give in to the unspoken promise that hung in the air.

The cab stopped and she handed the driver some money before exiting. Nealon followed as she unlocked the entrance to her building and went up the stairs. She could feel his gaze on her ass as they climbed the two flights of stairs, and her sex clenched. They were almost there. Her apartment was only steps away.

She unlocked the door and led him inside. A flick of her wrist had the lights on, and she kicked off her four-inch heels and shed her jacket. She met his gaze briefly and spoke clearly. "My bedroom is back there."

He nodded and turned down the hall.

Sarah took a deep breath and followed. He found her bedroom easily and turned on the lights. Sarah stepped into the walk-in closet and dropped her duffel bag next to the others.

She watched as Nealon's eyes traveled over the bags, taking in the names on each. When he raised his eyes to hers again, the fire in them made it clear he understood that each bag represented a man. She stepped out of the closet, toward him, and shut the door behind her.

"Strip for me," she ordered softly.

His movements were swift and sure, and Sarah's fingers itched to touch. Her breath came fast and her heart pounded as she watched.

He was beautiful.

A soldier's body for sure, scars marked previous wounds on his shoulder, hip, and thigh. She wanted to lick those scars, to show him that she was so grateful he'd survived them. The thick pelt on his chest eased as it went lower, light fuzz over a six-pack of muscle only to thicken between his thighs and give birth to a gloriously rigid cock that made her mouth water.

Sarah could wait no longer. She made quick work of her own clothes and was soon naked in front of him. She stepped forward, a minute trembling beginning deep inside as she reached out and finally touched.

Nealon's hands were on her hips and his mouth was on hers instantly. She pressed against him, her lips parting and her hands clutching at his shoulders. Tongues tangled and backs arched as they strained to get closer to one another.

"Yes," Sarah panted after tearing her mouth away from his to make her way over his jaw and down his throat. "God, yes!"

He felt so good, so right in her arms. Hot blood pounded through her system as her spirit rejoiced. They fit perfectly.

"Mine," Nealon growled, his hands roaming over her curves. "I'm here because you are mine."

Her heart sang. "Yes."

She lifted her mouth from his nipple and looked up at him. Raising a hand she cupped his rugged cheek. "I've waited for you for so long. I prayed for you, and finally wished for you, and you came. I'm yours, and you are mine."

He lowered his head and their lips touched lightly—oh so lightly. The emotion behind that precious touch saying more than any words ever could.

Then she pulled back and grinned wickedly. "Now get on your knees and serve me."

"With pleasure, Sarah mine." He knelt on the floor in front of her and she spread her thighs, knowing the scent of her arousal would tell him exactly what she wanted.

Firm hands stroked up her thighs and she bit back a groan. He had a real man's hands. Large, work roughened, and hot against her skin. She closed her eyes in pleasure as he leaned forward, making a show of inhaling her scent before his tongue darted between her thick lips and tasted the juices there. Sarah placed a hand on his head and threaded her fingers through his hair, holding him close.

He used his thumbs to spread her lips wider, giving his tongue easier access. He licked up and down her slit, drinking her in until she couldn't take it anymore and told him not to play around. "Just make me come."

As if he knew instinctively what she liked, he concentrated on her clit. Flicking his tongue back and forth, sucking it into his mouth, and nibbling gently as he thrust a finger deep inside her.

A second digit joined the first and began to pump in and out. Sarah couldn't hide her trembling any longer as her insides tightened, her orgasm approaching fast. His lips surrounded her clit and he sucked harder, rhythmically as he thrust a third finger in her pussy. Her chest tightened and she cried out as waves of pleasure washed over her.

When she released him, he sat back on his heels, licking his lips and waiting for further instruction.

Sarah couldn't believe her luck. The big fierce soldier that had appeared out of thin air was *hers*.

She stood and walked around him. Trailing her fingertips over his skin.

"Up."

He stood for her and she eyed the cushioned restraints peeking out from under the edge of her bed, but decided against them.

There would be time to get into that later, for tonight, she wanted to feel his hands on her as much as anything. She gently urged him backward until the backs of his legs hit the edge of the mattress, and then, with a forceful shove he was on the bed.

Sarah climbed on top of Nealon, straddling his hips she pulled his arms above his head and met his gaze. "Don't move."

She grabbed a bottle of massage oil from the bedside table and covered her hands with it. She began with his shoulders and arms, firmly rubbing the oil in. Moving down his body, Sarah massaged his chest and belly, loving the feel of his rumbling groans as she pinched his nipples and played with his belly button. She skipped past his hard cock and teasingly massaged his muscled thighs and calves.

Finally, unable to stand it anymore, she began to work her way back up his body, with her tongue.

Licking and nibbling the inside of his thigh, breathing heavily on his balls, on his straining cock, she teased him, and herself.

She skimmed over his belly and chest, to suck on the side of his neck before whispering in his ear. "I am going to ride you. I am going to show you what only I can give you."

Gripping his hard cock firmly in one hand she brushed it over her pussy lips. Slipping it in between her lips, Sarah stroked it up and down, flicking the head against her clit before sitting down and sheathing him completely.

Letting out a deep moan of pleasure, she started to rock gently.

A groan whispered from Nealon's lips. She knew he wanted her to ride him hard. But this was just the beginning so she continued to rock gently. She changed the angle so that her clit rubbed against his pubic bone and the delicious friction brought on a surprise orgasm. Nealon's groan matched hers as his hands came down to grip her hips, thrusting upward and burying himself deeper inside her throbbing sex.

When she could focus again, Sarah looked down at Nealon. His cock was still rock hard and throbbing inside of her, his eyes closed and mouth open a crack as he drew deep breaths in and out.

She leaned down and kissed him, thrusting her tongue into his mouth and letting him know how wonderful he was. She tightened her inner muscles and started to ride him again. But not so gently this time.

She leaned back and cupped her own breasts teasingly before raising one arm behind her head to release the clip holding her hair in a bun. Throwing her head back so her hair trailed down her back, she bounced wildly on his cock.

Nealon's groans mixed with her sighs and moans as she used him harshly. Her fingers pinched and pulled at his nipples while her cunt clutched hungrily at his cock with every bounce. Her belly tightened, signaling an oncoming orgasm, so she picked up the pace.

"Come on, soldier!" she shouted. "Keep it up!"

Nealon's chest rose and fell like a bellows, his hands shifting to cup her ass, his fingers slipping between the cheeks and spreading them as she dropped her hands to brace herself on his chest. Using one hand for balance, she rolled one of his nipples between thumb and forefinger of her free hand.

"Do you like this?" she asked. "Do you like to serve me?"

When there was only a groan in response she pinched his nipple harder. "Answer me!"

"Yes," he hissed out.

"Yes!" She repeated with another twist of his nipple.

"Yes!" he groaned loudly as he thrashed beneath her.

Her thighs tightened, she let go of his nipple and braced both hands firmly on the wall above his head . . . and kept fucking him hard. Her tits bounced in front of his face and his tongue kept darting out, trying to reach her. She leaned forward and cried out as his mouth latched onto a nipple. Her belly cramped and her cunt tightened as pleasure jolted through her system. "Come for me, Nealon. Come with me!"

She hadn't felt this alive in years. And she'd never felt so in sync with another person. *Ever.*

She cried out and ground down on him as he grunted and thrust upward, deeper into her. She collapsed on top of him as tremors ran through her body and her pussy milked every last drop from him.

When she could breathe again, she slid off his body to lie by his side. His arms immediately wrapped around her and held her tight to his body. A gentle kiss was pressed to her forehead, and his words made her chest fill with a satisfaction beyond sexual.

"Thank you."

They slept for a bit, holding each other tight. When Sarah awoke, Nealon was watching her sleep, a deep abiding tenderness clear in his eyes.

"Hello," she said.

"Hello," he replied.

"I'm Sarah Williams," she said, holding her hand out to him with a small smile.

"You're mine," he said.

Warmth that had nothing to do with the way Nealon radiated heat stole over Sarah. *His.* It was so archaic, yet she couldn't deny it was what she wanted. The strong, independent modern-day woman wanted nothing more than to belong to someone. And have him belong to her.

"That works both ways, you know. I'm yours, yes. But you're mine, too."

A blinding smile spread across his face. "Yes," he said simply.

Settling back in his arms, she asked about his home.

"Arista is a small planet," he said. "It is always warm and we have little vegetation above ground."

"Aboveground?"

"Yes. While we live aboveground, many of our resources are below ground. But don't think because we have little vegetation it is not beautiful. We have mountains and valleys and animals like you've never seen. There is magic on Arista and in all who are from there."

"I figured there had to be some sort of magic, otherwise how could you be here?"

He frowned. "You brought me here."

"Yes, but how?"

"I commanded a special unit in my King's army, made up of soldiers who are trained to travel through space to foreign planets to serve those that are pure of heart." He hugged Sarah tight and kissed her gently before continuing. "My king's bloodline is connected to the stars, and he receives the calls made by those who wish upon them. Most missions are of protection, guarding and protecting those that called for help in times of need. I'm not exactly sure how your call made it through, Sarah mine, but I am thankful it did."

Sarah recalled the way she felt when she was on the rooftop, staring down at the crowds of people; two by two and four by four. "I think maybe you were sent to protect me in a way that only you could," she said.

"Protect you from what?"

"From myself. From the loneliness that was starting to darken my soul. Only you could save me from that, Nealon." She gazed up at him. "You're not going to leave me here, are you? Arista sounds amazing, and I don't ever want to be without you again."

His arms tightened around her and his sigh of relief had Sarah laughing. "I would not leave you here."

A small bit of apprehension wormed its way into Sarah's happiness. "You're a commander, yet you were willing to get on your knees and serve me."

"I will always serve you. You are mine, and I yours. We will serve each other."

A heavy weight settled on her chest. "I'm not submissive, Nealon."

"Nor am I," he said. "I bow only to one, and that one is you. Strong women are revered on Arista, as it takes a strong woman to master a strong man. I've never met one whom I wanted to serve, but you . . . I *have* to. When I saw you with that other male tonight, my only desire was to replace him. I could sense your need for what you were doing, and I wanted to fill that need. Giving you what you need, being what you want, makes me complete. And as my life partner I will make you so happy you will never need to wish for anything again."

Nealon's smiling face lowered and his lips covered hers. Then with a groan he rolled over her and thrust his cock home. They were joined, as they should be.

Gifted with a salacious imagination, SASHA WHITE's brand of *Romance with Heat, and Erotica with Heart* is all about sassy women and sexy men. With a voice that is called "distinctive and delicious" by The Romance Studio, Sasha White has published over a dozen erotic stories in genres such as contemporary, paranormal, suspense, and science fiction and is going strong.

To learn more about her books, or send Sasha a message, please visit her website at www.sashawhite.net.

# That Old Black Magic

## Sylvia Day

*To Frauke Spanuth, my business partner*
*and promotional designer. You always amaze*
*and impress me, and I am grateful for*
*the time and attention you give*
*to everything you do.*
*Thank you!*

# Acknowledgments

Thanks go to my critique partner, Annette McCleave
(www.AnnetteMcCleave.com), for her friendship
and support. I treasure both.
And to the Allure Authors, for being my companions
on this sometimes arduous journey.

# One

*A Quarter to Midnight, the Witching Hour,*
*Christmas Eve*

*T*here was an indefinable *something* about the tall, darkly clad man traversing the sidewalk. That mysterious quality compelled lingering glances from every window-seat reveler in Richie's Diner. He appeared not to notice, his gaze direct and unwavering, his purpose set and immutable.

It was hard to pinpoint what it was that arrested attention. Was it the impressive breadth of his shoulders and the way his inky black locks hung past them like a mane? Was it the way he moved with sensual purpose, every stride elegant yet predatory? Or was it his face, classically yet brutally gorgeous, all hard planes and angles, rigid jaw combined with beautifully etched lips?

Perhaps it was simply that it was Christmas Eve, a time when he should be home, warm and safe with the ones he loved. Not out in the snow, alone and unsmiling.

He had eyes of gray, like a brewing storm, and an air of complete confidence that clearly stated he was not a man to be crossed without penalty.

"That man could fuck a gal to a screaming orgasm. Guaranteed," Richie's wife said breathlessly to her cousin.

"Where do I sign up?"

The diner was closed to customers, yet filled to capacity with Richard Bowes's family and friends. Children manned the soft serve machine, making shakes, while the men cooked and told bawdy jokes in the kitchen. Frank Sinatra sang holiday songs through the speakers, and laughter filled the air with the joy of the season.

Pausing at the corner, the hunk outside held out both arms, and a lithe black cat that had not been visible from the window booths jumped agilely into his embrace. It had been snowing hard earlier and featherlight flakes still drifted in the random gusts, yet the animal's luxurious ebony coat was unmarred by the weather. The man, too, did not appear to be wet or cold.

He held the feline with reverence, his fingers rubbing behind its ears and stroking down its arching spine. It climbed his chest and looked over his shoulder, emerald green eyes staring back at the diner occupants. Nuzzling the top of its head against his cheek, the cat seemed to smile smugly at the coveting gazes from women in the diner.

There wasn't a single Bowes female who didn't wish to be that cat.

For a long moment, the flashing Christmas lights in the windows cast rainbow hues on glossy fur and rich locks, creating a unique yet beautiful holiday scene. Then the man continued on.

He crossed the street and rounded a corner, disappearing.

Max Westin growled softly at the feel of a rough feline tongue stroking rhythmically across the sensitive skin behind his ear.

"Kitten . . . ," he warned.

*You're delicious,* Victoria purred in his mind.

"I can see why upper-level warlocks don't keep Familiars." He held her closer to ease the sting of his words. "You're a distraction."

*I'm necessary,* she retorted, laughing. *You couldn't live without me.*

He didn't reply; they both knew it was true. He loved her with a deep, saturating abandon and relished the bond they shared as warlock and Familiar. She was with him every moment, her thoughts and emotions melding with his, her power augmenting his. Even when physical distance separated them, they were always together. He couldn't breathe without her anymore. She was a part of him, and he wouldn't have it any other way.

Once a Hunter for the Council that ruled over all "magickind," he had been assigned only the most difficult of tasks—vanquishing those who had crossed over into black magic and could not be saved. He had been groomed to join the Council, an honor bestowed so rarely that few remembered the last time such a promotion had occurred.

Then, They'd tasked him with one last assignment—collar or kill Victoria St. John, a Familiar driven feral by grief over the loss of her warlock.

Max would never forget his first sighting of her and how powerfully she'd affected him. Slender and long legged, with green sloe eyes and cropped black hair, she had the inherent sensuality of a cat and the body of a woman built for sex.

A deeply rooted part of him had known she belonged to him from the moment they met. Some part of her had known it, too, yet they'd played a cat-and-mouse game until it could not be played any longer. Until the Council stepped in and forced them to make a choice—the Council's dictates or each other.

Neither of them had hesitated to choose their love, regardless of the penalty.

*I feel them,* she said, her throaty voice bereft of the teasing playfulness of a moment before.

"Me, too."

The Triumvirate. They were responsible for the death of Victoria's previous warlock, Darius. He, too, had been groomed for the Council, the last warlock so honored before Max had caught Their notice. Angered by Darius's decision to pair with Victoria instead of accepting a Council seat, They had retaliated by sending Darius and Victoria after the Triumvirate alone.

Darius should have refused, knowing his death would be the inevitable outcome of such an uneven match. He should have fought to stay with Victoria, to protect her from the machinations of the Council.

That's what Max would have done.

*Yet you hunt them now,* she murmured.

"For you."

It was the promise he'd made to her when he claimed her for his own—her submission in return for his destruction of the Triumvirate. She had not asked it of him until he insisted, but it was a Master's prerogative to ensure that his sub had what they needed to be happy. Victoria needed closure; he would give it to her.

*I love you.*

He felt the undeniable truth of her feelings deep in his soul. The shining brightness of Victoria's love was so powerful that it kept the darkness inside him in the shadows where it belonged. Skirting the edges of black magic was perilous, because the dark side was seductive. If he didn't have Victoria to anchor him, Max wasn't sure what he would have become over the centuries.

"I love you, too, kitten."

The snowfall picked up again, making it hard to see. The wind grew colder, blowing on the diagonal, pelting flurries at them from the side. They should be home, entangled naked before the fireplace, sweating from carnal exertion. Not shivering from a chill that came as much from the inside as the outside.

Shielding them in magic, Max kept them dry as they turned the street corner and then again into a trash-

strewn alley. The sudden blizzard was a show of force
from the Triumvirate, a reminder that the three brothers were forbiddingly powerful. It was two against three
as it was, but the odds were less favorable than even
that. The Triumvirate drew power from the Source of
All Evil. Max and Victoria had only each other. When
their resources were depleted, they would have no other
recourse. The Council would not help them. They'd
refused to sanction this battle, knowing it was what
Max and Victoria wanted more than anything. When
it came to holding grudges, the Council was in a class
by itself.

*Is it worth it?*

He paused midstep, startled by her thought.

Victoria leaped down from his shoulder to the wet
pavement. She altered form instantly, leaving her standing before him naked and endlessly alluring, her only
adornment a black ribbon around her neck.

His collar. The sight of it and the knowledge of what it
symbolized aroused him with violent alacrity.

"Gods, you're beautiful," he rasped, admiring the
ripe, curvy perfection of her lithe body. With a snap of
his fingers she was clothed from head to toe in form-
fitting black Lycra. Her figure was his to enjoy and no
other's.

When they met, she'd been too thin, a manifestation
of neglect wrought by centuries spent without a Master
to care for her. Familiars needed to be fed and groomed,
stroked and indulged. They also needed discipline, and
she'd had none, not even with Darius, who, despite his

extraordinary power and skill, had been too flexible to control a Familiar as willful as Victoria St. John.

"I'm not sure I want to do this, Max," she said, stepping into his arms.

Power pulsed through his veins at her nearness. He'd made love to her for hours today, using their bond to store much needed reserves for the battle ahead. Every time she climaxed, magic burst through him, enhancing and doubling before returning to her, creating a cycle that made them feel invincible together.

"But we aren't invincible," she argued against his unspoken thoughts. "And I can't lose you. Your life isn't worth the risk. I can survive in a world with the Triumvirate. I can't survive in a world without you."

"This is what you wanted."

"Not anymore." Her lush mouth thinned with determination. She was so beautiful, her eyes a brilliant green surrounded by thick, ebony lashes. "For a long time, my desire for vengeance was the only thing I had in my life. My only reason for living. You've changed that, Max."

His hand pushed into the super-short strands of her hair and cupped the back of her head. "Tonight is our best chance to vanquish the Triumvirate for the entire year."

The world was filled with joy and love, with celebration and happiness, with the prayers of the believers and the hope of the nonbelievers. Mortals felt the change, although they didn't understand how real it was. The Triumvirate's powers would be diminished, a tiny advantage Max and Victoria desperately needed.

"Forget this year, and the next," she said with tears in

her eyes. "Don't you see? I love you too much. Vanquishing the Triumvirate won't bring Darius back, and even if it could, it still wouldn't be worth it. That part of my life is over. You and I have a new life together, and it's more precious to me than anything."

"Kitten." Max's throat clenched tight. He hadn't thought it possible to love her more than he did, but the sudden ache in his chest proved him wrong. For centuries she'd sought a way to avenge Darius. Now she was willing to give up that quest. For him.

*"How touching."*

The grating voices of the Triumvirate swirled around them, rattling the protective bubble that shielded them from the snow. The force required to affect their warding spell was enormous, and Max inhaled sharply as Victoria was prompted to add her strength to his.

A shiver coursed down the length of her tense frame. Max felt it and soothed her with his touch, stroking along the curve of her spine.

"We can do this," he murmured, grimly determined.

Her hands fisted in his shirt. "Yes."

Max pressed a quick hard kiss to her forehead. She released him and took a place beside him, her fingers linking with his.

Before them in a line stood three hooded figures, their eyes glowing red from within the shadows of their cowls, their height well over seven feet tall, their frames rail thin but possessed of phenomenal power.

"Perhaps we'll take you this time, pretty kitty," one rasped at Victoria, laughing. His face was white as chalk and heavily lined, as if the skin were slowly melting off the underlayer of bones.

"Not on my life," Max challenged softly.

"Of course not," another cackled. "What would be the fun otherwise?"

The Triumvirate's unified front and appearance magnified the feeling that one faced a veritable army when they opposed them. While other demons and hellhounds were routinely discarded and removed from the Source's favor, these brethren had been immutable in the Order of Evil for centuries. Most magickind had come to see them as a fixture as permanent as Satan. They simply were and would always be.

In a lightning-quick movement, Victoria crouched and extended her arm, expelling a fiery ball of magic to hit the brother in the center. Almost instantly, two retaliatory strikes shot toward her from the left and right, the strength of the blows enough to rock her back on her feet despite the wards around her.

Max lunged forward, both hands out, returning fire. Victoria again attacked the one in the middle, resulting in the Triumvirate taking simultaneous hits.

If not for Darius's gift to her, Victoria would be unable to do more than stand beside Max and strengthen him, as she'd done the night Darius had been killed. But now she carried the strength of the fallen warlock inside her. Darius's power thrummed through her blood and enabled her to fight like a witch with Familiar augmentation. Max hoped that would be enough to save them both.

The Triumvirate retaliated as one, advancing one step

at a time, sending volley after volley of ice-cold black magic to batter Max and Victoria's defenses.

But they did not retreat. As they struggled to keep the wards in place and return fire, sweat dotted their brows despite the raging blizzard. The Triumvirate howled their fury, seemingly unaffected by the assault against them.

Victoria glanced at Max, saw the set of his jaw and the corded veins in his temples as he poured gray magic out of his fingertips in crackling arcs of energy. He focused on one brother, his shoulders curling inward with the force with which he projected the power inside him.

As the insidious streams penetrated dark robes and charred moon-pale skin, the targeted brother screamed in agony. His siblings rushed to his aid, concentrating their attention on Max. Victoria continued to attack in the hopes of attracting fire in her direction. But in the face of the possible loss of one, the Triumvirate took her hits with admirable resilience.

The wards around Max began to ripple and bend, bowing to the greater might levered against the exterior. Blood trickled from one of his nostrils and his pain invaded her chest like a white-hot spear. Victoria wept, her stomach clenching with mindless terror. Memories of the night she'd lost Darius mingled with the horror of the present moment, creating a nightmare unparalleled.

The Triumvirate was too strong. Max would die.

Victoria screamed, unable to bear losing him.

Centuries alone . . . Afflicted by grief . . . Then Max had entered her life. Changing everything. Changing her. Making her whole again. Soothing her restlessness. Loving her despite her faults.

*How will I live without you?*

Then, with alarming swiftness, a solution presented itself in her mind, offering a slender ray of hope.

She could repeat the spell Darius had used, transferring the bulk of her power to Max. He would be stronger then, able to save himself and get away.

*Do it.*

Summoning every drop of magic she possessed, Victoria began to incant the spell she'd never forgotten. Could never forget because they'd been the last words Darius had spoken.

Pulled by an invisible thread, her power drew up and gathered, the sensation dizzying in its strength and strangeness. Her lips moved faster, the words flowing more freely.

"Victoria!" Max yelled, his shields moving sinuously in a herald to their rapidly approaching destruction.

It was her fault he was here, fighting a battle that was hers alone. It was love for her that had brought him to this end. It would be her love for him that would spare him.

"*Max.*" Magic burst from Victoria in an explosion so powerful it brought her to her knees. It hit Max with such violence his body jerked as if physically struck. His wards restored to their rigid state and his bending arms straightened with renewed strength.

She gave all that she had to him, saving nothing for herself because her life would mean little without him.

She wouldn't survive his loss. She'd barely survived Darius.

Max roared in triumph at the sudden, heady rush. A thin layer of warding separated from the one that shielded Max. It grew in size, expanding outward, encompassing the Triumvirate and preventing reinforcing power from the Source from reaching the brothers.

Unable to recharge his depleting strength, Max's target fell to his knees, crying out at his impending vanquishing.

Victoria watched through tear-filled eyes.

*The Triumvirate draws strength from their numbers.*

Darius's voice drifted through her mind. She and Max weren't alone. There were three of them, just as there were three of the brothers. And it was Christmas Eve. They had a fighting chance.

Using the very last of her strength, she sent one last volley toward the nearest brother. The impotent force of the blast was barely enough to draw his attention. But as she sank to her knees, his laser-bright gaze locked fully on her. She felt the satisfaction that gripped him at the sight of her weakened state. He would assume her support of Max was affecting her. He didn't know it was already too late.

Steeled for the inevitable blow, Victoria made no sound when the piercing evil of his strike sank deep into her chest, chilling her heart and slowing its beat. She bit her lip and fell to her hands, holding back any cry that might distract Max at the moment of triumph.

The alley began to spin and writhe. Another punishing blast struck her full on the crown of her head, knocking her to her back. Her skull thudded against the gritty, potted asphalt, and her sight dimmed and narrowed. Her ears rang, drowning out the sound of her racing pulse.

"Max . . . ," she whispered, tasting the coppery flavor of blood on her tongue.

A blinding explosion of light turned the night into day. Sulfur filled her nostrils and burned her throat. The buildings around them shook with the impact, freeing a cloud of minute debris that mingled with the falling snow.

*You did it, my love,* she thought as her limbs chilled.

*"Victoria, no!"*

Max's agonized cry broke her heart.

Icy snowdrops mingled with hot tears. In the sudden stillness, the distant sounds of Christmas songs and jingling bells tried to spread cheer. Instead it was a mournful requiem.

Her chest rose on a last breath.

*I love you.*

With Max on her mind and in her heart, Victoria died.

## Two

*Six hours earlier . . .*

He was there, in the darkness. Watching her. Circling her.

His hunger wrapped around her, sharp and biting. Insatiable. It startled her sometimes, how ravenous he was. She could not temper or appease his desires.

She could only surrender. Submit. To them, to him.

Arching her back, her arms stretched the distance allowed by the silken bonds at her wrists, and her eyelids fluttered behind the red satin blindfold. Victoria stood, anchored, spread-eagled, her hands fisted around the forest green velvet ropes that extended from the ceiling. The colors of the season. More than mere sentimentality, it was a testament to Max's attention to detail. The same intense attention he paid to her body. He knew her inside and out, every curve and crevice, every dream and secret.

The sudden sharp smack of the crop against her bare buttocks made her hiss like the feline she was. The sting lingered, grew hot, made her writhe.

"Don't move, kitten," Max rumbled, his deep voice a husky caress.

If only she could see him. Her feline sight could drink him in, worship him. He was so beautiful. So delicious. Her warlock. Hers.

His lust was a potent scent in the air, dark and alluring, powerful. It beaded her nipples, swelled her breasts, slicked her sex. Her mouth watered for the taste of his cock and she purred, the low rumble an unmistakable plea for more. Always more.

She was as insatiable as he, driven by a love so consuming and vital she wondered how she'd ever lived without it.

"Max," she whispered, licking her lips. "I need you inside me."

Magic rose in the air between them, his considerable power augmented by her Familiar gifts. Her collar tingled around her neck. It was invisible to mortals, but to other magickind it was a blatant and unmistakable symbol of Max's ownership. A simple black ribbon that proclaimed she was owned, loved, looked after, protected. She'd rejected that symbol of submission for centuries after Darius had perished. Then Max Westin hunted her, and she learned to love supplication.

Now they were rogues, tasked with only the most unwanted assignments, punished by the Council at every turn. The adversity only made their bond stronger, deepening their connection.

"I love you," she breathed, arching in an effort to relieve the agonizing lust that consumed her. Her skin was hot and misted with sweat, desperate for the feel of his powerful body pressed to hers.

The scorching lash of a tongue on her beaded nipple made her cry out in near mindless longing.

"I love you, too," he murmured, his breath humid against her newly dampened skin. She heard the crop clatter on the floor just before his large hands cupped her hips.

"Y-yes." She swallowed hard. "Yes, Max."

As his heated face pressed into the valley between her breasts, his hands slid around to cup her buttocks, his fingers kneading into the firm flesh. His touch was gentle and reverent, despite the savage need she smelled on him. He loved her so much, enough to temper his passion and control it. There was nothing in the world like being made love to with such ferocious intensity and focus. Victoria was addicted to the pleasure he bestowed with such expert detail.

"Fuck me," she whispered through dry lips. "Gods, Max . . . I need your cock."

"Not yet, kitten. I'm not done playing."

She shuddered as his hot mouth wrapped around the aching tip of her breast. Panting, she writhed in his arms. "Damn you . . . you're killing me."

The sound of the Boston Pops playing holiday songs flowed in from the living room stereo, mingling with the sound of rushing blood in her ears. Outside, the snow continued to fall unabated, blanketing the city in a pristine layer. It was beautiful, but deceptive. The hair on Victoria's nape rose and a trickle of sweat coursed down her temple. Dark, insidious magic lay in wait for them. The whistling of the wind against the windows gave proof of that.

*We're waiting,* it whispered.

The sneering challenge of the Triumvirate given voice by the storm.

But here inside Max's vast loft apartment, she was shielded in a cocoon of desire and love. Together, their magic was a powerful force to be reckoned with. So far, they were undefeated. But they had never battled against any demon as close to the Source as the Triumvirate.

*Think about me,* Max snarled, his fingers tightening on her delicate skin.

His words echoed through her mind, a manifestation of the soul-deep connection between Master and Familiar. Their tie had to be at its strongest, its deepest, if they had any hope of succeeding tonight.

*Always,* she husked, wrapping her long legs around his lean waist. "It's always you."

She was lifted by his power, raised high into the air as if supported by a harness. The blindfold fell away, leaving her blinking, her sight adjusting into the feline night vision that allowed her to see her lover in all his glory.

Max stood between her spread thighs, his dark hair

dampened by sweat and clinging to his arrogant brow. His eyes were dark and shining, his skin golden, his musculature made visible by sharp sexual tension.

As his head lowered and his lips approached her quivering cunt, the depth of his desire flooded her mind in a ferocious growl that made her jolt within her bonds.

*My beautiful kitty has a beautiful pussy,* he crooned. *Soft, sweet, and delicious.*

Then his mouth was between her legs, his tongue slipping through the slick folds and stroking across her swollen clitoris. She arched into his grip, her body shivering with the delightful torment.

With dazed, heavy-lidded eyes, Victoria took in the view of a gorgeous man eating her out with helpless fascination. Their love only added to the eroticism of the moment. Max relished having her this way, craving the taste of her so strongly that he sucked her off daily, his enjoyment obvious in the hungry snarls that vibrated against her tender flesh. His pleasure spurred hers until it rode her hard, tearing her apart.

Her power rose with the ecstasy he dispensed with wicked skill, augmenting his, filling the loft until the wooden ceiling beams and floorboards creaked with the effort to contain it.

"Let me touch you," she begged, her hands clenching and releasing restlessly. She could free herself easily, but she didn't. That made her submission even more valuable to him. He cherished her because of it, and she adored him for seeing it as the strength it was and not a weakness.

*I want you like this.*

She gasped as his lips circled her clitoris and he sucked, the pleasure radiating through her body in rolling waves. His tongue stroked rhythmically across the hardened bundle of nerves, making her pussy clench desperately in a silent plea to be filled.

"Max . . ."

His head tilted and he lifted her higher, his tongue thrusting deep, fucking hard and fast into the melting, spasming depths of her.

Victoria keened, coming hard, her back bowing as the orgasm stole her sight. Magic exploded from her like ripples on water, pouring into Max until he shook as savagely as she did.

But he didn't stop.

His lips, tongue, and teeth continued to feast on her, groans spilling from his throat as he drank her down. The silky curtain of his hair brushed against her inner thighs, adding to the overwhelming barrage of sensation that assailed her. It would all be too much if not for his love, which anchored her in the maelstrom and prevented her from losing her mind.

"Oh gods, Max," she whimpered, shivering with the aftershocks.

She'd never known sex could be so . . . *fervent* until she met Max. He took her body to places she hadn't known it could go. He allowed no barriers between them, no resistance.

Max released her wrists and she sank limply into his arms, her cheek falling to his shoulder and her lips touching his skin. The taste of him was an aphrodisiac, keeping her hot and wet. Hungry.

He set her carefully on her feet, then applied gentle but insistent pressure to her shoulders. "Suck my cock, kitten."

She sank gracefully and gratefully to her knees, her mouth watering for the taste of him and the feel of that heavy, vein-lined shaft sliding over her tongue. She was desperate for it, her throat clenching in anticipation.

He held the weighty length in one tightfisted hand and guided the flushed, glistening head to her parted lips.

"Yeah," he groaned, his chest heaving. "You look so beautiful when you're giving me head, baby."

Hot and throbbing, Max's cock slid inexorably into her drenched mouth. Her hands cupped his buttocks and drew him closer, her throat working to swallow and lure him deeper.

He kept one hand fisted around the base so he didn't feed her too much. The other hand cupped her cheek, feeling her mouth worshiping his cock from the outside.

"Gods," he gasped, his buttocks clenching against her palms as her tongue fluttered over the sensitive spot beneath the crown. "Slow down, kitten."

Victoria pulled free with a wet pop, her lips curving in a catlike smile. Tilting her head, she followed a throbbing vein with the tip of her tongue, then circled his grasping hand. She backtracked, sucking softly as she moved upward, her emotions entangled with her physical responses.

"Fuck," he growled, his thighs quaking. "Suck it, baby. Don't play."

Pressing her lips to the tiny hole at the tip, she barely parted them, then flowed over him in a rapid dip of her head.

His hand left her cheek and cupped the back of her head, holding her still as he fucked her mouth in rapid, shallow digs. She moaned in delight, her thighs squeezed tightly together to fight the ache of emptiness in her pussy.

"Suck it hard, kitten."

Her cheeks hollowed on a drawing pull and his fierce shout of triumph swelled upward through the exposed ductwork, combating the sounds of the Triumvirate's challenge in the wind outside.

Shuddering, he spurted hot and thick, the creamy wash of his semen flowing over her tongue and down her throat. His fist stroked from the thick base of his cock to meet her lips, pumping his cum hard and fast along the jerking shaft into her waiting, willing mouth.

The power she'd given him with her climax flowed back into her, hotter and more powerful, a deluge so intense she wouldn't have been able to take it if not for the gift Darius gave her. She felt Max in her mind, his love flowing through her in a saturating embrace, his pleasure as necessary to her as breathing.

He pulled free of her suckling. The next instant cool, crushed velvet cushioned her back and Max was over her, kneeing her legs wider so his hips could sink between them. She purred at the feel of the slick head of his cock notching into place at the tiny slitted entrance of her pussy.

With a powerful lunge, he was deep inside her, his still-rigid cock thrusting through her swollen tissues until he'd hit the end of her.

"Max!" His name was a breathless cry on her lips, her toes curling with the delight of having him pulsing within her, stretching her to her limits in the most delicious way possible.

"Naughty kitten," he rumbled, nuzzling his cheek against hers. "You almost finished me with your mouth."

"I love your cock, Max."

"As much as you can take." His head lifted and his gaze promised hours of joy ahead of her. "I'll always give you as much as you can handle, kitten."

"Give it to me now," she purred. "Hard and deep."

Fists clenched in the coverlet, Max obliged her, pounding her into the mattress with the heated length of his magnificent cock. He whispered lewd praise in her ear, describing how she felt around him, how he loved her hot pussy and greedy cries for more.

Victoria clawed at his back, her long legs wrapping around his pumping hips, her cunt tightening on every withdraw and quivering on every plunge. Gluttonously relishing the brutality of his passion.

There was a desperation in his taking, a primal urge to sink as deep into her as possible so that they could never be separated. They faced the greatest foe of their lives tonight and they might not survive it.

*I love you . . . so beautiful . . . mine . . .*

As his emotions filled her mind and heart, tears coursed down her temples to wet her hair. She embraced his sweat-slick back and spread her legs wider, sobbing with the mind-numbing pleasure of his possession, trembling violently from an orgasm more fierce than anything she'd ever experienced before.

His climax followed hers, his cum spurting in scorching

skeins, his cock jerking inside her with every wrenching pulse. Their combined magic swelled, shaking every item in the loft. The windows creaked, whined, barely able to contain the power they created as one. On this night.

Victoria clung to Max, crying. She wouldn't lose him. She couldn't.

If the end approached, it would be her life for his.

She would ensure it.

# Three

*Midnight, the Witching Hour*

*H*e was going to die.

The hot trickle of blood from Max's nostril assured him of that fact. His veins felt scorched by acid, his chest burned with every gasping breath, his skull felt as if it were being squeezed in a vice. Every blow to his warding spell felt like a physical one and they were incessant, coming from two sides.

"Victoria!" Max yelled, his shields rippling sinuously in testament to their swiftly approaching collapse. She had to turn and flee, before his strength waned and left her vulnerable.

*Run!*

Just as his vision began to dim and he feared slipping

into unconsciousness, a surge of power almost too potent to contain tore through him in a scalding rush.

Victoria. So visceral it felt as if her very soul had entered his body. Her augmentation whipped around and through him, strengthening and protecting him from harm.

As his target sank to his knees and victory was at hand, an invasive chill spread outward from the center of Max's chest and gripped his heart. The icy fist tightened, then spread insidiously through his veins. The sudden dearth of Victoria in his mind was like a scream in silence, piercing and terrifying.

Turning his head, he looked for her and found her sprawled on the pavement, a smoldering hole in her beautiful chest.

"Victoria, NO!"

Her beloved voice with its soft, throaty purr whispered through his mind. *I love you.*

Max roared into the storm. His hands began to lower, his need to be with her a driving impulse that he couldn't deny.

But she wouldn't allow him to give up.

Her strength of will straightened his arms and increased the flow of gray magic he sent into the falling brother. His quivering arms shot forward and magic poured from the tips of his fingers in white-hot streams, arcing through the air like lightning, sinking deep into the collapsing body of the middle Triumvirate brother. The wards around him thickened, shielding him from the blows that pelted his frontal perimeter.

His body and magic were no longer his own. They were possessed by a force greater than himself. Something strange and new penetrated deep into his bones, embracing his grief and fury. Magnifying them and sending them outward in a shockwave of power so destructive it shattered his wards and sliced through the center of the Triumvirate brethren like a guillotine blade.

Their screams echoed through the alley, rising like banshees' cries, ripping apart the sky in a thunderous boom. As one, the Triumvirate exploded in a blinding flash, rocking Max back on his heels and quaking the very ground beneath him. The buildings shook with such violence they threatened to topple, and animals across the city protested in a sudden cacophony. Dogs whined and howled. Cats screeched. Birds fled their warm nests in a riot of flapping wings and caws.

Then the alley fell silent. The only sounds that broke the stillness were the jingling of distant sleigh bells and Max's own tortured sobbing.

He dropped to the snow on his knees, the emptiness inside him a gaping, yawning hole he knew he couldn't survive. He needed Victoria. Couldn't live without her.

Centuries he'd spent alone, focused on his primary mission—enforcing the will of the Council by death. Victoria had brought light into his life, warmth with the heat of her passion, and love into the emptiness of his heart.

"Damn you," he said hoarsely, crawling toward her as debris rattled down and mingled with the snowflakes. "You can't leave me here alone."

Max caught her up and pulled her into his lap. Chanting one spell after another. Trying everything he knew, black and white magic, *anything* at all to heal her and bring her back to him.

But she didn't move, her chest did not rise and fall with breath, her eyelids didn't flutter over the brilliant emerald irises he adored.

"Kitten . . . ," he sobbed. "You can't leave me here alone . . . you can't leave me . . ."

Rocking her, Max pressed shaking lips to her forehead and felt his sanity slipping from him like sands through an hourglass.

"Heal her!" His command cracked through the night, reaching out to the Council who heard and saw everything. "Heal her or I will hunt you down," he hissed. "Every last one of you. I'll kill you all. I swear it."

*We told you this would happen,* They crowed. *Her loss is the penalty for your arrogance.*

Max's jaw tightened. His gaze narrowed on Victoria, who looked beautiful and oddly peaceful. Her skin pale and luminous like a pearl, her thick lashes spiked from tears and melting snow. She glowed. Softly, faintly. With an inner radiance.

Stilling, Max took in that hint of illumination. And what it signified.

The magic within her still lived. Darius's magic.

*You can't have her,* Max growled, fury overtaking his crushing grief. *She's mine.*

There were consequences for penetrating the Transcendual Realm. Dire penalties.

He didn't care.

He would be stained, marked. Some would hunt him as a rogue. Peace would be ephemeral with a price on his head.

Max didn't hesitate. It would all be worth it. *If* he had Victoria.

Slicing across his wrist with a sliver of magic, he held his arm above the wounds in Victoria's chest. The crimson of his blood blended with the snow and dripped onto her charred flesh. The mixture sizzled atop her skin and smoke rose.

Max closed his eyes and began to incant.

Victoria woke with a gasp and found herself lying in a field of yellow flowers. The air was redolent of lilies and sun-warmed grass, and butterflies flitted through the air in rarely seen numbers.

Pushing up to a seated position, she perused her surroundings with greater care, attempting to reconcile the beauty of the summer day with the snow-covered alley she'd occupied just a moment before. She looked down, noting the simple linen shift she wore, cleanly cut and unadorned. Her hand lifted to her unmarred chest and she frowned.

Where was Max? And where was she?

A masculine hand penetrated her vision.

Her gaze lifted and came to rest on a beloved face she thought she would never see again.

"Darius."

"Hello, Vicky." His beautiful mouth curved in a

loving smile. The sunlight lit his golden hair with a luminousness that stole her breath and tightened her chest. Her favorite dimple dotted his cheek and brought back a flood of treasured memories.

"Where are we?"

She accepted the hand he held out to her, allowing him to pull her to her feet.

"Together," he said simply. "Although I've always been with you."

Darius linked his fingers with hers. "Walk with me?"

"Am I dead?"

His head tilted to the side, as if listening to something she couldn't hear. His handsome features took on a thoughtful cast and his lips pursed. Then he set off, pulling her along with him, forgetting to answer her. Or choosing not to.

As they strolled, recognition of their location came to her—the south of France. One of the many places they'd visited and enjoyed as a couple.

"Have you been here the whole time?" she asked.

"No. I switch it up every now and then."

" 'Switch it up'?"

He glanced aside at her with a familiar twinkle in his eye. "I'm keeping up with vernacular."

As flowers crushed beneath their feet, sweetly alluring fragrances filled the air. It was paradise, in a fashion, but echoes of pain and longing turned down the corners of her mouth.

*Max.* Her fear for him was paramount in her mind.

"Where are we, Darius?"

"You know where we are." He looked straight ahead, revealing no more than the classical elegance of his profile.

"Is it over for me, then?"

"It can be." With a gesture of his hand, he directed her to sit upon a half-moon bench that hugged a tree. A tree that had not been there just a second ago.

"You still have magic," she said.

"It is ingrained in us."

Victoria sat, her fingers moving restlessly over the edge of her skirt. The urgency inside her grew with every breath she took, sparking a driving need to act. For her, the clock was ticking double time, a jarring contrast to the pervasive leisure she felt in the Transcendual Realm.

Darius sat beside her and picked up one of her hands in his. "When I first saw you," he said softly, "I knew you were the only woman for me. The sensation was lightning in a bottle, an instantaneous awareness. I was certain, prior to exchanging a word with you, that you would make me happier than I had ever been or could ever be without you."

Her eyes stung as her vision blurred with tears. "I felt the same."

"I always knew you loved me."

"Yes . . ."

"I also knew that I was not your soul mate."

Victoria stilled. Darius smiled, but his handsome features were marred by sorrow.

"What are you saying?"

"You were all I needed, Vicky, but I couldn't be all you needed. I didn't have a firm enough hand. You were content with me, but not thriving."

"No," she protested, canting to face him directly. "That's not true."

"It is." He cupped her cheek, his thumb following the line of her cheekbone. "That's why I gifted my power to you. I wanted you to have a choice. I wanted to give you the opportunity to get it right the next time."

"It was right the first time," she insisted. "I will always care for you, always love you."

"I know." The sadness left his blue eyes, replaced by the mischievous twinkle she'd fallen in love with. "What we had was perfect . . . but now you have something even more perfect. I wish I could have been that for you. Still, I'm grateful for what we did have. I know we had something wonderful."

"Yes. We did." Victoria glanced at the field of flowers around them. "What happens now?"

"Now, you decide." He squeezed her hand. "Stay with me or live the rest of your eight lives."

She bumped his shoulder with hers. "That's a myth."

Darius grinned. "Is it?" he teased, standing.

Victoria rose to her feet and stared up at him. "Are you happy?"

"Of course." His dimple flashed. "I'm with you always. There's nothing more I could ask for."

"Do you want me to stay?"

"I want you to be happy," he said, in a low ardent tone.

"Whether that's with me or with Westin. He loves you. Almost as much as I do. He's fighting to bring you back as we speak."

"I love him." Her tears flowed freely.

"I'm glad, Vicky."

"I love you, too."

"I know you do."

His golden head lowered, bringing his mouth to hers. His advance was slow, yet heartrendingly familiar. The press of his lips soothed a long restless part of her heart. She hadn't had the chance to say good-bye; he'd been ripped from her too quickly. That lack of closure had haunted her for centuries.

Victoria's hands fisted in Darius's linen shirt and she kissed him desperately. Not with the passion she felt for Max, but with the lingering love they'd once shared. It was a bittersweet parting, but one that felt absolutely right. Her life was with Max now. So was her heart.

"Thank you," she whispered. "I couldn't have saved him without you."

"I'll see you on the flip side, love," Darius replied softly. "Stay out of trouble until then."

She tried to open her eyes, but sank into darkness instead.

Victoria woke to the feel of snow falling on her face. Warmth cradled her right side and she rolled into it, groaning as searing agony burned through her chest.

"Kitten?" Even from a perceived distance, the aching wonder in Max's voice could not be mistaken.

"Hi." She pressed her cheek to his soaked shirt. "Miss me?"

"Don't tease, damn you. I could kill you for putting me through that." He caught her close, his large frame quaking with the violence of his emotions. "What a shitty stunt to pull on a man. Especially on Christmas."

"I'm sorry, baby." Her hand curled around his side.

*Take good care of her, Westin.*

Darius's voice moved through her like a tangible caress.

"I will," Max assured hoarsely.

Turning her head, Victoria found Darius standing a few feet away. Translucent and glowing, he watched her with warm, loving eyes.

*Live for yourself now,* he admonished gently. *You've lived enough centuries for me.*

She nodded.

With a wave, he was gone.

And with a snapping of Max's fingers, so were Victoria and Max.

# Epilogue

*Six days later . . .*

"If you ever do that again," Max growled, rising over her in his velvet-covered bed, "I'll spank your ass red."

"Is that supposed to be a threat?"

She purred as he rolled his hips and pushed his magnificent cock into her.

"Kitten, you have no idea." He withdrew and thrust deep, the wide-flared head of his cock stroking across a sensitive spot inside her. "I thought I was losing my mind in that alley. I would have, if Darius hadn't brought you back to me."

"I'll always come for you, Max."

Holding her hip with one hand, he responded to her

teasing by shafting her pussy in hard, fierce drives. "Come for me now," he bit out.

She climaxed with a mewl, gasping as heated pleasure exploded across her senses with dazzling brightness.

An edgy rumble vibrated in his chest. "Fuck, that sound makes me hot as hell."

"After nearly a week of nothing but showers, food, and sex?" she asked breathlessly. "You're insatiable."

"I'm just enjoying my Christmas present, kitten. Besides, you love it."

Max stared down at her with his stormy gray eyes and she knew she'd never loved him more. He'd kept her within touching distance for the last week; cooking her favorite meals, feeding her by hand, and washing her hair and body. For a Familiar, it was heaven, and she soaked it up like sunshine after a long, dreary winter.

"Max . . ."

He thrust rhythmically, plunging deep and slow to give her time to recover, making her feel every throbbing inch of him.

Her neck arched, her nails dug into his back, and her pussy fluttered in helpless delight around him.

"Oh yeah," he rumbled, a wicked smile curving one side of his gorgeous mouth. "You definitely love it."

"I love you." She offered her mouth and he took it with breathtaking passion.

"I love you back."

Finally content, Victoria's lips curved against his in a catlike smile.

# *Author Note*

*Dear Readers,*

*I hope you enjoyed the continuation of Max and Victoria's romance from the first* Alluring Tales *collection. Their world fascinates me, so I'm grateful that cats have nine lives.*

*With love,*
*Sylvia*

SYLVIA DAY is the national best-selling, award-winning author of over a dozen novels. A wife and mother of two, she is a former Russian linguist for the U.S. Army Military Intelligence. Called "wonderful and passionate" by WNBC.com and "wickedly entertaining" by *Booklist*, her stories frequently garner Readers' Choice and Reviewers' Choice accolades. She's been honored with the EPPIE award and has been named a finalist for Romance Writers of America's prestigious RITA® Award of Excellence multiple times.

Visit with her at www.SylviaDay.com

# Silver Waters

## Vivi Anna

# One

The heat of the Caribbean sun razed Sangria Silver's back as she swam along the surface of the pristine azure waters. Swimming in the ocean—even in November the water was still warm—was one of her favorite pastimes now. She did it whenever she got a chance, morning, noon, or night. All she had to do was open the back door of her quaint beach cottage, nestled contently among thick grass and brush, and walk out onto the soft white sand skirting the expanse of blue water.

She could do it for the rest of her life and planned on doing just that. Two years on the run was long enough. Escaping the long reach of First Lady Maxine Madison and her goons had been difficult, but Sangria had pulled it off and gotten both her and Vance safe.

She was tired after that long run and just wanted her piece of paradise. So far, she'd been enjoying it to the fullest.

Rising to the surface, she made her way to shore. She had a thirst for something cold and sweet to drink. As she walked up the sandy beach, her gaze rested on a beautifully sculpted man in nothing but a towel lying on a beach chair on the deck of a quaint cottage, her cottage. Vance Verona never failed to arouse her. The man was pure unadulterated sex on a stick and she was hungry for just that after her long swim.

The corners of his full sensuous mouth turned up as she walked toward him, her swimsuit top forgotten on the sand behind her.

Raising his sunglasses to the top of his head, Vance grinned.

"Girl, I think you lost something during your swim."

"And I'm about to lose something else as well." Hooking her thumbs into the band of her bathing suit bottoms, Sangria pulled them down her hips and shucked them off her legs as she walked. Despite the impending holiday season there was no one else on the beach. They had a small strip of utopia all to themselves.

A year ago she wouldn't have thought to do such a brazen act, but life on the small Caribbean island had changed her. Vance had changed her. For the better, she liked to think.

She was much more relaxed now and didn't constantly look over her shoulder for that ominous something to crash down on her. A month ago, she had finally stopped sleeping with her gun under her pillow. It now rested in the drawer of the nightstand beside the bed. A small move to some, but to Sangria it meant trust was wriggling its way back into her life. Trust in the world that it wasn't always out to get her.

As she neared Vance, he sat up and reached for her, dragging her closer. With a satisfied sigh, he pressed an open mouth kiss to her stomach just above her navel.

She thrilled from the stroke of his lips. After two years of being together, his touch hadn't lost its fire, its excitement. His heated gaze alone could make her tingle in all the right places. The man was a gift from the sex gods. And he was all hers to play with.

"*Mmm*, salty." He trailed his tongue over her stomach, dipping the tip into her navel.

Burying her hands in his unruly dark hair, she yanked his head back and grinned down at him. "Let's take it inside."

"Why? There's no one around. We can fuck right here without being bothered." His hands molded her ass cheeks, the tips of his fingers brushing lightly against the slope between them.

Her thighs clenched at his words. She loved it when he talked dirty to her. His tongue was delicious no matter what it was doing.

Gripping her thigh in his hands, he pushed her leg up and set her foot on the edge of the beach chair. She wrapped her hands in his hair to hold on but he barely gave her a chance to take a breath before he slid his tongue into her throbbing pussy, parting her slick lips with one deft stroke.

Fiery, unbridled heat radiated over her flesh. Her entire body quivered from the inside out as Vance feasted on her. She wanted him to explore every slope and fold of her flesh again and again. He was a skilled lover always showing her new ways to find pleasure. No wonder he had been in such high demand back in the New States of America, a prized stud in Maxine Madison's illegal sex-trading harem.

Again he stroked her, stopping at her clit to circle it with the tip of his tongue. She could hardly breathe as her belly flipped over and over, like a roller coaster, and the muscles in her thighs tightened. An explosive orgasm built like a raging inferno at her center. It wouldn't take much more to push her over into orgasmic euphoria.

Gripping his hair for support, Sangria looked down at Vance as he licked and suckled on her sex. He was feral in his pleasuring of her and reveled in driving her mad with desire. She'd never been with a man who cared so much about her pleasure, but she knew he found his power in the ability to make her feel . . . everything. For a woman who had taught herself over the years to have ice for blood, that was saying something.

As if sensing her need, Vance raised his head and locked eyes with her. His eyes were dark and dangerous.

"You taste so damn good," he growled, his lips glistening with her lust. Then he went back down and settled his lips over her again, suckling gently.

Sweat trickled down her back. Her thighs tightened with anticipation. Sangria bit down on her lip as she felt the beginning flutters of orgasm.

Vance increased the pressure of his strokes, alternating between teasing her clit and sliding his tongue in deep. One final flick on her nub was all it took for her to come crashing down.

Moaning, Sangria squeezed her eyes shut. Her climax was intense and violent. It clutched her tightly as wave after wave of ecstasy crashed over her like a typhoon.

Releasing his intimate grip on her sex, Vance leaned back and grinned up at her. "Woman you come like you do everything else, with fierce determination."

She chuckled while tremors continued to cascade up and down her thighs. He was right. Everything she ever did she tackled with intense purpose, and that included fucking. The bonus was with Vance it was just so damn enjoyable.

"*Mmm,* it must be because you're so good at making me come."

"That could be it." Still grinning, he feathered kisses to her belly and slowly made his way up, standing to reach her mouth.

Wrapping his arms around her, he kissed her hard, his tongue dancing around hers. He tasted like mango and rum and sunshine. Everything she'd been starting to associate with happiness. It'd been a long time since she'd considered herself happy. But right now in this place, with this man, she was blissfully content.

It was a long way from conveying illegal shipments around the country for unsavory characters. But she couldn't be too sad about her past situation, because if she hadn't taken that job from Maxine Madison, she'd never have met Vance. She'd never have found him tied up in a steel case in the back of her Hummer.

As he nibbled on her chin, his hands streaked down her back. "Damn woman, you have the finest ass in the Caribbean."

"So, you keep telling me."

"Turn around. I want to marvel at it again."

She swiveled on the balls of her feet and stuck out her rear end, wiggling it back and forth, teasing him. She knew he loved it. She enjoyed it, too. So much, a new wave of tingles radiated deep inside her core. Vance liked to play and she had to admit, so did she, especially with the wicked games he imaginatively invented.

He rubbed his hands over her backside, molding and squeezing her cheeks. "*Mmm,* firm, yet subtle."

She chuckled, but what he was doing to her was making her pussy purr with delight.

Then he slapped her one cheek smartly with the palm of his hand. She gasped, shocked at his action and her body's reaction to it. She liked it. A lot. This was a new game and she wanted to play.

Pleasure licked at the inside of her thighs. She had to part her legs to release the insistent ache between them.

He rubbed her flesh again, squeezing the spot where

he had spanked her. "I think someone likes it rough." He slapped her again, this time on the other cheek.

She glanced over her shoulder at him and gave him a heated look. "Maybe."

Arching a brow, he grabbed her around the upper arms and steered her toward the beach chair. "Put your hands on it, give me your ass."

His command made her squirm. She was usually the one that made the decisions. She'd been the one that had gotten them out of a jam and into safety. Vance had happily followed her behind, without comment, without argument. She liked that about him. But she also knew that he could be lethal if needed.

During their run from the States, they had to deal with some unsavory types. One such type took it upon himself to try and steal their money, and he made the mistake of thinking that Vance would be an easy target. That was the man's last mistake he ever made. And that made her feel safe with him.

Leaning forward, she placed her hands on the far end of the chair. The motion tilted her pelvis and pushed her ass into the air.

He moved a leg between hers and kicked them apart. The violence of it made sweet come trickle down the inside of her thigh.

Vance noticed it. He drew his finger over her flesh gathering it onto the tip. He slid his finger into his mouth and moaned. "Fucking delicious."

Losing the towel, he positioned himself behind her and rubbed the tip of his cock in between her cheeks.

Back and forth. Lazy strokes. She pushed back at him, urging him to end her suffering. He just chuckled and continued to tease her.

Gripping her hips, he slid the head of his cock into her opening, and then without pause he finally plunged into her. Wave after wave of scorching heat seemed to burn her from the inside out as he stroked her with his cock. Here there were no gentle strokes, no teasing. Vance continued to plunge into her pussy mercilessly, relentlessly.

Her whole body quivered and quaked from his pounding desire. But she never thought to ask him to stop. Even as she felt herself teeter on the edge of delirium, she shouted for more.

"Harder!" she shouted, pushing back into him even as he shoved into her again and again. This was passion. This was hunger. The kind she had been dreaming about, the kind she'd only experienced with Vance.

She reveled in his groans as he pounded into her. His flesh slapped against hers, sparking thoughts of the slight spanking she received. New desire ripe and hungry wrapped itself around her body, igniting fresh ripples of pure unadulterated fervor.

She lowered her face to the chair and pushed back with her ass. If he could completely bury himself inside her, she wished he would. Every orifice burned for his touch.

Like a blessing from above, Sangria felt a sharp pressure at her anus. She clamped her eyes shut and bit her lip as Vance slid his lubricated finger into her puckered hole. Another wave of glorious pleasure washed over her as he pumped both his cock and his finger into her repeatedly.

Every muscle in her body began to contract as another intense orgasm surged through her. She screamed out, unable to contain her pleasure. She clenched down in her sex and squeezed his cock with her velvety flesh. Vance pressed his fingers into her hip as he rammed himself deep into her and came. She could feel pulse after pulse of hot liquid filling her until she thought she'd drown.

Spent, Vance pulled out and wrapped his arms around her, nuzzling contentedly into her back. She could feel the thump of his heart on her skin.

"Let's go dancing," Vance murmured into the back of her neck, pressing his lips to her skin. "There's a masquerade band playing in the market square."

Sangria could hardly breathe. "Are you kidding? I need to rest."

He chuckled. "Okay, how about we compromise." His fingers played at her nipples, squeezing and tweaking playfully. "We'll shower, get dressed, eat and go dancing, then come back here and fuck until sunrise."

He pulled on her taut peak with enthusiasm. Sharp jolts of pleasure zinged up her form. "Okay. But this time I get to ride you."

# Two

Sangria was startled awake.

The scented ocean air blowing in from the open window tickled her bare shoulders, causing shivers to race up and down her back. She pulled the light blanket up to her chin and snuggled in against Vance's warm body. A content smile curled her lips.

They had danced for hours, eaten great food, drunk copious amounts of alcohol, and had stumbled back to their cottage, passion brimming like wildfire between them. They didn't quite make it until sunrise. Somewhere after the third orgasm, both Vance and Sangria fell asleep.

But something had jerked her from her deep sleep. Had she had a bad dream? A memory from her past coming to haunt her?

Lying still, she listened to the night sounds surrounding the cottage. She could hear the gentle lap of the ocean waves, the crickets singing from the nearby grass, and Vance's steady breathing. All seemed normal. Sounds she heard every night.

Despite all that, the hair on the back of her neck rose.

Sitting up, she scanned the dark room. It was never fully black, not with the moonlight streaming in through the windows. But nothing looked out of place. No unusual shadows moving about.

Maybe she was being paranoid. It was going on two years now since they had escaped First Lady Maxine Madison's clutches. After taking the money that Sangria had received for transporting Vance from L.A. to Las Vegas, Leon, the hired goon, hadn't come looking for them. She imagined that he had faced his own set of dire circumstances when he returned to Washington without his intended targets. He seemed like the type that would hold a grudge.

With the little money Sangria had stashed in various locations and by calling in a few favors, she had managed to make herself and Vance invisible. At least, she had hoped they were still flying under the radar. She had only one more favor to cash in if they had to go on the run again. And she didn't ever want to use it. The man who owed her was meaner and nastier than anyone they'd dealt with before.

Tilting her head, she strained to listen once more. She'd be damned if she was going to be caught with her pants literally down.

And then she heard it. Just the faintest *ping* of something metal just outside the far window.

She covered Vance's mouth with her hand and leaned down to his ear. "Someone's here. We need to go."

His eyes snapped open but he didn't struggle against her hand. They had talked about the drill in the event that someone came looking for them. Eyes wide, he nodded, letting her know he had heard her loud and clear.

After removing her hand, Sangria rolled over the bed and quietly opened the side table drawer. Lifting out the gun and ammunition clip, she set them beside her on the pillow, then pulled on the discarded skirt and tank top that she had worn earlier to go dancing. She forewent her sandals, as they would just slow her down. And she had a feeling she was going to need all the speed she could muster.

Picking up the gun and sliding in the clip as quietly as she could, Sangria glanced over her shoulder at Vance. He was dressed, had their prepacked bag of necessities, previously stashed under their bed, looped over his neck and shoulder and was looking at her expectantly.

Nodding, she pointed to the back door that led to the beach and to the boat dock. If they could make it to their small powerboat, they might just be able to escape without too much trouble. It all depended on who was after them and how much trouble they were looking for.

Without a word, Vance moved across the room and toward the back door. Gun lifted toward the front of the cottage, she waited until he passed her, and then followed him to the exit. Cautiously, he opened the back door.

Sangria winced, hoping the hinges didn't squeak. Vance told her he would take care of it when she told him about it last week. When the door opened with no noise, she let out her breath.

Vance peered out into the night, then glanced over his shoulder at her, giving her the thumbs-up. Relieved, she patted him in the back and he went through the door and out onto the beach.

Surveying the room one last time, Sangria turned to rush through the door. Splinters of wood peppered her face before she passed the threshold. The popping sound of the muffled shot echoed throughout the cottage, following in her wake.

Heart pounding, she raced after Vance. She'd been lucky. An inch to the left and Sangria's face would've been plastered by a 9 mm slug, putting a very nice hole in her forehead. A professional was after them, one with a silencer.

"Find something to hide behind," she called to Vance. "Our visitor is armed."

An explosion of sand near her feet punctuated her statement quite effectively.

Nearing a rusted-out discarded metal rowboat perched on its side, Vance zigzagged across the side and dived for cover behind it. Sangria was right on his tail.

"Who's after us?" he asked.

"I don't know yet." Hunkering down behind the boat, she peeked over the side, gun pointed.

A dark shadow flitted by the side of the cottage, making its way toward them.

Sangria fired three shots in a row, and then ducked back down. A bullet pierced the side of the cottage, the other two hopefully finding their mark. Holding her breath, she waited to hear the telltale signs of injury, like groaning or yelping. Nothing.

She cursed and cautioned to peer over the boat again, this time from the other side. Vance stayed alongside her, ready to do what she asked when she asked. Once she had tried to train him to shoot, but he abhorred guns and refused to use one. He preferred to work close to the people he knew, whether they were friends or enemies. The blade strapped to his leg was evident of that. Unfortunately, it wouldn't stop a bullet.

"Ms. Silver, you're not a very good shot."

The gravelly voice came from the side of the cottage, near the deck. And Sangria knew exactly who it belonged to.

Shaking her head, she glanced at Vance. He had the same concern in his eyes, which she knew was swimming in hers.

"How did he find us?" he whispered.

"He's one persistent bastard, our Leon."

"Hey, Vance. Sangria. I don't want to kill you, just to talk."

"Yeah, right," she said under her breath as she turned to survey the distance between where they were holed up to the boat tied to the dock. "Do you think you can make it to the boat?"

Vance took in the boat and the path to it. He nodded. "Yeah, but not without you, sugar."

She grabbed his hand and squeezed. "I'll distract him and you make a run for it." He opened his mouth to protest, but she finished for him. "I'll be only a few seconds behind you. I promise."

"You better be, girl, or I'm going to give you the hardest spanking of your life."

She chuckled and pulled him to her so she could press her lips to his. "I'll hold you to it."

After one final kiss, she released his hand and readied herself at the side of the boat. "One, two, three . . . go!"

Standing, she fired off three more shots as Vance raced down the beach toward the dock. She hunkered back down and watched as he ran toward the boat. She'd wait a few more seconds, fire more rounds and join him.

But she didn't get a chance to do any of that.

Horrified, she watched as Vance took a shot to the leg and went down. She hadn't even heard Leon's gun fire.

Tears welled in her eyes. She hadn't cared for someone in so long that her heart nearly burst from the pain of it. Standing, she screamed as she fired her gun, emptying the entire clip in rapid succession.

The press of cold metal in the back of her neck forced the weapon from her hands. Her whole body vibrated with fury.

"Hey, I said I wasn't going to kill you, but I didn't say anything about shooting."

"Fuck you," she growled.

"It might come to that, sweetheart, so I'd be nice to

me if I were you." He nudged her with the gun. "Turn around, nice and slow."

Seething beyond reason, Sangria put her hands out and turned to face the hit man. He was just as she remembered him, big and mean looking.

He smiled at her. "Nice to see you again, Sangria."

"I can't say the same."

"Hey, don't worry, darling, Vance isn't dead. I like him too much to do that to him."

"What do you want?" she bit out between clenched teeth.

"What I've always wanted. Money." He took a few steps back and aimed his weapon at her chest. "And the two of you are worth quite a lot."

"I can get you money."

He shook his head. "Not this time, sweetheart. Not the kind I can get from Ms. Madison."

"How much?"

"Three hundred grand."

"Wow, who knew I was worth that much?"

He grinned. "You're not, that's just for Vance."

"How do you feel about selling out your friend?"

His eyes twitched. "I'm not."

"Really? That's not what Vance tells me."

He slapped her across the face. It was hard. Sangria knew she'd have a big bruise on her cheekbone if she lived to see it.

"I'm going to kill you, Leon, just so you know."

Chuckling, he shook his head. "Okay, darling. But first you're going to sleep."

He pulled the trigger. Stinging pain radiated over her chest.

Staggering back, she put a hand up to her breasts. She pulled a tranquilizer dart from her skin. It fell from her fingers as she looked up at Leon.

He finger waved at her. "Nightie-night, angel."

Everything began to spin and her tongue felt thick, sticking to the roof of her mouth. Wobbling to the left, she fell on her back, landing on a bed of soft sand. Eyes heavy, she closed them. Her last thought was one of ocean waves, and the gentle sway in her mind.

# Three

Sangria woke to the sound of something moving beside her. Blinking back waking tears; she opened her eyes and surveyed her surroundings. A rat the size of her forearm stared back at her and she suddenly wished she hadn't opened her eyes at all. It peered at her, sniffed a few times, and then moved on, thankfully not finding what it was looking for.

Moaning, Sangria tried to move her arms. But she found them too leaden to lift. She didn't think they were bound as she didn't feel any rope around them, but she looked down to check. Nope, she was unbound, but unfortunately the drug that Leon pumped into her was still affecting her limbs.

As she moved her head, she noticed that she was lying on the cool hard cement of a large warehouse. She couldn't be sure if she was still in the Caribbean. For all she knew,

Leon had taken them back to America and back into the First Lady's lecherous hands. By the humidity in the air, there was a slight possibility that they were still somewhere on the islands likely in one of the big cities. She hoped.

Straining, Sangria moved her shoulders and tried to pull herself up into a sit. She needed to see where Vance was. He wasn't on the floor next to her, or anywhere in the immediate vicinity that she could tell. Yanking hard, she managed to bend her arms and rest up on her elbows. At least this way she could see all around her.

The first thing she saw was movement behind frosted glass in what appeared to be an office of some kind. Three shadows moved about. Vance, Leon, and the First Lady?

She shut her eyes, considering what they were doing to Vance. She knew he'd been abused a few times under Ms. Madison's iron-fisted rule. Some of his clients hadn't been gentle with him; some had been quite vicious, thinking they could do whatever they had wanted to him because they had paid their money.

The next thing she noticed was the steel pipe lying on the ground near the office door. If she could crawl over there, she could grab it, burst into the office and take Leon out, then Maxine.

Struggling, she managed to roll over and onto her hands and knees. She moved one hand then the other, dragging her legs behind her. She wished she knew what drug Leon had used, then maybe she'd have some idea how long they'd been in the warehouse and how much longer it would be until she had full use of her limbs again. She was itching to kick some ass.

More minutes than she had hoped ticked by before she was within grasping distance of the metal pipe. Crawling fast proved more difficult than she had thought. The skin on her knees felt raw from scraping against the dirty, chipped cement floor.

With a sigh of relief, Sangria reached over and grabbed the pipe. The door to the office opened at that exact moment. Leon stepped out and looked down at her.

She was expecting him to be smiling, triumphant in his coup, but his eyes were dark, and his lips were pressed into a tight line. He didn't seem relieved or happy at all. Was there an edge of guilt there somewhere?

"What do you think you're going to do with that?" He gestured toward the metal clutched in her fist.

"Bash your head in."

He smirked but made no smart-mouthed remark in return or attempts to relieve her of it. Interesting.

"Is Vance alive?" she asked, her tongue still thick and coated.

He nodded.

"She'll eventually kill him, you know."

Leon dug into his pants pocket and came away with a pack of cigarettes. He took one out, put it in between his lips, and lit it. He blew out a smoke ring. "He's worth too much alive."

"Whatever makes you sleep at night. But we both know that she can't afford to keep him alive for long. Her reputation is more valuable than he's worth."

He shrugged. "Maybe."

Sangria could see the tension in his neck and around

his eyes. Something about this wasn't sitting too well with him. And she had a feeling it had everything to do with what was happening to Vance right now in the office under the depraved hand of Maxine Madison.

She knew that Leon had feelings for Vance. She'd used them before when they first had been tracked and she'd use them again. Maybe, just maybe, she could convince Leon to let them go again. But this time she knew she had to give him more than money. She had to give him what he truly wanted—Vance.

Sitting, she kept the pipe clutched in her hand, since Leon still made no attempt to take it from her. She eyed him carefully. "He cares for you, you know?"

His right eye twitched. He rubbed at it with the side of his hand but she caught it regardless. He took another drag on his cigarette. "Quit talking. It's not going to do you any good."

"He didn't tell me exactly what happened between the two of you, but I know something did."

"Doesn't matter. It's history."

Licking her lips, she chose her next words carefully. "Come with us, Leon. Get us out of here and we can all disappear together."

He cocked an eyebrow and laughed, blowing smoke out as he did. "You're something else, sweetheart."

"I mean it. If its money you want, we can get that no problem. People like us are never out of money. But I can offer you more than that. Companionship, friendship, trust. You can have that, too."

"Trust," he snorted. "Ha! The moment you were able, you'd slit my throat."

Sangria shook her head. "Not if Vance didn't want me to."

He flicked his cigarette butt across the room. "What makes you think Vance wouldn't want you to?"

"Because he has feelings for you, like I said before. And you know as well as I do that Vance is fierce about those he cares for."

Leon studied her for a long moment. She knew he was mulling over her words, considering them, trying to decide if she was telling him the truth or not and how he felt about it if it was true. Sangria had seen the emotion between the two men the first time Leon had come after them. It was there like a solid entity. Time didn't break that, whatever it was.

Did she think they had been together physically? Oh yeah. A person didn't develop feelings like that without intimacy. And she had no issue with it if it aided their escape. She could live with sharing Vance, if only they could live. If Vance wanted to be with Leon, she wouldn't complain. She had no delusions in thinking that their relationship would be forever.

A loud cry coming from behind the office door made both Leon and Sangria flinch. She cringed to think what Maxine was doing to Vance. She knew the First Lady wouldn't permanently damage him, as damaged goods weren't good for the sex business. But whatever she was doing was hurting him both physically and mentally. She remembered the haunted look in his eyes when he had told her about some of things he had gone through working for her.

Sangria thrummed with fury. If given the chance she'd gut Maxine Madison like the pig she was.

She locked gazes with Leon and pleaded with him to give her that chance. "Make your decision. It doesn't sound like Vance has much more time."

Licking his lips nervously, Leon glanced at the door, then back to Sangria. "I'll kill you if you betray me."

She nodded. "I wouldn't expect anything less."

Sighing, he moved toward her and offered his hand. She took it and he pulled her up. Her knees were like rubber and she nearly fell again, but Leon kept her upright.

"How do you want to play it?" he asked.

"The old double-cross?"

He nodded.

"Okay, you'll have to help me in though. I'm not sure if I can walk so well."

With an arm wrapped around her waist, Leon opened the office door and dragged her through.

Sangria had to bite her lip to stifle a yelp when she saw Vance. He was tied to a metal chair, naked, gagged and bleeding from various places: nose, mouth, a few places on his chest and legs. It was the blood dribbling down his thigh that made her stomach roil. Maxine had cut him, not enough to damage him but enough to send a brutal message.

The First Lady looked up from where she knelt in front of Vance, a spot of red on her pointy chin and lips. Sangria didn't even want to consider why there was blood on the woman's mouth. The thought made her sick.

"Why are you interrupting me?"

"Change of plans, bitch." Sangria pushed out of Leon's grip and brought the metal pipe around to smack Leon in the face. "Sorry, Leon."

Her aim was savage and it only took one blow to make her point. Leon dropped to the ground. Blood weeping from the wound in his forehead.

Maxine Madison jumped up and wheeled on Sangria with the blade in her bony hand. "I should've killed you first."

"Yes, you should've." She sized up her opponent in a matter of seconds. The First Lady was a tall, frail-looking woman with high cheekbones and sharklike eyes—dead and unfeeling. Sangria knew the woman would kill without hesitation and suspected she had on more than one occasion.

Maxine's gaze flicked from Sangria to Vance and back to the metal pipe in Sangria's hand. "This doesn't have to end badly for any of us."

Sangria squeezed the pipe tighter. "I know, but it's going to, at least for you."

"Don't be a fool, Sangria. I can make you a rich woman."

"I don't want your money," she spat.

"He's not worth it. He's a whore and nothing more than that."

Sangria looked at Vance. He was watching her, his expressive eyes telling her everything she needed to know about him. He had a beautiful soul and she'd been blessed to spend the time with him that she did. For two years he made her happy. Something no one else in her life had ever done for her. He was worth more than any amount of money Maxine could bribe her with.

"Well, I know one thing, Maxine; he's worth a hell of a lot more than you." Gripping the pipe tight, she rushed the First Lady, feinting to the left, then going right with her arm hefted high.

The metal found its intended target, and the First Lady slumped to the ground, an impressive indentation in her skull.

Dropping her weapon, Sangria rushed to Vance's side and removed his gag. A strong sense of déjà vu came over her. This was the same situation they had been in the first time they had met. Vance had been tied up and gagged and Sangria had been rescuing him.

His lips lifted in a grin, obviously remembering the same thing. "What is it about you, that I keep getting tied up over?"

She pressed a soft kiss to his forehead. "Not sure." She reached for Maxine's knife and cut Vance free.

When he stood, he massaged his wrists and gave Maxine's body a fleeting glance, then dismissed her. Sangria was glad to see it.

She found his clothes and helped him dress. Afterward, he stood over Leon's prone form and shook his head. "Too bad about Leon."

She grabbed his arm to steer him out of the room. "Oh, he'll live." Reaching down, she dug into Leon's pants pocket for a set of keys. She found them on the first try.

It was time they disappeared again. And if she could help it, they'd never be found again. At least, Ms. Madison would no longer be on their tail. But Sangria was certain there would be someone to replace her. A person didn't kill the First Lady of the New States of America without paying the price.

## Four

$\mathscr{M}$exico was a perfect country to get lost in. For the right amount of money and a few favors, both Sangria Silver and Vance Verona had officially disappeared off the map, and it had only taken a little over two weeks. In their places returned Sofia Santos and Chico Cortez with birth certificates, and driver's licenses to prove it.

Vance had always wanted to be called Chico. And so now Sangria called him that whenever she got a chance.

"Oh yeah, Chico, right there."

Sangria sighed as Vance pressed on her right shoulder blade and massaged the knot out. He had set up a massage therapy practice in the coastal Mexican town. Most of his clients came from the luxury all-inclusive resort just down the beach from where they lived. It was lucrative to say the least. Vance had the best hands in the Mexican Riviera.

Sangria was just lucky she didn't have to pay for them. She got to experience them on a regular basis.

Smoothing his oiled hands over her skin she could feel all the tension seeping out of her body. Quite possibly from between her legs. It couldn't be helped that massages led to sex. She was just wired that way, and Vance was just that good at what he did.

While she lay on her stomach, she squirmed on the table and spread her legs a bit to accommodate the first flutters of desire starting in her pussy.

Vance chuckled as his hands moved down her spine. "Is that all you think about?" His fingers brushed against the rise of her buttocks barely covered by a small cotton towel. "I'm not a machine, you know?"

"You could've fooled me," she sighed while flipping over onto her back.

She grabbed his hands and placed them on her breasts. "Massage these, Chico."

He smiled and pressed a kiss to her mouth. "Well when you put it like that . . ." He pinched her nipples between forefingers and thumbs.

She closed her eyes as he squeezed and massaged her taut peaks. Soon, the wet press of his mouth joined his fingers on her breasts. Opening her eyes, she watched as he took one rigid nipple into his mouth and suckled it.

"*Mmm,* is this what you do for all your massage clients?" she teased; it was an ongoing banter between them since he started the business.

"No, just for my special clients," he murmured around her nipple, as he stroked it with his tongue and teeth.

The pulling sensations went straight to her pussy. Every time he drew on her nipple it was if he sucked on her clit. The feeling was explosive. Already an orgasm was building between her thighs.

Lifting his head, he let her breast pop out of his mouth. He moved around the table, his fingers feathering against her legs. When he reached the end, Vance grabbed a leg in each hand and pulled her down the length of the table.

She squealed as she slid. The towel covering her pelvis floated down to the floor.

"What are you doing?" she yelped.

"The deluxe special."

He tugged her to the edge, spread her legs and stepped in between them. He nuzzled his cotton clad erection into her pussy and ground against her exposed flesh.

Sangria cried out as the material scraped the sensitive folds of her sex. Maybe if he'd grind harder, she'd find a quick release. She pushed into him, rubbing herself on his rigid length.

Vance chuckled and backed up. "You can't have it until you tell me what you want."

"Fuck me."

"Not good enough. Tell me more." He flicked a finger over her clit.

Sangria bowed her back and moaned loudly.

"Do you like this?"

"Oh yeah, you know I do."

"Do you want more?" he asked, licking his lips.

"Yes."

"Yes, what?"

"Yes, Chico, I want more.

Chuckling, Vance pressed his thumb against the swollen nub and rubbed it around in circles. "Like this."

"Yes, harder."

He pressed down hard and rubbed faster. "Like this."

Sangria could barely speak as jolts of pleasure surged through her pussy and over her body.

He pinched her clit between his finger and thumb and pulled sharply on it. She cried out as her orgasm pounded into her belly and radiated up and down her thighs. Her muscles contracted and quivered as waves of pleasure crashed over her and threatened to drown her under their sublime grip.

She kicked out, forcing Vance to back up. But he still held on to her clit, rubbing and jiggling it, pulling more from her. More than she'd ever given to any man.

"Ah, no more," she panted. "No more."

Vance relinquished his hold on her clit, and gazed down at her, his eyes dark and slitted with desire.

"You're amazing, especially when you come."

Sangria could finally feel the ripples of orgasm quieting. She relaxed her body and took in a deep breath.

"I want to see that look again and again."

Vance yanked his cotton pants down and released the erection that must have been painfully constricted inside. Sangria marveled at the size of him. He was wide and long, like the rest of his body. She loved looking at him.

He chuckled as he stroked a hand over himself, squeezing the end where a droplet of come dribbled from the tip. He gathered the lust on his fingers and brought his hand to her lips.

Sangria opened her mouth and let him rub his come over her lips. She stuck out her tongue and tasted him, eagerly licking at his fingers.

He groaned low as he watched her, restraint deeply etched on his face.

Gripping his cock, he rubbed the head up and down her slick channel. He settled the tip into the entrance of her pussy, pushing a little in, and then pulling back.

"Grab your legs. Spread yourself as wide as you can. I want to see my cock go all the way in."

Sangria did as he asked, reveling in his position to take control. His words commanded her. He could do what he wanted with her. She wouldn't stop him. She'd never given any man that kind of power over her before.

She hooked her hands around her knees and pulled her legs back and apart. Her knees touched her breasts. She could feel herself stretch wide and open. Lust dribbled down the crack of her ass.

Vance gripped his cock in one hand and gently touched her clit with the other. She bolted a little, as she was still sensitive. But soon the pain crossed over to pleasure and she felt herself go lax as he pushed his penis into her slowly, stopping every so often to catch his breath.

Inch by glorious inch of Vance slid into her until the entire length of him was buried deep inside. She was afraid to move as another orgasm quickened deep within her belly. She feared she would not be able to control the descent down if she let go. She wanted it to last as long as possible.

Vance pressed his thumb down on her clit as he began to move, finding a slow tortuous pace to tease her with. He clenched his teeth and groaned. Sangria knew he struggled with his control. She could plainly see it on his sweating face, the quivering muscles of his forearms as he held her down.

She closed her eyes against the assault of intense pleasure that swept over her. Her whole body vibrated ablaze with delight as she crested the waves of release.

"Open your eyes," Vance groaned.

Sangria slowly opened them.

"Watch me fuck you."

He moved faster, sliding in and out with quick hard thrusts. Sangria gasped as her muscles tightened around him. She could feel her orgasm quicken and harden. Her breath hitched in her throat.

He slid his cock out slowly then thrust back in hard. Sangria gasped, almost losing her breath as jolts of pleasure radiated up her body. He slid out again and thrust in fast and hard. He dug his fingers into her legs and picked up his pace, panting wildly as he pumped into her again and again. Sweat poured off his face and neck and dripped down on her belly.

Sangria let herself go. She stopped fighting the jolts and let them ripple over her unhindered. She cried out as her orgasm slammed into her, taking her over the edge into a free fall.

Vance turned his head to the side as he ground into her, his gaze focused on something else, something that drove him hard. She followed his line of sight and gasped, not expecting to see what she did. Now she knew why he took her so fiercely.

Vance was always giving to her. And she wanted to give something back to him. Maybe her Christmas gift to him just walked through the door.

With a loud grunt, he fell forward, grabbing onto her shoulders and burying his face in her breasts and came. She wrapped her arms around him and stroked his back until his violent surge ended.

After he quieted, she took his face in her hands and kissed him hard. "You definitely worked my kinks out."

He laughed, and pressed a final kiss to the top of her nose. Slipping out of her, he tucked himself back into his pants and leaned against the table, affecting a cavalier air, as if a ghost hadn't just appeared in their room.

"You changed your name to Chico? What were you thinking?"

"Hey, Leon," Sangria said.

The big man sat in a chair beside the small decorated tree Vance had put up in the corner for the holidays. He waved his fingers at them. "Sorry to interrupt."

Sangria sat up on the table, swung her legs over, and stood to get her robe hanging over the chair. When she was covered, she walked over to Leon and smiled. "What took you so damn long?"

He patted the big black bag he had set on the table next to him. "Couldn't forget the Christmas presents, now could I?"

She unzipped the bag and pulled it open. Ten thick stacks of one-hundred-dollar bills stared back at her.

Glancing at him, she trailed her finger over the scar that lined his forehead. "Sorry about that, Leon, but I had to make it look authentic when her people came. Didn't want them to think that you helped us escape or anything."

"No worries. It was worth it."

Sangria looked over her shoulder at Vance. He had yet to move and his gaze was fixed on their unexpected guest. She could see the emotion in his face. It was a cross between desire and fury. He had never given her that look. She supposed the two of them had a lot to work out.

Tying her robe tighter, she padded toward the open deck door. "I'm going outside for some air and wine. It should give you two enough time to work your shit out."

She sat on one of the deck chairs and sipped from her glass of red wine. It was definitely going to be an interesting evening. She wasn't sure if they were going to fuck or fight. Either way, it would be fascinating to watch.

She wasn't sure if the three of them could live together without conflict, but she was never one to shy away from discord. The next few years were going to be an adventure, that was for sure. Frankly, she couldn't wait to get started, and she had always thought Christmastime was the best time to start something new.

A bad girl at heart, VIVI ANNA likes to burn up the pages with her unique brand of fantasy fiction. Whether it's in ancient Egypt or in an apocalyptic future, Vivi Anna always writes fast-paced action-adventure with strong independent women that can kick some butt, and dark delicious heroes to kill for.